Mountain Refuge

Surviving The Collapse

K J Godsey

Spanish Peaks Publishing

For my best friend Kevin. Your unwavering friendship, laughter, and wisdom are gifts I cherish every day. Thank you for always being a constant source of encouragement and inspiration. This book is dedicated to you with heartfelt gratitude. "You taught me nothing, and I learned it all."

Mountain Refuge

Chapter 1

Just Another Day

Morning light crept across Overlook Ridge, painting the pine trees in shades of amber and gold. The first rays caught the dewdrops clinging to the scrub oak leaves, transforming them into countless tiny prisms. A gentle breeze stirred the branches of the juniper trees, carrying the crisp scent of pine needles and wild sage through the Colorado wilderness.

The three-story house stood sentinel against the backdrop of untamed landscape, its windows reflecting the sunrise like sheets of polished copper. Shadow and light played across the concrete siding, emphasizing the building's commanding presence on the grounds.

Detached from the main house, the four-car garage remained dark, its doors closed against the morning chill. The structure's clean lines contrasted with the organic shapes of the surrounding wilderness, a reminder of human presence in this remote corner of the world.

The winding dirt road that connected Overlook Ridge to Blackhawk Ranch snaked through the property like a dusty ribbon. Morning mist clung to its curves, softening the edges of the landscape. The road disappeared into a stand of pines, the only lifeline to civilization from this isolated sanctuary.

Beyond the developed area, the rest of the seventy acres stretched wild and untouched. The rising sun revealed layers of terrain - rocky outcrops jutting through blankets of pine forest, patches of scrub oak creating natural barriers, and clusters of juniper adding their blue-green hue to the palette of the morning.

The underground storage bunker remained mostly invisible from above, its presence marked only by one end, exposed and subtle changes in the terrain. Native grasses and wildflowers had long since reclaimed its roof, maintaining the illusion of undisturbed wilderness.

As the sun climbed higher, shadows retreated across the property. Light filtered through the pine canopy, creating patterns on the needle-strewn ground. A hawk circled overhead, riding the thermal currents that rose from the warming earth. Its cry echoed across the ridge, a lone voice in the morning quiet.

The property's elevation offered unobstructed views of the surrounding wilderness. To the west, endless waves of forested hills rolled toward the next mountain range, untouched by human development. The morning light emphasized every ridge and valley, creating a tapestry of light and shadow that stretched as far as the eye could see.

The air grew warmer as the sun rose higher, burning away the last wisps of morning mist. Pine needles released their sharp, sweet scent in the heat. A gentle breeze stirred the branches, creating a soft whisper that blended with the calls of waking birds.

The property's natural boundaries became more distinct in the full light of morning. Dense stands of pine marked the edges of clearings, while rocky outcrops created natural barriers. The wilderness beyond Overlook Ridge stretched unbroken to the horizon, a reminder of the vast solitude that surrounded this pocket of civilization.

Small signs of wildlife appeared as the day warmed. A mule deer emerged from the cover of scrub oak, moving cautiously through the morning light. Squirrels chattered in the pine branches, and a pair of Steller Jays swooped between the trees, their blue and white plumage flashing in the sunlight.

The dirt road caught the morning light differently now, its surface taking on the color of worn leather. Seven miles of twists and turns separated this sanctuary from the entrance to Blackhawk Ranch, ensuring privacy and isolation. The morning sun emphasized every rut and ridge on its surface, telling stories of past travels and weather.

Around the main house, native grasses swayed in the strengthening breeze. The movement created waves of light and shadow across the ground, a natural counterpoint to the solid presence of the building in the middle. The house's windows continued to reflect the changing light, now showing glimpses of blue sky and passing clouds.

The landscape of Overlook Ridge revealed itself fully in the morning light - a careful balance of human presence and wild nature. The property's seventy acres provided a buffer between civilization and wilderness, a transition zone where the ordered world of human construction met the chaos of untamed Colorado landscape.

Todd Blodsey's eyes snapped open, his internal clock attuned to the first light of dawn filtering through the top floor bedroom window. He lay still for a moment, listening to the familiar creaks and settles of the three-story house, his sanctuary nestled on Overlook Ridge. The walls, stained a warm honey by the rising sun, bore witness to his solitary mornings.

He swung his legs over the edge of the bed, the cool carpet floor greeting his bare feet. His body protested slightly, a reminder of the decades it had served him. Stretching, he reached towards the ceiling, working out the kinks from a night's rest. His joints popped, the sound echoing in the quiet room.

"Another day, Blodsey," he muttered to himself, a ritualistic incantation to start the day. His voice, rough with sleep, filled the silence.

Todd padded to the kitchen, the house revealing itself in the growing light. Pictures lined the walls, chronicling his life in stark black and white - government service, his daughter's childhood, the construction of this retreat. Each step was a testament to his history, his journey to this isolated haven.

In the kitchen, he filled the red coffee maker, the whisper of water warming in the internal reservoir breaking the morning hush. He set his cup underneath the spout and hit the start button. While waiting, he stood at the sink, looking out at the sprawling hill to his south beyond the window.

Bear and Buttercup, his two German Shepherds, stirred from their beds in the corner. They stretched, mirroring Todd's earlier actions, before trotting to his side. Bear nudged his hand, her cold nose pressing against his skin.

"Morning, girls," he greeted, scratching behind their ears. Their tags jingled softly, a peaceful melody in the quiet kitchen.

The coffee maker hissed as it finished, piercing the tranquil atmosphere. Todd poured what seemed like a pound of creamer into a mug, the aroma of instant coffee filling the air. He preferred the simplicity of it, the predictability. It was one less variable in his carefully controlled world.

Mug in hand, he stepped onto the front deck. The chill mountain air nipped at his exposed skin, but he welcomed it. It was invigorating, a reminder of his vitality. He leaned against the railing, sipping his coffee, the heat a stark contrast to the crisp morning.

Overlook Ridge stretched before him, a tapestry of greens and golds. The sun cast long shadows; the light changing rapidly as it continued its ascent. He took a deep breath, the cool air rushing into his lungs, carrying with it the scent of pine and damp earth.

Below, a mule deer picked its way through the scrub oak, its ears flicking nervously. Todd watched it, his eyes tracking its progress across the landscape. He found peace in these moments, the silent communion with nature. It was a stark contrast to his past life, the noise and chaos of working in the city every day.

Buttercup whined softly, pushing her head under his hand. He obliged, rubbing her coarse fur. Bear sat beside him, her eyes scanning the vista, ever the vigilant sentinel. Luckily, they didn't notice the deer, or they would have gone nuts.

Todd finished his coffee, setting the mug down on the railing with a soft thud. He closed his eyes, taking another deep breath. The world was silent, save for the rustle of leaves and the distant cry of a hawk. In this moment, he was at peace.

But his mind was never still for long. As he stood there, he mentally reviewed his tasks for the day. Check the perimeter, work on the treehouse, perhaps figure out why all his tools keep going missing. There was always something to be done, always a way to improve his sanctuary.

He shifted his eyes, his gaze falling on the winding dirt driveway leading to his property. It was his lifeline to the world, the tenuous connection he maintained with civilization. But it was also a potential threat, a vulnerability. He made a mental note to maybe one day build a gate.

Turning, he reentered the house; the dogs following close at his heels. He deposited the mug in the sink, the clink of ceramic against metal echoing in the small room. His reflection stared back at him in the window above the sink, a ghostly apparition against the brightening landscape.

Todd Blodsey was a man of ritual, of habit. It was how he had survived this long, how he had carved out this sanctuary in the wild Colorado landscape. And as he stood there, the morning light casting his reflection in sharp relief, he was ready to face whatever the day might bring.

Todd settled into his favorite seat on the couch, the frame creaking beneath his weight. Bear flopped next to him, her black coat gleaming. Buttercup, ever the vigilant one, positioned herself at the back sliding door, her ears perked and alert.

"What do you say, girls? Ready for our morning routine?" His weathered hand found the sweet spot behind Bear's ear, and her leg thumped against the couch in response.

Buttercup was up with his voice and pressed her nose into his palm, her brown eyes fixed on his face. The intelligence in her gaze never failed to impress him. She'd proven herself repeatedly, warning him of approaching vehicles long before they reached the property line.

Bear rolled onto her back, exposing her belly for rubs. Her tail wagged lazily, thumping against the couch in a steady rhythm. Despite her size, she believed herself to be a lap dog, often trying to squeeze onto the couch with Todd no matter if someone was sitting next to him.

"You're getting heavy, girl." He chuckled as Bear attempted to crawl into his lap. She settled for resting her head on his knee, drool dampening his pants leg. The weight was comforting, familiar.

Buttercup nudged his other hand, demanding her share of attention. Her fur was silky under his fingers, well-maintained despite their rugged lifestyle. She'd always looked groomed even though she rarely was, unlike Bear, who treated mud puddles like personal spa treatments.

The morning light shifted, throwing shadows across the room. Todd reached for his book on the side table, but Buttercup intercepted his hand, demanding more pets, or maybe a bone. Her tail wagged in victory when he complied.

"Five more minutes," he said as he held out five fingers and flashed them in front of her face. The words carried no reproach, only direction. They'd earned their comfort, these loyal companions who guarded his solitude.

Bear's snoring filled the quiet room, her bulk warm against his legs. Buttercup remained alert, dividing her attention between Todd's scratches and her self-appointed watch duty. Every few minutes, she'd pause to listen to some distant sound, her ears swiveling like radar dishes.

Todd ran his hand along Bear's side, feeling the rise and fall of her breathing. Despite her less strategic approach to guard duty, she'd proven herself a fierce protector when needed. Her size and bark alone deterred most unwanted visitors.

Buttercup pressed closer, sandwiching Todd between the two dogs. Her presence was different from Bear's - less physical weight but more focused attention. She tracked his movements, anticipating his needs with an almost uncanny awareness.

"What would I do without you two?" He spoke softly, not expecting an answer. Bear snuffled in her sleep, while Buttercup tilted her head at his words.

The morning stretched on, measured in belly rubs and ear scratches. These quiet moments grounded him, reminded him why he'd chosen this life. The dogs' unconditional companionship filled the solitude of Overlook Ridge with purpose.

Bear stirred, her head lifting from Todd's knee as she yawned widely. Her tongue lolled out, and she fixed him with a hopeful stare that he recognized all too well.

Buttercup noticed the change in her companion's demeanor and stood, her tail wagging with renewed energy. She knew the routine as well as Todd did.

"Outside? You guys need to go outside?" Todd glanced at his watch, though he hardly needed to. The dogs' internal clocks were as reliable as any timepiece.

The word 'outside' transformed both dogs from lazy companions to alert sentinels. Even Bear managed to shake off her drowsiness, her tail now wagging with enthusiasm, beating anything it made contact with. These quiet moments would soon transition into their daily activities, but for now, Todd savored the simple joy of their company.

Todd stepped out of the door underneath the upper deck, his boots scuffling against the gravel. Around him, the property stretched out in careful sections, each zone maintained with military precision. The gravel path connecting the house to the four-car garage gleamed with rock and dirt mixed. Not a single blade of grass breaking through the landscaping. Grass wasn't an option at this altitude. It either grew naturally, or it didn't keep.

His eyes traced the natural flow of the land where he'd positioned his structures. The house commanded the center point, its windows offering clear sightlines in all directions. The garage sat at a calculated angle, its green metal roof reflecting the morning sun, the distance providing a tactical buffer while remaining convenient.

Between stands of ponderosa pines, carefully maintained clearings created natural firebreaks. He'd trimmed back the scrub oak and juniper, maintaining visibility while preserving the property's wild character. Native grasses swayed in the morning breeze, camouflaging the subtle changes in elevation that marked his underground storage.

The bunker's entrance blended seamlessly with the landscape. Unless someone knew exactly where to look, they'd walk right past it if it wasn't for the one open side, thinking it was nothing more than another small hill among the natural formations dotting the property. Todd had spent years trying to perfect its concealment, moving dirt on top and letting the wildlife take over, encouraging natural growth on the shipping containers.

A small vegetable garden occupied the south-facing slope, its raised beds arranged in tidy rows. The surrounding fence kept deer at bay while matching the property's rustic aesthetic. Every element served multiple purposes - beauty, function, and security working in harmony.

The driveway curved through the trees, its route carefully planned to slow approaching vehicles while providing multiple observation points from the house. Todd had installed subtle drainage channels along its length, preventing erosion from compromising this critical access point.

Todd knelt in the raised garden bed, his calloused hands working the soil with practiced efficiency. The morning sun warmed his back as he inspected the tomato plants, adjusting the wire cages he'd fabricated from old fencing material. His modifications had outlasted any store-bought alternative.

"Look at that, girls. Perfect spacing." He brushed the dirt from his knees and moved to the garage, Bear and Buttercup trailing behind.

Inside the garage, tools lined the walls in meticulous order. Each implement hung from custom brackets he'd welded himself, the metal work clean and precise. The workbench bore the marks of countless projects - nicks and stains that told stories of problems solved and innovations made.

He picked up the chainsaw that he'd been attempting to repair, examining his handiwork. The carburetor had given him trouble, but he'd rebuilt it with parts he'd machined himself when the manufacturer's replacements proved subpar. The engine purred to life on the first pull.

"That's how it's done." He shut it off and moved to his latest project.

The solar panel control system spread across his workbench, a maze of wires and circuits he'd modified to improve efficiency. Store-bought systems worked fine for most people, but Todd had enhanced this one with backup redundancies and surge protection that exceeded military specs.

His fingers traced the connection points, checking each solder joint. The work was neat, methodical - each wire precisely stripped and positioned. He'd developed these skills over decades, from his days as an engineer.

Buttercup watched from her spot in the center of the driveway as Todd tested the voltage output. The meter displayed exactly the readings he'd calculated, confirming his modifications had achieved the desired results.

"See this?" He pointed to a custom circuit board he'd etched himself. "That's what reliability looks like." The board housed his own design, improving on the original with features the manufacturers hadn't thought to include.

Todd made his way to the underground bunker and opened the door, the LED lights flickering to life automatically. The temperature dropped ten degrees as he moved deeper into the container. Bear and Buttercup followed, their nails clicking against the reinforced floor.

He pulled out his inventory clipboard, its pages worn from monthly checks. The first section housed floor-to-ceiling metal shelving, each section labeled and organized by an expiration date. Canned goods occupied the front rows - vegetables, fruits, and meats stacked in neat columns. Behind them, vacuum-sealed bags of rice, beans, and pasta filled the middle shelves.

"Getting low on the vitamin C supplements." He marked the clipboard, noting to rotate the older bottles forward. The pharmaceutical section rivaled a small clinic - fish antibiotics, pain relievers, and specialized medications stored in climate-controlled containers.

The water filtration system hummed quietly in the back corner, feeding into a series of interconnected tanks. Clear pipes showed the water's journey through charcoal, ceramic, and UV purification stages. Spare filters lined the adjacent shelf, each component cataloged and dated.

Todd moved to the back portion of the container. Tactical gear hung on custom racks - plate carriers, night vision equipment, and communication devices arranged by purpose. Solar-powered radios sat beside hand-cranked alternatives. A cabinet of tools contained everything from basic wrenches to specialized electronic repair kits.

"Need to check the seals on these." He ran his hand along the rubber gaskets of the chemical protection suits. The material remained supple, properly preserved in the controlled environment.

The ammunition storage, separated by plastic containers, showed the same attention to detail. Rounds were organized by caliber, with primers and powder stored separately. Reloading equipment waited on a sturdy bench, tools arranged in the order of use.

Buttercup nosed at a box of emergency rations while Bear investigated a corner for a mouse, their presence part of the weekly routine. Todd checked off each section methodically, his engineer's mind always calculating supply levels against potential scenarios.

The bunker represented years of careful planning, each item chosen for durability and multiple uses. Nothing frivolous occupied the precious space. Even the recreation materials served practical purposes - even playing cards included in survival kits for their morale value. He loved to play cards even though he was terrible at it.

Todd stepped out from the container, inhaling deeply. The late morning sun filtered through the towering ponderosa pines, their bark a patchwork of russet plates that reminded him of puzzle pieces.

A gentle breeze carried the sweet scent of pine, unique to these ancient sentinels.

Scrub oak clustered in dense thickets between the larger trees, their leaves casting intricate shadows on the ground. The gnarled branches twisted and turned, creating natural barriers across the landscape. In spring, these same oaks would burst with fresh green growth, but now their leaves had taken on the deep, mature green of late summer.

A flash of movement caught his eye. A western tanager perched on a juniper branch, its red head and yellow body bright against the blue-green foliage. The bird pecked at the aromatic berries, unconcerned by his presence. Bear watched it with mild interest, but remained at Todd's side.

Buttercup's ears perked up as a mule deer emerged from the tree line, its coat dappled by shadows. The doe moved with delicate steps through the native grasses, pausing to browse on tender shoots. More wildlife had returned to the property since Todd had started managing the land, proof that his efforts worked with nature rather than against it.

A nasty old turkey buzzard circled overhead. The bird rode the thermal currents with barely a wing movement, scanning the ground below. Todd watched its effortless flight, appreciating how each creature here had its place, its purpose. He'd learned to read these signs over the years - the birds' behavior, the movement of deer, the changing patterns of vegetation. They told him more about his property's health than any sensor could.

Todd filled the dogs' metal bowls with measured portions of premium kibble, adding a spoonful of supplements to each - his own recipe for maintaining their coat health. Bear dove in immediately while Buttercup waited for hers to be delivered to the deck before eating with more restraint.

"Easy there, Bear. No one's going to steal it." He shook his head at her enthusiasm.

The morning routine continued in the garden, where Todd checked the soil moisture with calloused fingers. The tomatoes needed staking, their heavy fruit pulling the vines earthward. He worked methodically down the rows, testing each support, adjusting ties, and removing yellowing leaves.

Sweat beaded on his forehead as he moved to the potato patch. The plants were ready for hilling, and he mounded soil around their bases with practiced movements. Each sweep of the hoe was precise, creating uniform rows that would maximize the yield.

Bear patrolled the garden's perimeter while Buttercup sprawled in a patch of shade, watching through half-closed eyes. The morning warmed quickly, and Todd paused to drink from his plastic water bottle, checking items off his mental list.

The property's fence line needed inspection. Todd loaded tools into his ATV and drove the trails to the perimeter, stopping to repair a section where winter storms had loosened posts. He worked efficiently, using techniques refined over years of maintenance.

Back at the house, he cleaned and oiled his tools before storage. Everything had its place in his workshop, arranged for maximum efficiency. The dogs followed him through each task, their presence a constant in his carefully structured day.

Todd sat at his workbench, spreading out the week's maintenance logs. He'd developed his own tracking system with engineering efficiency. Each column represented a critical system - water, power, security - broken down into subsystems and individual components.

His fingers traced the power consumption patterns, noting subtle variations. The solar array's output dropped three percent on Tuesday. He pulled up the weather data he'd recorded, cross-referencing cloud cover and temperature. The numbers didn't align with environmental factors.

"Something's drawing extra power." He sketched a quick diagram, breaking down the electrical system into its components. The backup batteries showed normal cycling, and the inverter readings remained consistent.

Buttercup watched as he moved to the breaker panel, multimeter in hand. Todd measured each circuit methodically, recording values in his notebook. The garage workshop drew standard amperage, the house systems matched historical data, but the perimeter sensors...

"There it is." He plotted the readings on graph paper, the line revealing a pattern invisible in raw numbers. One section of the security system pulled additional current every four hours. Not enough to trigger alarms, but the deviation bothered him.

Todd retrieved his laptop, pulling up the sensor schematics he'd designed. Each component had redundant power paths - a feature he'd added after a lightning strike took out the water pump power panel four years ago. The current draw matched the profile of a failing redundancy switch.

He traced the circuit in his mind, visualizing electron flow through the backup paths. The mathematical model formed naturally - resistance, voltage drops, capacitor charge rates. The solution crystallized: the switching circuit needed a higher threshold to prevent micro-oscillations.

"I've done this before." He remembered solving a similar issue with the chemical sniffer equipment, where desert heat caused component values to drift. The same principles applied here, just on a smaller scale.

Todd sketched the modified circuit, adding a hysteresis buffer to prevent false triggers. The elegant solution satisfied both his engineering standards and redundancy requirements. He'd need to update his maintenance protocols to check for similar issues in other sectors.

"Soon it's gonna be colder than a witch's tit in a brass bra soon. Let's go inside, come on!" he called, his breath almost in the chilly air as he rubbed his hands together. The dogs glanced up at him, ears perked, tails wagging in anticipation of his movement.

Inside Todd's kitchen table was a sprawl of maps, charts, and lists, each one meticulously organized and color-coded. He marked the day's temperature and weather conditions on a homemade calendar, his handwriting so terrible that only he could decipher it. Then, he flipped to his inventory, a detailed log of all his supplies. His eyes scanned the columns: food, water, medicine, fuel. Each category meticulously tracked, every supply accounted for, with detailed notes on usage and expiration dates.

He tapped his finger on the paper, his brow furrowing in concentration. "We're low on canned goods. And I need to check the generator's fuel line. Don't want any surprises when the snow hits."

The dogs followed him into the pantry, watching with keen interest as he counted cans, jars, and boxes, his lips moving silently as he tallied the supplies. He jotted down notes, calculating how much more he'd need to last through the harsh Colorado winter. Bear whined softly, her tail thumping against the floor, eyes hopeful for a treat.

"I know, girl," Todd said, giving her ear a scratch. "We'll make a run to the store later. Gotta make sure we're stocked up."

Outside, the wind picked up, sending leaves scattering across the ground in a dance of red and gold. Todd watched them, his mind calculating wind speed and direction, always assessing his environment. His gaze shifted to the woodpile stacked neatly below. The chopping block stood tall, the ax embedded on its surface, ready for the next task.

"Time to earn our keep," he said, getting up from the table and striding towards the shed. The dogs bounded ahead, tails wagging with excitement, eager to assist in their own canine way.

Todd hefted the ax, feeling the solid, familiar weight in his hands. He set a log on the block, swung the ax, and split the wood cleanly in two with a satisfying thunk. The rhythm was comforting, the physical exertion warming his muscles and focusing his mind. Bear chased after the scattered wood chips, her black fur blending with the earth, while Buttercup lay in the sun, her eyes never leaving Todd, always the vigilant protector.

As the sun dipped lower, casting shadows across the yard, Todd retreated to the house, his arms laden with freshly chopped firewood. In the kitchen, Todd opened a can of beef stew for dinner, pouring some into bowls for Bear and Buttercup. As they ate, he sat at the table, flipping through a worn almanac, its pages yellowed with age and use. He cross-referenced the weather patterns with his own observations, nodding as they matched up, his predictions proving accurate once again.

"Colder nights, shorter days," he read aloud, tracing the lines with his finger. "First frost any time now. We'll need to be ready."

After dinner, Todd loaded the dogs into his old, reliable truck. They drove to the nearby grocery store, the sun already setting behind the mountains, painting the sky in hues of orange and pink. Inside, he pushed a cart down the aisles, Bear and

Buttercup nervously waiting in the truck, their eyes scanning the darkening parking lot. People gave them a wide berth, the sight of the two large dogs enough to deter any would-be troublemakers.

He stocked up on canned goods, rice, and beans, then moved on to batteries, candles, and matches. At the checkout, the cashier eyed his purchases warily, her eyebrows raised in curiosity.

"Someone's ready for the apocalypse," she joked nervously, trying to lighten the mood.

Todd just smiled, handing her cash. "Never hurts to be prepared. You never know what's around the corner."

The last rays of sunlight painted the Colorado mountains in shades of gold, casting a warm glow over the landscape. Todd settled into his deck chair once more, the frame creaking the familiar sound beneath him. Bear flopped down next to him with a heavy sigh, her black coat blending with the growing darkness, her body warmth a comforting presence. Buttercup sat alert at his side, her ears swiveling to catch the evening sounds, her protective instinct always on guard.

Todd pulled his flannel shirt closer, savoring the peaceful moment. His day's work was done - the woodpile stacked high, supplies organized and stocked, equipment maintained and ready. This was his life now, this constant preparation, this vigilance. And he wouldn't have it any other way.

"Good girls," he said, reaching down to scratch Bear's belly. Her tail thumped against the deck boards, her eyes closing in contentment. Buttercup pressed her head against his knee, and he ran his fingers through her thick fur, the gesture as much of a comfort to him as it was to her.

Todd sat quietly, watching the TV and changing the channels rapidly, the flickering light casting shifting shadows across the room. The mountains stood like silent guardians, their peaks still catching the last light, their presence a steady reassurance. A gentle breeze rustled through the open windows, their leaves sounding like tiny applauses, nature's own symphony.

He breathed in deeply, letting the mountain air fill his lungs, the crisp scent of pine and earth grounding him. This was what he'd worked for - this peace, this freedom, this sense of security in an uncertain world. Bear snored softly next to him while Buttercup kept her quiet vigil, both dogs content in their evening routine, their presence a comforting constant in Todd's well-ordered world.

Chapter 2

The Early Warnings

Todd leaned forward from his favorite seat on the couch, the TV remote clutched tightly in his hand. The local news station had been taken over by a special report, the banner screaming:

"UNPRECEDENTED NATURAL DISASTERS SWEEP EAST COAST."

He turned up the volume, his eyebrows furrowing into a single line.

"...hurricanes, tornadoes, and massive flooding have left the East Coast in shambles," the news anchor reported, her voice uncharacteristically grave. "Ports from Florida to North Carolina have been severely damaged, bringing global supply chains to a screeching halt. Experts warn that this could lead to widespread shortages and economic instability."

Buttercup, the taller of the two German Shepherds, sensed his tension. She lifted her head from her paws, ears perked forward. Todd didn't notice, his eyes glued to the screen. The footage was grim: oil tankers capsized in harbors, spilling oil in the bays, oil and gas refineries destroyed, massive power outages, and warehouses submerged under murky water.

"What a mess," Todd muttered, his inner prepper kicking in. His mind started to race, calculating the domino effect of such widespread devastation.

The anchor switched to an interview with a supply chain expert. "We're looking at months, if not a year, of delays," the man said, his face pale under the harsh studio lights. "Gas, food, medicine, goods of all kinds—they're all going to be in short supply until we can get these ports and refineries functioning again."

Todd's grip tightened around the remote. His genius-level intelligence, always a blessing and a curse, spun out potential scenarios. None of them were good.

Bear, sensing the shift in the room, stood up from her spot by the kitchen table. She walked over to Todd, nuzzling his hand. He absently stroked her fur, his mind miles away, assessing, analyzing.

"...urging citizens not to panic," the anchor continued, but Todd could read between the lines. He'd seen firsthand how quickly things could spiral out of control during the COVID pandemic. It was a matter of time before the panic set in, as if it wasn't already in full swing.

He flicked off the TV, the room suddenly silent except for the soft hum of the house. He stood up. Both dogs immediately came to attention.

"Alright, girls," he said, his voice steady with resolve. "Looks like we need to step up our game."

Todd strode into the kitchen, the dogs on his heels. He grabbed a notepad and pen from the counter, his movements swift and efficient. He started to make lists, his mind like a steel trap of information.

"Food, water, medical supplies..." he murmured, the pen scratching against the paper. "We've got a good start, but we'll need more. Much more."

He paused, looking out the window at the sprawling wilderness surrounding his isolated property. He'd chosen this spot for a reason, away from the noise and chaos of the world. Now, it seemed, the chaos might be finally catching up.

Bear nudged his hand, a soft whine echoing from her throat. Todd looked down, his stern gaze softening. "You're right, girl," he said. "We're not waiting around for trouble to find us. We'll be ready."

With renewed determination, Todd ripped the top page off the notepad and tucked it into his pocket. He headed towards the basement door;

the dogs following close behind. Their nails clicked against the tiled floor, a rhythmic cadence echoing through the house.

The basement was cool and dry, stocked floor to ceiling with shelves of supplies. Todd had been preparing for years, always adding, always improving. He scanned the room with a critical eye, his analytical mind already running through potential improvements and additions.

As he started rearranging the supplies, his movements were brisk and efficient. There was no room for doubt or hesitation in Todd's world. Not when there was work to be done.

Back upstairs, the TV screen was dark, but the news anchor's words still echoed in the room. Todd didn't need to hear them again. He knew what was coming. And he knew what he had to do.

He opened the cabinet beneath the kitchen sink, pulling out a large plastic tub. He handed it to Buttercup, who eagerly sniffed it before trotting back to the basement. Todd grabbed a second tub, following her with Bear at his side.

Together, they began the meticulous task of reinforcing their supplies, their movements synchronized like a well-oiled machine. The dogs followed Todd's lead, their instincts sharp and but always seemingly waiting for a treat. There was a storm coming. He could feel it in his bones.

As Todd worked, his mind drifted to his daughter. She was safe, living in a small town far from the chaos, or so he hoped. He made a mental note to call her, to warn her. But for now, there was work to be done.

The hours ticked by, the clock's steady rhythm a constant reminder of the time slipping away. Todd didn't falter, his resolve unshakable. He was a man on a mission, driven by instinct and intelligence, fueled by a burning need to protect what was his.

By the time the sun set, dark shadows filled the wilderness. Todd had organized his already impressive stockpile into a veritable fortress of supplies. He stood back, surveying his work with a critical eye. It was good, but it wasn't enough. It would never be enough.

Todd climbed the basement stairs, his steps heavy with fatigue and determination. The dogs trailed behind him, their tails wagging softly, their eyes watching his every move.

As he reached the top of the stairs, Todd paused, looking out the window towards the mountains. Complete dark sky. There was a storm coming, and it was going to be a big one. But he was ready. He had to be. There was no other choice.

With a last nod to the gathering darkness, Todd turned away from the window, his mind already racing with the next task. There was no time to waste.

The next few days brought little news. All bad. Todd was keeping up with the news at least twice a day to watch the development of the east coast disaster. As he sat on the couch, the TV's glare illuminating his furrowed brow another day in a row. Bear and Buttercup lay at his feet, their ears twitching as the news anchor's voice filled the room. The stock ticker at the bottom of the screen bled red, a grim parade of falling numbers.

"In a historic plunge today, the Dow Jones Industrial Average dropped over three thousand points, marking the worst single-day loss in U.S. market history," the anchor reported, her voice steady despite the grim news.

Todd's fingers drummed on the armrest, his gaze flicking from the television to the laptop balanced on his lap. Refreshing the page, he watched as world markets followed suit, a cascade of failures echoing across the globe. London, Frankfurt, Tokyo—all crumbling like dominoes.

His phone buzzed on the side table. A glance revealed his friend's concerned text: "You seeing this, bro?"

"Yeah," he typed back, his thumbs moving swiftly over the keyboard. "Been tracking it all day. Stay alert!"

Setting the phone down, he turned his attention back to the news. The anchor switched to a correspondent standing outside a bank, where a line of panicked customers snaked around the block.

"Reports are coming in from across the country," the correspondent said, microphone gripped tight. "People are rushing to withdraw their savings, fearing a collapse of the banking system."

Todd's jaw clenched. He'd seen this coming too, the writing on the wall clear as day. Governments printing money like it was going out of style, debt piled so high it blocked out the sun. Now the house of cards was tumbling down.

He stood, Bear and Buttercup lifting their heads in unison. "Come on, girls," he muttered, and headed for the garage.

Flipping on the fluorescent lights, Todd surveyed his preparations. Shelves lined the walls, filled with tools and gear. Gasoline cans sat in the corner, ready to provide power when the grid inevitably failed. He'd installed solar panels too, a backup for his backup.

Bear whined softly, giving a soft yelp. Absently, he scratched behind her ear, his mind racing. What else? What had he missed?

He pulled out a notebook from his back pocket, flipping through pages filled with his terrible handwriting. Inventory lists, plans for fortifying the house, evacuation routes. He'd spent years preparing, but there was always more to do.

Back inside, the news played on, a grim soundtrack to his preparations. "Protests have erupted in major cities worldwide," the anchor said, her composure finally slipping. "Citizens are demanding action from their governments as economies continue to spiral out of control."

Todd paused at the kitchen island, eyes locked on the screen. Fire and smoke billowed behind protesters clashing with riot police. He'd seen similar scenes before, but never on this scale. Never here, in the heart of America.

His phone rang, his friend's name flashing across the screen. He answered, putting him on speaker as he continued his work.

"Dude, Should I be scared?" he asked, voice uncertain. "They're talking about martial law, curfew s... What if—"

"No what-ifs," he cut him off, firm but gentle. "You know what to do. Grab your bug-out bag and check it. Make sure you've got enough supplies for a week. If things get any worse, head up to the ranch. You'll might wanna leave now before they start blocking roads."

Silence stretched over the line. Then, a, "Roger that."

Hanging up, Todd looked down at Bear and Buttercup, their dark eyes watching him intently. They sensed it too; the tension coiling around him like a spring ready to snap.

Over the next few days, the news worsened. Banks closed their doors, ATMs ran dry, and supermarkets were stripped bare by panicked shoppers. Todd watched it all unfold from his safe-haven, venturing out only once to top off his tanks with what little fuel remained at the station.

Each night, he called his daughter, checking in, ensuring she was safe. Each night, her voice grew more frightened, the chaos outside her city window escalating.

Meanwhile, Todd prepared. He double checked his wood supply, drew a plan for some type of motion sensors around the property, and checked his firearms, cleaning and oiling them until they gleamed under the harsh garage lights.

On the fourth day, the television showed pictures of all out civil unrest. Todd switched channels, but each one greeted him with different versions of the same story. Internet was blowing up with first person videos being uploaded of the chaos, his laptop displaying unsettling images that the major news channels weren't showing.

He sat back, staring at the screens. This was it. The storm is coming. Soon, the unrest would spread here, away from the cities and into the suburbs. And when it did, he'd be ready.

Standing, he whistled for Bear and Buttercup. Together, they stepped out into the cool evening air together, the sun setting behind the mountains. His property was isolated, chosen specifically for its distance from major roads and neighbors. Out here, it was just him, his dogs, and the wilderness.

Todd breathed deep, the scent of fresh air filling his lungs. Worried about the uncertainty. He'd fight to protect what was his, to survive the storm barreling towards them.

As darkness fell, Todd sat on the deck looking at the stars as he ran scenarios through his mind, his dogs by his side, waiting to see what the next day would bring.

Todd flipped between news channels, each showing different angles of the same nightmare. Smoke rose from downtown Colorado Springs, barely a hundred miles away. Crowds swarmed around gas stations, fists flying over the last drops of fuel. Outside a bank in Pueblo, a mob smashed through plate-glass windows.

Bear pressed against his leg while Buttercup paced by the window. Todd muted the TV, focusing on the police scanner app on his phone. Reports crackled through: looting at King Soopers, fights breaking out at Walmart, shots fired near the mall.

"Multiple units responding to First National," the dispatcher's voice cut through static. "Be advised, situation escalating. Large crowd, possible weapons."

His phone buzzed - a text from his daughter. "Dad, it's getting bad here. People are breaking into houses."

Todd's fingers hovered over the keypad. The roads between the two of them would be chaos. Assuming there was still gas to make the trip.

On the screen, a reporter ducked as a Molotov cocktail arced behind her, flames spreading across the pavement. The camera panned across faces twisted with desperation and rage. These weren't strangers anymore - these were people that lived there, normal folks driven to violence by fear.

The scanner squawked again. "All units, be advised. Multiple fires reported downtown. Fire response is delayed because of blocked streets."

Todd switched to another local station. Aerial footage showed the spread of violence from city centers into residential areas. Cars jammed the highways leading out of Colorado Springs, while others abandoned their vehicles to flee on foot.

The proximity hit him hard. He'd prepared for this, planned for it, but seeing it unfold so close to home made his mouth go dry. These weren't distant cities anymore - this was his backyard. The thin veneer of civilization was peeling away just miles from his front door.

Bear whined, pressing closer as Todd watched columns of smoke rise in the distance. The violence was spreading outward like ripples in a pond. Soon, those ripples would reach even the outskirts and beyond, bringing desperate people looking for food, fuel, shelter. Looking for places like his.

Todd's fingers moved across his phone's keypad. "Amy, where are you right now? Home?"

"Yeah, but Dad, I can hear gunshots. The Hendersons next door just packed their car and left."

"Listen carefully. Check your doors and windows. Stay away from them." Todd paced the living room while Bear and Buttercup tracked his movements. "How's your food situation?"

"I've got some stuff. Maybe three days' worth?"

"That's not enough. What about water?"

"Just what's in the tap." Her voice cracked. "Mom called. She wants me to come stay with her."

Todd stopped pacing. Carol's place sat twenty miles from the closest city, potentially far enough away from the spreading chaos of Amy's area. "Your mother's area would work. They have a good setup there on the farm. Can you get there?"

"I think so. They haven't shut down any roads yet."

"This isn't a drill, Amy. Remember what I told you about-"

"About bug-out bags and emergency protocols? Dad, I got it."

Todd pressed his forehead against the cool window glass. "Your life matters more than your things. Your mother's place is in the country. That community will take care of their own."

"Do you want me to come to you? I could-"

"No. Absolutely not. Streets aren't safe." Todd's free hand clenched. "Amy, you need to grab your supplies, and get into the car and leave as soon as possible?"

Silence stretched across the line.

"I would love to have you here with me, but I don't think there's enough time. We will both get through this. Try to call me when you get there."

"OK, Dad. You sure you are ok there by yourself?"

"I don't think I'll be alone for long. Jason and his family are heading up, I think."

"Well, that's good." Her voice steadied.

"Pack light. Essential documents, medications, warm clothes. Use the checklist we made."

"The one in the red folder?"

"That's right. And Amy? Don't tell anyone where you're going. No one," he stressed. "I love you."

"Love you too, dad."

Todd ended the call with Amy and stared out the large sliding glass door. All quiet for now. Bear stretched out at his feet while Buttercup kept watch by the stairs.

The isolation pressed in around him. Years of preparing, stockpiling, planning - all focused on self-sufficiency. But watching the chaos spread made him question his lone wolf strategy.

He pulled up the Blackhawk Ranch property map on his computer. Several parcels belonged to people he'd pegged as fellow preppers. The Knolls on Lot 47 had a greenhouse setup that rivaled his own. Old Jim Cooper, over on the east ridge, bred horses and knew every trail in the county. He'd seen other properties with chicken coops and such. Not to mention the crazy fella at the entrance to the Ranch. He seemed the type to have explosives.

All of them had skills. Resources. Knowledge that could be pooled.

Todd zoomed in on the satellite view on his laptop, studying the natural choke points between properties. Working together, they could establish a perimeter, coordinate watches, share specialized equipment. His engineering background could complement their agricultural expertise.

But cooperation meant trust. Trust meant vulnerability. Todd had spent years building systems that didn't rely on anyone else.

Bear lifted her head, sensing his unease. The dog's steady presence reminded him that even he hadn't chosen complete isolation. He'd always kept family close - Amy, his friends, the dogs. Maybe it was time to expand that circle carefully.

He picked up his ham radio, the one he used to monitor ranch-wide emergency frequencies. Several property owners maintained similar setups. They'd never discussed it openly, but they all knew why they had them. He was pretty sure no one had a license to operate, but everyone felt the same. If it had to be used, no one is going to care about someone not having a license to transmit.

His finger hovered over the transmit button. The strength in numbers argument made tactical sense. But once you let people in, you couldn't easily cut them loose. Every addition multiplied the complexity, the potential for conflict. He decided to hold off until he knew if Jason would make it or not.

The police scanner crackled with another report of violence in town. Soon, desperate people would look to the hills. To isolated properties like Blackhawk Ranch, where it was out of the way of chaos and wildlife was abundant.

Chapter 3

An Unexpected Visitor

The afternoon sun sat low through the pines as Todd tinkered with his ham radio setup in the garage. The constant hum of equipment filled the space, broken only by the occasional static crackle from the speakers. Bear and Buttercup lounged near the open garage door, their ears perking up at every chipmunk or bird that dared venture too close.

A sharp bark from Buttercup cut through the quiet. Bear jumped to her feet, the fur on her back raised. Both German Shepherds fixed their attention toward the winding dirt driveway leading to the property.

Todd set down his soldering iron. "What's got you two worked up?"

The dogs' low growls deepened as a figure emerged from between the trees. The person stumbled, catching themselves against a pine trunk. Their clothes hung in disarray, covered in dirt and pine needles.

"Bear, Buttercup, hold." Todd stepped between his dogs and the approaching stranger, keeping one hand on Bear's collar. The closer the figure got, the more details emerged - a middle-aged man with a scraggly beard, his face red from exertion and streaked with sweat.

The stranger raised a trembling hand. "Need... need help." His voice came out as a rasp.

"Stay right there." Todd maintained his grip on Bear, who continued to rumble deep in her chest. "Where'd you come from?"

"Other side... ridge." The man slumped against another tree. "Car broke down... tried to find... shortcut."

Todd studied the stranger's appearance - expensive hiking boots caked with mud, torn designer pants, a North Face jacket that had seen better days. Not your typical drifter, but experience had taught Todd to stay cautious.

"You're about ten miles from the main road. No shortcuts out here."

"Didn't know... got turned around." The man wiped his forehead with a dirty sleeve. "Phone's dead. I walked here."

Buttercup inched forward, her nose working overtime as she assessed the newcomer. Her posture remained rigid, but the aggressive growling became more subdued.

"What's your name?" Todd kept his tone neutral.

"James... James Marshall. Got a place... over on Elk Ridge." He gestured vaguely eastward. "New here. Moved in last month."

Todd remembered hearing about a new property sale on that side of Blackhawk Ranch but didn't recall there being an Elk Ridge. The dogs' behavior had shifted from protective to curious - a good sign, but not enough to lower his guard completely.

"You're looking rough, James. When's the last time you had water?"

"Few hours?" James swayed slightly. "Everything started looking the same after a while. These hills..."

"Stay put." Todd turned to his dogs. "Bear, Buttercup, watch." The shepherds sat at attention, eyes locked on James as Todd disappeared into the garage. He returned with a bottle of water and tossed it underhand.

James caught it with shaking hands, cracking it open and turned the bottle to the sky to drink. Water dribbled down his chin and neck.

"Easy there. Small sips, or you'll make yourself sick."

James lowered the bottle, gasping. "Thanks. Don't know what I was thinking, trying to cut through these woods."

"Nobody ever does." Todd crossed his arms. "Blackhawk's terrain isn't forgiving to folks who don't know it. Even with GPS, it's easy to get turned around in these trees."

"Learning that the hard way." James capped the water bottle, some color returning to his face. "Don't suppose you could point me in the right direction? Or maybe call someone?"

Todd glanced at his dogs, who had relaxed their stance but maintained their vigilant watch. Years of preparation had taught him to balance caution with humanity - and his instincts weren't raising any red flags about this particular stranger.

"Got a cellphone. You can make a call, but stay where you are for now. These dogs take their job seriously."

"Appreciate it." James managed a weak smile. "Promise I'm not usually this much of a mess. City folk still learning mountain life, I guess."

Todd reached for the cell phone, keeping one eye on their unexpected visitor. "Welcome to Colorado. First lesson's free - always carry extra water and a compass."

Todd tossed the phone in a gentle arc. James fumbled but caught it, his hands still unsteady. The dogs tracked the movement, their muscles tense and ready.

From his position by the garage door, Todd studied the stranger's body language as James punched in numbers. The way James held himself, his mannerisms, the subtle tells - Todd's instinct kicked in automatically. The expensive clothes suggested money, but the wear patterns showed they weren't just for show. Working hands, despite the manicured appearance. A wedding ring. The slight favor of his left leg hinted at an old injury.

James spoke into the phone, his voice clearer now. "Hey, it's me. Yeah, I'm okay. Got lost in the woods." He paused, listening. "No, I'm at..." He looked at Todd questioningly.

"The last cul-de-sac," Todd supplied, noting how James' posture shifted - relief mixed with embarrassment rather than the calculation of someone marking a target. However, not giving out too much detail was prudent at this point.

"The last cul-de-sac," James repeated into the phone. "Some guy named Todd and his dogs found me. Can you..." Another pause. "Yeah, that'd be great. Thanks." James gently tossed the phone back to Todd, the dog's heads following the arc.

Bear's tail wagged slightly - the first actual sign of acceptance from either dog. Buttercup maintained her guard position, but had settled into a more relaxed stance. Todd had learned to trust their judgment over the years. Dogs sensed things humans missed.

The whole situation pulled at Todd's analytical mind. A new neighbor, lost in the woods, stumbling onto his property - it could be coincidence or something more. The timing, with everything else going on in the world, made him wary. But his gut wasn't screaming danger, just urging caution.

Todd kept his distance, one hand resting casually near his concealed holster, while his mind ran through scenarios and contingencies. The dogs would give warning if anything felt wrong. For now, he'd watch and wait, gathering more data before deciding how to handle this unexpected addition to his carefully maintained world.

Buttercup's ears suddenly flattened against her head. The change came without warning - one moment relaxed, the next rigid with tension. Bear's hair rose, a deep growl rumbling from her chest.

James shifted his weight, reaching into his jacket pocket. The motion sent both dogs into a frenzy of barking and snarling, their bodies coiled like springs.

"Whoa, easy." Todd's hand tightened on his holster. "Whatever you're reaching for, do it slow."

James froze, his hand still inside his jacket. Sweat beaded on his forehead despite the cool mountain air. "Just getting my wallet-"

"Leave it where it is." Todd's voice hardened. Bear lunged forward, stopped only by Todd's sharp command. "Dogs don't react like this to wallets."

The change in James was subtle, but unmistakable. The exhausted stumble vanished from his posture. His eyes darted between Todd and the dogs, calculating.

"Look, there's been a misunderstanding-"

Buttercup cut him off with a savage bark, her teeth bared. She positioned herself between Todd and James; her muscled body coiled and ready.

"Only misunderstanding is you thinking my dogs wouldn't notice." Todd stepped back, creating distance. "Bear, Buttercup, hold position."

James' hand remained in his jacket, his friendly demeanor evaporating like morning dew. "Your dogs are just spooked. I can explain-"

Todd looked at his phone. "The phone call wasn't real." Todd's mind raced through the signs he'd missed. "You never actually dialed."

A thin smile crossed James' face. "Observant."

Bear's growl deepened, her black fur standing on end. Buttercup matched her sister's aggression, both dogs forming a barrier between Todd and the stranger, who was no longer stumbling or confused.

Todd's hand moved in one fluid motion, drawing his pistol from its holster. The familiar weight settled into his grip as he leveled it at James's chest.

"Take your hand out of that jacket. Slow." Todd's voice carried the weight of his military years. "Whatever you're reaching for stays where it is."

James's eyes narrowed, focusing on the pistol's barrel. His hand emerged empty, held palm-out at shoulder level. The friendly mask had completely fallen away, revealing cold calculation beneath.

"Back up." Todd shifted his stance, maintaining his sight picture. "You're going to turn around and walk back the way you came."

"This isn't necessary." James took a step backward, his boots crunching on pine needles. "We could have a profitable conversation-"

Bear's snarl cut through his words. Both shepherds advanced with their handler, maintaining their protective formation.

"Eight more steps." Todd's trigger finger rested along the frame, muscle memory from countless hours on his range. "Whatever you're selling, I'm not buying."

James continued his retreat, each step measured and precise - not the movements of someone who'd been lost in the woods. His expensive hiking boots barely made a sound on the gravel.

"You're making a mistake." James' voice dropped an octave, all pretense gone. "This property has potential. The location, the resources - people would pay well to be here."

"No thanks," Todd advanced, matching James' pace. "Keep moving."

A branch snapped under James's foot. His hand twitched toward his jacket again, but Buttercup's warning growl froze him in place.

"Six." Todd's aim never wavered. "Touch that jacket again. You'll leave here with more holes than you arrived with."

James's lips curled into a cold smile. "You're not the only one who's prepared, Todd. There are others who've noticed this place."

"I'm running out of patience."

"Think about it. The world's changing. When things fall apart, places like this will be worth-"

Todd squeezed off a round, sending dirt spraying next to James' foot. The gunshot echoed through the trees, setting birds to flight.

"Next one won't miss."

James backpedaled faster, his composure cracking. Sweat darkened his designer jacket despite the cool mountain air.

"You're dead wrong if you think more people ain't coming." James' voice carried equal parts fury and frustration.

Bear lunged forward, her teeth snapping inches from James's leg. He stumbled backward, catching himself against a pine trunk.

"One more word, and I let them do what they want to do."

The dogs moved like shadows, their muscled bodies coiled with barely contained aggression. James glanced between them and Todd's unwavering pistol.

James took his final step back onto the road, his expensive boots now coated in genuine mountain dirt. The facade of the lost hiker had completely dissolved, leaving something harder and more dangerous in its place.

"I'll be back." His words carried the weight of a promise.

Todd's finger tightened fractionally on the trigger. "Turn around. Walk away. Don't look back."

James held his gaze for one more moment, calculation and rage warring in his expression. Then he turned, his movements stiff with suppressed anger, and began walking down the road.

Todd maintained his aim until James's figure disappeared as he went around the curve at the top of the hill. Bear and Buttercup remained rigid, their ears forward, tracking sounds Todd couldn't hear.

The afternoon sun had dipped lower. The forest seemed to hold its breath, waiting to see if the intruder would truly leave or if this was just the opening move in a longer game. Todd knew he had to be careful of his surroundings now and expect the unexpected.

As he stood there reflecting on the perceived threat. His mind wondered what he would have done if he'd shot James. The morbid thought of having to dispose of him somewhere on the property made Todd's mind race about where and how.

Chapter 4

TWO IS BETTER THAN ONE

A white Chevy Suburban and a heavy-duty truck pulled up and stopped in front of Todd Blodsey's residence. Jason switched off the engine, exhaling as he leaned back in the driver's seat. His wife, Bobbie, did likewise, shifting the Suburban into park behind Jason's truck. She glanced over from the driver's side, dark circles visible under her eyes. In the rear, their five children stirred, awakening from a restless sleep.

Todd stood on his upper deck, his hair shimmering in the late afternoon sunlight as he looked down. He stood slightly hunched, fatigue evident in his posture. Bear and Buttercup, his German Shepherds, flanked him, barking incessantly. Todd observed the family exiting their vehicles, his sharp gaze taking in their exhausted expressions and the dust-coated car.

"Hey!," Jason nodded, too weary to say more than a single word.

Todd descended the stairs and stepped out through the basement door, the dogs rushing to greet them. "Jason. You made it." He looked at Bobbie, at the kids, and back to Jason. "All of you."

Bobbie offered him a small smile. "Thank goodness."

Jason ran a hand through his thinning hair. "It was tough, man. The roads... they weren't safe."

Todd's eyes narrowed. "Come inside. You must be hungry." He led them in, the dogs following closely.

The house was warm, filled with an aroma of meat on the dehydrator. Bobbie directed the children to the bathroom to wash up, then everyone gathered around the kitchen table. He served them his renowned hotdogs and chips, watching with satisfaction as they ate.

Jason swallowed a mouthful, following it with a sip of bottled water. "We saw some terrible things, Todd. Gangs on the highways, people desperate for food and gas."

Todd leaned back in his chair, arms crossed. "Tell me."

Jason looked at Bobbie, then back to Todd. "We left Texas just in time. The cities were in chaos. Stores looted, hospitals overflowing. We stuck to the back roads when we could. But even those weren't safe. The rural folks are starting to block off the farm-to-market roads too. And they have the equipment to do it."

Bobbie added, "We saw a group of men attacking another family. They were taking their car, their supplies..." she trailed off, shuddering.

Jason placed a comforting hand on her shoulder. "We managed to avoid them, but it was close. Too close."

Todd's expression darkened. "And the kids? How did they handle it?"

Hyden, Bruce, and Jake looked up at the mention, their eyes wide. Jake, at 16, tapped his chest. "I was ready. I was ready to fire some shots."

Todd raised an eyebrow. "And you, Hyden?"

Hyden, older and wiser, pursed his lips. "I was a little scared. But I was ready if something happened. So was Bruce." Bruce nodded in agreement.

Jason continued, "We ran into a roadblock outside of Sweetwater. Local police, trying to keep people out. They had rifles and all the gear. Crazy."

Bobbie's voice was barely above a whisper. "They told us to turn back. Said they couldn't take in any more refugees. Jason had to lead us off-road to get around them."

Todd's jaw tightened, his gaze hardening. "They're turning people away? Damn smart. It's going to get ugly out there."

Jason nodded, his expression grave. "We lost a tire driving through a field. Had to change it while the boys kept watch with the rifle. They were steady, reliable." He looked at his sons, pride shining in his eyes. Jason glanced over at Bobbie, his voice softening. "She was amazing, Todd. Never complained, never faltered. Followed perfectly behind me, kept the kids calm and quiet."

Todd looked at Bobbie, his gaze filled with newfound respect. "You did well, Bobbie. Both of you. I'm glad you made it. We'll be a lot safer together."

Jason looked around the cozy kitchen, taking in the warmth and safety it offered, then back to Todd. "What's the situation here? Is the property getting secured?"

Todd nodded, his expression serious. "A little slower than I'd like. But we've got a good group here, people looking out for each other. I thought about a neighborhood watch with the neighbors, pooling resources. It may not be perfect, but would be a start. I figured I'd wait to see if you made it before reaching out on the radio. Now that you're here, let's give it some thought."

The family began to settle into their rooms, all five kids barely able to keep their eyes open. Todd and Jason watched them go, a mix of relief and concern on their faces. Bear came over and jumped up between them on the couch, her enormous frame forcing Jason to move seats with a chuckle.

After Bobbie and the kids had settled in, Todd and Jason retreated to the deck to sit and talk under the starlit night. Jason recounted the trip, sharing the genuine dangers that only he had noticed or seen. The treacherous roads filled with desperate people, cities descending into chaos. Todd sighed heavily, running a hand through his thick head of hair. He shared his experience with the stranger that showed up with Jason. They both had a feeling that things would get worse before they got better.

Todd reached into his pocket and produced a relaxant from a small plastic cylinder, offering it to Jason. Jason took it with a grateful smile, hoping there was a supply of them. But for tonight, they were safe. And in that moment, that was enough.

Dawn crept over Outlook Ridge, painting the mountains to the west in harsh relief. Todd stepped onto his front deck, Bear and Buttercup flanking him. The morning air carried the acrid scent of wet pine trees.

Jason emerged from the house, a notepad in hand. "We need to catalog everything we've got. Food, water, ammunition-"

"Already ahead of you." Todd pulled out his own worn leather journal. "Been keeping inventory since day one. But we should double-check, account for what we used yesterday."

The two men moved through Todd's property with military precision, years of thinking of this day clear in their methodical approach. They started with the main house, checking the windows and doors for any compromise.

"Water pumps are good," Jason called from the basement, checking the breakers. "Your well system's holding up."

"Solar panels are intact too." Todd flipped through his notebook. "Battery bank's at eighty-seven percent. We can run essentials for weeks, maybe months, if we're careful."

As they made their way to the bunker, Bear's ears perked up, and she trotted ahead. Todd followed her gaze but saw only the normalcy.

"Ammo count?" Jason looking at the list.

"About twenty-five thousand rounds for the ARs, plenty of stuff for the handguns. Plus another two thousand rounds loose of shotgun and whatnot." Todd moved to his storage room. "Foods where we might have issues long-term. I've got six months' worth. We might could get more out of it if we start rationing now."

Jason nodded, making notes. "We could stretch it to maybe nine months between us if Bobbie is in charge. She can make anything taste good. Your greenhouse still looks good."

They stepped outside to inspect the garden beds and greenhouse. Todd's years of preparation had yielded a productive setup - tomatoes, peppers, cannabis, and leafy greens grew in neat rows.

"Irrigation system's automated," Todd explained, checking the soil moisture. "But we'll need to protect it. Keeping the wild animals away is one thing. Keeping people away when they are desperate and hungry is another story."

Jason chuckled, "At this point, we shoot on sight. Speaking of which-" he pointed to a fencepost on the garden where a section of wood had splintered. "Is that new?"

Todd whistled, and Buttercup bounded over. "Good girl, keep watch." He examined the damage. "Someone must have tested it last night. Didn't get through the fence, though. Looks like they grabbed what they could through the fence."

"We should set up a patrol schedule." Jason sketched a quick diagram. "Four-hour shifts, alternating. Put the two older boys on it and the dogs can help."

They moved to the garage where Todd's workshop occupied half the space. Workbenches lined the walls, tools organized with precision. A ham radio sat in one corner, its display dark.

"Still no signals?" Jason asked.

Todd shook his head. "Nothing but static since yesterday morning. Either the repeaters are down, or-"

"Or no one's broadcasting." Jason stepped out and scanned the nearby hills where he knew houses to be. "Your neighbors' houses are empty. Robert's family's gone. The old vet's place up the hill also looks empty."

"They all bugged out." Todd checked his list again. "Fuel situation's decent. Five hundred gallons of diesel, three hundred of gas. Both treated with stabilizer."

"Vehicle status?"

"My truck's ready, full tank. Got the bug-out trailer positioned to be hitched, just in case. Your vehicles have three-quarters."

They spent the next hour checking the perimeter, noting vulnerable points and planning defensive positions. The dogs followed their patrol, alert to every sound.

"Medical supplies?" Jason seemed to be just naming things out as they came to mind.

"Full trauma kits, antibiotics, basic surgical supplies." Todd stopped to think. "Even got some dental equipment. Figure if things go south long enough, we might need it."

"Oh geez. I'm betting I'll be the first one getting a tooth pulled. I knew I should have taken care of this cavity sooner. Your prepper paranoia's paying off."

"Not paranoia if they're really out to get you." Todd's humor made Jason laugh, as most of the things Todd said made him at least chuckle. He'd heard every punch line a million times, but to Jason, it was still funny.

Back in the kitchen, they spread their notes across the table. Maps of the area covered one end, marked with potential escape routes and rally points.

"We've got shelter, security, water, food for months." Jason tapped his pen against the paper. "Power, medical supplies, communications capability, even if it's not useful right now."

"Question is, do we take over the house on the hill?" Todd watched Bear's reaction to something outside - just a bird this time.

"Well, I think we give it another day or two. If they don't show up by then, chances are they won't be showing up at all with all the roadblocks taking place. That is the perfect spot to snipe down the road. We'd be able to see someone coming down the roadway before they get here." Jason circled their location on the map. "But we need to plan for variables. More people showing up. More supplies if we can, weather changes and such. Have you heard from our other friends?"

"Nope. Tried calling them. I figure they'd either show up like you did, or try to weather it out at home. They have supplies and are out of the city. Hopefully, it won't get too bad there." Todd marked potential cache locations on the map. "We should distribute supplies, not keep everything in one place. Set up some backup positions in case we have to evacuate the house, or re-take it in the event we get pushed out."

Todd and Jason spent the next hour marking potential cache locations on their maps. The weight of their conversations wasn't lost on them. This wasn't a planning session for 'what-ifs'. This was now potentially life or death.

Chapter 5

Cut Off from the World

The next morning, as the sun peeked over the horizon, Todd Blodsey reached for his iPhone. The screen's cold glow illuminated the dimly lit kitchen, casting an eerie blue hue on his bushy blonde hair. He checked for any signal, but there were no bars to be seen. He tapped the screen, trying to refresh the signal, but to no avail.

Jason walked into the kitchen, pouring himself a cup of coffee. "Still out?" he asked, noticing Todd's furrowed brow.

Todd nodded, setting the phone down on the counter with a sigh. "Could be the towers or the lines. Who knows?"

Jason handed Todd a steaming mug of coffee. "Let's check the radio," he suggested, his hand running through his mostly gray hair.

The two men huddled around the old AM/FM set, Todd carefully twisting the dial. The static crackled through the speaker, the needle jumping from one end of the spectrum to the other. They listened intently, but there were no voices or music, just the unnerving sound of white noise.

Jason leaned back in his chair, a worried look etched on his face. "That's not good," he muttered.

Todd switched to the shortwave bands, his notebook filled with frequencies open beside him. He tried each one, pausing and listening carefully. Still, there was nothing but static. He flipped through the pages, his brow furrowing further as he realized they were completely cut off from the outside world.

"Internet?" Todd asked, turning to Jason.

Jason grabbed his laptop from the counter, flipping it open. "Satellite Internet is still working," he said, "But..." He clicked through his bookmarks, shaking his head. "News sites aren't updating. Last posts are from two days ago."

Todd leaned over Jason's shoulder, scanning the headlines. "That's when things started getting really bad," he said, his voice barely above a whisper.

Jason clicked on a few more sites, checking social media and forums. "Some people are posting, but it's all local stuff. Nothing big. Nothing worldwide."

Todd leaned against the counter, sipping his coffee as he tried to process the information. "We're cut off then," he said finally.

"Looks like it," Jason agreed, his eyes scanning the screen. "No phone, no radio, no news. We're on our own."

Todd let out a deep sigh, his mind racing as he tried to come up with a plan. He had always been a prepper at heart, believing in being prepared in the event society breaks down. But now it was real. This was something he never wanted to see happen.

He looked over at Jason, his eyes filled with determination. "We'll figure this out," he said, his voice steady. "We've talked about this for years. Just never thought it would actually happen. Honestly."

Bear whined, nudging Todd's hand. He scratched her ears, looking out the window at the empty road. "Guess we need to focus on what we can control. Ourselves. This place."

Jason closed the laptop. "Agreed. Let's get to work."

Todd stared into his coffee, the dark liquid reflecting fragments of memories from the past week's news broadcasts. "Remember that report about the power grid failures in California?"

"The cascading blackouts." Jason leaned back in his chair, his coffee half gone. "Started in San Francisco, spread down the coast."

"Then Chicago went dark." Todd traced the rim of his mug. "New York right after. No explanations, just darkness."

Bear's nails clicked against the floor as she paced between them, her black coat blending with the shadows in the kitchen corners.

"The markets hit the breakers the day before that and completely crashed the next day." Jason's fingers drummed against the table. "All of them. Worldwide."

"Banks froze accounts." Todd stood, walking to the window. The morning sun beaming across his property, the tree wall shining in the distance. "People couldn't access their money, which means ATMs stop working..."

"The riots started that night." Jason's voice dropped. "Los Angeles, Houston, Miami. I saw that footage, and that's when we decided to come up."

Todd turned back to his friend. "Police couldn't contain it. National Guard deployed in probably all the states."

"Even Hawaii." Jason pulled out his phone, checked the screen again. Still dead. "Georgia called them in right before everything went quiet."

Todd disappeared to his office, returning with a map spread across the kitchen table. Red marks dotted major cities, each one representing a reported incident. "Look at the pattern."

Jason leaned forward, studying the marks. "Coastal areas first. Then inland. Moving like-"

"Like a wave." Todd circled several points with his finger. "These blackouts are putting stress on all the power grids because they are all interconnected. I'm shocked we still have power."

"Yep, even Texas' infrastructure is connected now." Jason traced lines between the states. "If a large system fails, the entire system fails. I bet they wouldn't design it like now."

Bear growled low, her ears perked toward the window. Todd glanced outside but saw only empty fields.

"We're twenty miles from the nearest town, and sixty from a city of any size." Todd pulled another map from his office, this one showing local topography. "Got the solar panels, well water, propane, the garden, several generators. We should be able to last months if needed."

"Assuming no one comes looking." Jason replied with a non-asked for assessment. "These roads are the only way in or out. Easy to monitor, easy to defend."

"After that guy just walked up, I have some wireless cameras set up on the driveway entrance, but they are battery powered, so we'll have to keep charging them." Todd clicked through feeds on his tablet, showing the property's perimeter. "Motion sensors too. Nothing gets near the house without us knowing, unless they come through the thickets. If they do, we should hear them cursing from all the thorns." They both chuckled, knowing that the thorns are brutal when it's mixed in with scrub oak.

Bear's growl turned to a bark, sharp and alert. Both men froze, listening. The sound echoed once, then the silence returned.

"Probably deer." Todd checked the app on his iPhone. "Nothing on the sensors."

"Still." Jason moved to the window, scanning the tree line. "Might want to start regular patrols. Set up a schedule."

"Yeah, every few hours, maybe?" Todd grabbed a notepad, sketching out a rotation. "Or once in the morning, one before dark?"

"Man, staying up here is like old times." Jason's mouth tightened into a grim smile. "Never thought we'd have to actually be doing this."

"Yeah, who would have thought?"

Chapter 6

Weathering the First Storm

G ray clouds loomed over Outlook Ridge as Todd peered through his workshop window, his weathered hands resting on the worn wooden workbench. The temperature had dropped twenty degrees since sunrise, and the clouds building up over the mountains showed the first winter storm was about to roll in. His German Shepherds, Bear and Buttercup, paced restlessly behind him, their nails clicking against the concrete floor as they sensed the changing weather.

"By the looks of it, I'd say we've got about four hours before it hits." Todd traced his finger at arm's distance across the mountain outline in the distance, his engineering mind already calculating the work ahead. He'd seen enough Colorado winters to read the signs. "That greenhouse isn't going to heat itself." His preparations for winter had been methodical, as always, but there were always last-minute adjustments to be made to ensure his carefully cultivated plants would survive the coming freeze.

Jason stood at the workbench, measuring lengths of steel pipe with practiced precision, his weathered hands steady on the tape measure. "Good thing you have those old fifty-five-gallon drums from the scrapyard. Should make decent wood stoves once we're done with them. Better heat distribution than those fancy store-bought ones, if you ask me."

"Bear, get out of there!" Todd shooed his German Shepherd away from a pile of scrap metal, his voice carrying equal parts concern and exasperation. "Those damn dogs are so obsessed with mice. Plus, the last thing we need is for one of them to cut their paw on scrap metal. Come on, girl, leave the rodents alone for now."

The two men worked in sync, years of friendship evident in their movements, a well-oiled machine born from decades of collaboration. Jason marked cutting lines on the first drum with a white grease pencil, double-checking his measurements, while Todd prepped the plasma cutter, adjusting the settings with the expertise that came from years of metalwork. The familiar scent of metal and machine oil filled the workshop as they settled into their routine.

"Remember that winter in 2004 or so?" Todd positioned the fifty-five-gallon drum for the first cut, his weathered hands steady on the metal surface. "Depot shut down, cows froze, that was a bad one. I hope this one isn't like that."

"Yeah, remember when Dan shut the Depot down because of the pending blizzard, and the following day was like 70 degrees?" Jason and Todd laughed hard, their voices echoing off the workshop walls. "Good ol' Dan. He never lived that one down."

The plasma cutter sliced through steel like butter, sending brilliant orange sparks cascading to the concrete floor in mesmerizing patterns. Todd carved out the door panel with practiced ease, the years of metalwork clear in his precise movements, then moved to the top for the chimney hole. The acrid smell of hot metal filled their nostrils.

"Bobby's going to kill me if these tomatoes don't make it through winter." Jason test-fitted the heavy-duty hinges against the freshly cut edge, checking the alignment carefully. "She's already planned our whole spring garden. Got the seed catalogs spread all over the kitchen table, marking everything with sticky notes like she's planning an invasion."

"Bobbie always was the optimistic type." Todd grabbed his angle grinder, checking the worn disc before flipping the power switch. "Need to smooth these edges before someone loses a finger. Last thing we need is for someone to get an infection. A simple cut could get infected, then we'd have a real problem."

Metal shrieked against metal as Todd worked the rough cuts, sending a fresh shower of sparks dancing across his heavy leather apron. Outside, Buttercup's deep, insistent bark echoed across the property, followed by a second, more urgent volley.

"Buttercup has spotted something." Jason stepped out of the garage, wiping tiny his face with his sleeve as he peer into the gathering gloom.

"Probably that mountain lion again. She's been hanging around since the deer moved down from higher ground." Todd switched tools, reaching for his smaller file. "Hand me that quarter-inch plate. We need air control on these things if we want them to burn efficiently through the night."

They fabricated damper plates for both stoves, adjusting the mechanisms until they moved smooth as silk, testing and retesting the action. The workshop filled with the sharp tang of hot metal and grinding dust, the air thick with the scent of their labor.

"How's Amy doing with that new job?" Jason drilled mounting holes for the legs, carefully measuring each mark twice before punching the bit through.

"Teaching suits her. Kids actually pay attention when she talks about engineering." Todd wiped sweat from his brow with a shop rag that had seen better days. "Unlike her old man - I could never get interested in teaching anyone anything. I just can't suffer fools. Never had the patience for it."

The wind picked up outside, rattling the shop's metal siding like someone shaking a tin can. Todd checked his watch, frowning at the darkening sky visible through the high windows.

"Storm's moving faster than predicted. We need to get these mounted before the snow hits, or we'll be doing this in the dark with flashlights."

They loaded the finished wood-burning stoves onto Todd's mud-spattered ATV, securing them with heavy-duty straps. Bear and Buttercup bounded alongside as they drove to the greenhouse, their breath visible in puffs of white vapor in the cooling air, paws kicking up loose gravel from the path.

"You really think we can keep it above freezing in there?" Jason helped unload the first stove, grunting with the effort as they maneuvered the heavy steel unit down from the cargo bed.

"These walls are double-layered polycarbonate." Todd positioned the unit carefully in the corner, checking its level with practiced eyes. "With both stoves running, we should maintain sixty degrees, easy. Maybe even warmer on sunny days."

They anchored the stoves to bricks that he had salvaged from his previous job site, then ran galvanized pipe through carefully measured holes in the greenhouse wall for the chimneys. Jason stacked split oak methodically near each unit, making sure the wood was elevated off the damp ground, while Todd meticulously checked the seals around the pipe penetrations with a bead of high-temperature silicone.

"Where the hell are your kids? Why aren't they doing this?" Todd said, slightly short of breath.

"Thought you said you hated to teach? We need to test these before the temperature drops." Jason crumpled the newspaper for kindling. "Last thing we want is smoke backing up into the growing space."

The first stove caught quickly, drawing air through the damper with a healthy roar that echoed softly in the enclosed space. Heat radiated from the barrel's surface, creating a warm pocket in the corner that made the nearby seedlings rustle slightly in the rising air current. They repeated the process with the second unit, moving with the practiced efficiency of longtime collaborators.

"There's your thermal zone." Todd pointed to the natural air circulation developing between the stoves, his engineering mindset showing in his satisfied expression. "Hot air rises, creates convection current. Basic thermodynamics. See how it's already affecting the humidity?"

"Always the engineer." Jason adjusted both dampers to quarter-open, his movements precise and deliberate. "Bobbie would say we're overthinking it. Do you think we are over engineering it?"

"Bobbie's never had to calculate heat loss through transparent surfaces." Todd checked the thermometer mounted between the plant beds, squinting at the reading through his glasses. "We'll need to feed these every four hours to maintain temperature. Better set up a rotation schedule."

The first snowflakes drifted past the greenhouse panels, tiny white crystals dancing in the strengthening wind. Bear pressed her nose against the polycarbonate, her black form a stark contrast as she watched the white specks accumulate with typical canine fascination.

"Think we'll get much accumulation?" Jason stacked the last of the firewood, arranging it with precision against the wall.

"Maybe a few inches, but I've been wrong before." Todd brushed woodchips from his jacket, glancing up at the darkening sky through the greenhouse panels. "At least the tomatoes will survive. Might even get some peppers through if we're lucky."

"Bobbie will be pleased." Jason patted the nearest stove, his calloused hand lingering on the warm metal surface. "She hates cold weather. Being able to spend time in the greenhouse with it heated will make her day."

"Better overboard than underwater." Todd checked the stove temperatures one last time, methodically noting the readings on each gauge. "Speaking of which, we should get that rainwater collection system set up before spring. Those fifty-five-gallon drums aren't doing us much good just sitting empty."

"Agreed," Jason nodded, already mentally calculating the work involved. "Could probably knock it out this weekend if the weather holds."

Todd and Jason made their way back to the shop, their boots crunching against the dirt and gravel. Buttercup maintained her vigilant post by the entrance, her ears perked forward and tail straight as she watched the tree line and sniffed the air for any signs of strangeness. Her black and tan coat ruffled slightly in the increasing wind.

Chapter 7

Signs Of Trouble

Todd wiped sweat from his brow as he and Jason crested the final hill leading to the vacant house that sat on a hill above them to the south. The afternoon sun cast shadows across the overgrown hillside, highlighting the property's terrain.

"Perfect vantage point." Todd pointed to where the main road curved around the base of the hill. "You can see vehicles approaching for at least a mile."

Jason nodded, scanning the terrain through narrowed eyes. "Good natural barriers, too. That thicket on the south side would slow down anyone trying to come up on foot."

The two men picked their way through scrub oak toward the weathered, one-story structure. The house sat empty almost all year, expect for about two weeks in the summer. A small house, but built well.

"Water tank is intact." Todd knocked against one of the support posts on the wraparound porch. "No mold that I can see."

"How long has it been empty?"

"Going on five months now. The old man passed, I think, and none of his kids wanted the place. Too remote for most folks' taste. They are from way out of state. Even they wanted to be here, it's probably too late."

Jason circled to the back of the house, boots crunching on gravel. "Got a sewer holding tank?"

"Yeah, it's probably empty, which is good. Place looks pretty secure, shutters on the windows, solid doors." Todd joined his friend at the rear of the property. "A few solar panels wouldn't be hard to install on that south-facing roof."

"Defensible position." Jason gestured to the rolling hills that surrounded them. "High ground, clear fields of fire. Anyone trying to approach would be completely exposed."

Todd pulled out a small pair of binoculars and studied the valley below. "Main road's the only real access point unless someone knows these hills well. We could set up a type of trip wire for a vehicle, early warning system."

"What about the basement?"

"No basement, but the garage has plenty of storage space."

They made their way down the overgrown path to the garage door. Todd yanked on the handle, but it had a padlock on the latch.

"We need some bolt cutters." He walked around the water tank. "But check this out."

He pointed to the tank and roof like, pointing as if drawing in mid air.

"We could put a rain water runoff system on the roof and tie it into the cistern." Todd's voice filled with hope. "Natural rain feeds can feed the cistern in the rainy season. Previous owner wasn't big on self-sufficiency."

"Yeah, this was a summer get-a-way." Jason ran his hand along the back of neck to remove an insect. "We could actually use this as one of the caches in the event we have to retreat."

"Living space looks good." Trying to peer through the window, hands coupled to the window to block the light. "The structure's sound. New windows, insulation, reinforced doors - place would make a good defensive position."

Jason pulled out a topographical map of the entire ranch and spread it across the back of Todd's ATV. "Show me those alternate routes you mentioned."

Todd traced his finger along a faint line. "Old jeep road here connects to Forest Service land through the peaks, I think. There's also an escape route that the ranch put in a few years back in the event folks had to escape a forest fire. The problem is, it's basically a back door. If someone wanted to, they could drive up from the highway and bypass the main entrance."

"Speaking of that, you think it would be wise to spend the gas to talk to the crazy guy that owns the first lot? Would love to understand what he's doing to prepare for unwanted visitors." Jason made several notations on the map. "What about the other neighbors, like the brick house on the turn a mile from here?"

"Nearest one's three miles that way." Todd pointed east. "Retired couple, keep to themselves. Next closest is down in the valley, but you can't see their place from here. There's also a few more on the other side of this hill to the south. I think it would be worth our while to ride down the road to have a look around and see what ol' crazy Italian is doing at the entrance."

"Great, I'll bring a pair of pliers with us," Jason said, laughing. They both chuckled at the inside joke.

They spent the next hour walking the property perimeter, noting natural choke points and discussing potential security measures. The sun had dropped considerably when they finally returned to the ATV.

"Just a matter of time before the power goes off on these lines." Todd squinted at the weathered utility pole. "Once it does, I don't expect it to come back on for a while."

"Been thinking about the wind turbine." Todd sketched a quick diagram in his notebook. "Ridge gets good airflow year-round. Combine that with solar, might give us all the power we need in the winter when the sun is behind the clouds for days on end."

Jason nodded, taking one last look at the house silhouetted against the darkening sky. "Place is a good spot. Real potential. Have to think about manning it. In a way, I hope a few more of our friends show up. It's going to take about ten men to really secure this place comfortably. Otherwise, we might have to depend on the older boys. I just don't know about them in that position."

"That's what I was thinking." Todd folded his notebook and tucked it away into his flannel shirt. "Just need to continue to spitball it and think about a plan."

The morning sun was peaking over the horizon to the east, lighting just the tips of the distant mountain peaks to the west. Todd pulled out tactical vests from a storage locker. The weight of the Kevlar vest brought thoughts of how serious things are getting. He tossed one to Jason, who caught it with practiced ease.

"Just like Iraq." Jason slipped the vest over his head, adjusting the straps with muscle memory that hadn't faded in the fifteen years since that deployment.

Todd grabbed his AR-15 from the gun safe, along with extra magazines. "Never thought we'd be gearing up like this on American soil." He handed Jason four clips of his short-barreled assault rifle. Jason smacked each clip on the back of the ATV before putting them in his vest front pockets. Todd doubled checked the pistol on his hip while Jason racked his 10mm, dropped the hammer and slipped it back into the leg holster he was wearing on his right leg.

"World's gone crazy." Todd checked the chamber of his AR-15, his movements precise. "I hope we don't need all this firepower for a reconnaissance run. If we do, it's probably going to be a bad day."

Jason pulled a med kit from his prep supplies and secured it to his vest. "Rather have it and not need it. Those gunshots we heard last night weren't exactly welcoming. I'm really hoping someone was just shooting a deer and not your neighbors."

"Point taken." Todd zipped up his vest. "But two armed men on an ATV might draw attention that we don't want."

"Better than being sitting ducks." Jason grabbed a pair of binoculars and stuffed them in a side pocket. "We stick to the road, keep our distance from any structures. I just hope we don't look gay riding this thing together."

The ATV's engine rumbled to life in the crisp morning air. Bobbie, Bear and Buttercup watched from the upper deck, their ears perked forward at the familiar sound. Even though it was a common theme for Todd to ride around alone, Bear always took an exception any time she wasn't invited and let it be known through a series of pleading barks.

"Shuuuut Uuup!," Todd commanded in musical tones. The shepherds sat obediently, but their whines made clear their disapproval of being left behind.

Jason climbed on behind Todd, his rifle slung across his back. "Your dogs giving us the guilt trip?"

"They'll get over it. Rather not have them giving away our position if we need to stay quiet."

"By the way, that's my pistol you feel," Jason whispering in Todd's ear.

"Yeah, I figured. Otherwise, I wouldn't have felt it at all." The statement made them laugh. A slight break from the seriousness of the situation.

The ATV rolled down the gravel driveway, Todd keeping the speed low to minimize the noise. Morning dew sparkled on the grass, and birds called from the trees - nature carrying on as if nothing had changed. But everything had changed.

"Stop." Jason tapped Todd's shoulder. "Movement in those trees."

Todd cut the engine, and they sat motionless. A deer emerged from the forest edge, its tail flicking as it grazed. Both men released held breaths.

"Jumpy as hell," Jason muttered.

"Can you blame us?"

They continued down the road, Todd staying close to the right side of the road as if there were a ton of cars on the road. The morning silence felt heavy, broken only by the ATV's low rumble and the crunch of tires on gravel.

"Hold up." Todd slowed near the intersection of the main road. "That's not right."

A pickup truck sat abandoned across both lanes, its driver's door hanging open. Todd kept their distance, cutting the engine.

Jason raised his binoculars. "No movement. But look at the windshield."

Todd squinted through his own pair. Spider-web cracks spread across the glass, centered on what could only be bullet holes.

"Recent?" Jason whispered.

"Well, it wasn't there when you drove through here two days ago, was it?"

"Yeah, I guess that was a stupid question. Should we check it out?"

Todd studied the surrounding tree line. "Too exposed. Anyone watching would have us dead to rights."

"Agreed. IT'S A TRAP!" Jason imitating Admiral Ackbar from Star Wars. "But that truck's blocking the main road out. Only other option is the fire road, and that's not exactly discrete in an emergency."

Todd backed the ATV slowly away from the intersection. "We'll mark it on the map, maybe come back better prepared. Right now, we need to-"

A distant engine sound cut through the morning quiet. Todd gunned the ATV into the tree line, killing the engine behind thick brush. They dismounted the ATV. Todd ducking behind the ATV while Jason took cover ten feet away behind a thicket of scrub oak, weapons at the ready.

The sound grew louder - multiple vehicles approaching from the direction they'd come from. Todd and Jason exchanged glances, years of shared experiences communicating without words. They needed better cover.

Jason pointed to a drainage ditch twenty yards back. Todd nodded, and they moved quickly but carefully through the underbrush, staying low.

The vehicles drew closer. From their hidden position, they watched three SUV's speed past, headed toward the blocked intersection. The vehicles' windows were tinted black, making it impossible to see the occupants.

"Government?" Jason whispered.

Todd shook his head. "No markings. And look at how they're driving - no convoy discipline. These guys are civilians."

"Armed civilians, based on those make shift gun ports cut in the rear doors."

"This keeps getting better and better." Todd waited until the engine sounds faded. "Let's work our way back, stick to the trees. I've seen enough for one morning."

Chapter 8

RE-ACTION VERSUS NO-ACTION

Dark clouds rolled across the sky, casting a grayness over the valley below Outlook Ridge, as the first light of day struggled to pierce the overcast. Todd and Jason were up with the dawn, their breaths misting in the cool morning air, and back on the ATV. The road was dark from the overnight moisture, which worked in their favor, preventing the dust from billowing up as they traversed the normally dusty road.

As they approached the intersection where the abandoned vehicle sat, they pulled off into the tree line and dismounted, ensuring they were far enough away to remain unseen and unheard. They approached the vehicle through the woods, their footsteps muffled by the damp earth, and stopped a hundred yards from the road. Jason traced his finger along his trigger, with his thumb on the safety switch ready to release if required, his brow furrowed in concentration.

"Doesn't look like anything has changed," he remarked, turning to Todd, who was squatting beside him, weapon in hand. "No movement, no lights, nothing."

Todd took a quick glance at his own safety switch and flipped it down, his eyes scanning the area for any sign of life. "Could be bait," he suggested, his voice low and cautious.

"My thoughts exactly," Jason agreed, stepping back behind the tree and crouching next to Todd. "That house on the hill is just out of view, which means we really can't see it from here. But if anyone decides to come down this road towards us, we could throw a few rounds through the truck to get them stopped or turned around. It's a better defensive position than anywhere else on the property."

Todd set his rifle down and pulled his map out, spreading it on the ground between them. "House sits here." he pointed to the map with his index finger, tracing the lines with a calloused hand. "That line of sight would cover almost all the way to about where we are standing."

"Plus, it would cover the west side if someone decides to come over the land in a vehicle," Jason added, his finger tracing the perimeter of the west property line. "We really need to figure out what's going on with that black truck running around. I'm pretty sure they don't belong here."

"Agreed. I would really like to get to the brick house and check on them. But I'm not sure that's wise with that truck rolling around," Todd replied, his gaze lifting to the horizon, contemplating their next move.

"You still have that ghillie suit?" Jason asked, looking at Todd with a spark of an idea in his eyes.

Todd straightened up and looked to the sky for the answer, mentally rifling through his well-organized supplies. "I'm pretty sure I do. Down in the basement in a box, I think. Why?"

"I could position myself near the intersection this afternoon and just watch what traffic we have. Get a sense of what's going on down this road," Jason explained, pulling out a Black and Mild cigar, a habit he'd tried to kick but found comfort in during these uncertain times. "If I see that black SUV again, I can see if I can put a round through one of the tires as they drive away from me. If they stop and get out, then we can see who or what we are dealing with."

"I thought you stopped smoking those," Todd remarked, raising an eyebrow at the cigar.

"Well, I tried, but I figure with the situation we are in, might as well start again. May not live long enough to reap the negative benefits they bring anyway," Jason said, a hint of remorse in his voice as he held up his lighter, ready to ignite the cigar. But he paused, reconsidering the wisdom of his action. "On second thought, probably not a good idea to light up here. I would hate to waste it if I had to shoot someone right now. I'll wait, I guess." He pocketed the lighter and placed the cigar back in his breast pocket, a sense of resignation in his movements.

Todd and Jason had seen enough. The roads were quiet, and the usual sounds of the forest seemed muted, as if nature itself was holding its breath. They retreated to the ATV, Jason mounting backwards to keep watch in case a vehicle drove up on them while they escaped back home.

Once back at the house, Bobbie had a small but healthy breakfast waiting for them, the aroma of fresh coffee and warm food filling the air. They sat at the kitchen table, and for a small time, it was like old times. The enjoyment of just being together and sharing stories at the kitchen table was a welcome respite from the tension that had become their new normal.

The aroma of bacon lingered in the kitchen as Todd scraped the last bits from his plate. His German Shepherds lay at his feet, their tails thumping against the heated tile floor whenever Bobbie passed by.

"Best breakfast I've had in days." Jason patted his stomach. "Nothing like your pancakes, honey."

Bobbie collected their empty plates. "Well, someone's got to keep you boys fed if you're running around playing soldier all day."

"Speaking of which-" Todd pushed back from the table. "Let me grab that suit from downstairs."

The basement stairs thumped under his boots as he descended into the cool basement. Bear and Buttercup followed, their nails clicking against each concrete floor at the bottom of the stairs. Todd navigated past rows of storage shelves until he reached a sealed trunk tucked in the corner.

The lock clicked open and musty air escaped as he lifted the lid. Inside, wrapped in plastic, lay the woodland ghillie suit - a masterpiece of burlap strips and synthetic materials he'd had for years but never used.

"Found it." Todd carried the bundle upstairs, where Jason waited with his tactical backpack open.

"This'll do perfectly." Jason examined the suit's intricate camouflage pattern. "Light enough to pack, too."

They carefully folded the suit and slipped it into Jason's backpack between his water bottle and first aid kit.

"I'll be completely invisible with this?" Jason zipped the pack closed.

"Just don't be smoking out there. Dead give away."

"True." Jason laughed as he helped Bobbie clear the last dishes from the table.

Todd and Jason moved to the garage where the ham radio station was producing a quite static, their boots scuffing against the gravel driveway. The garage was a haven of organized chaos, filled with tools, spare parts, and the faint scent of motor oil. The ham radio station occupied a corner work-bench, surrounded by an array of tools and elec-tronic components.

"Been a while since I've seen one of these." Jason ran his fingers along the vintage Kenwood trans-ceiver, a hint of nostalgia in his voice. Todd flipped switches and adjusted dials with practiced ease, bringing the radio to life.

The radio hummed, its display casting a soft green glow across the workbench. Static crackled through the speaker as Todd fine-tuned the frequency, the noise filling the garage with a sense of anticipation.

"This is Overlook Ridge, testing transmission. Anyone copying?" Todd's voice remained steady and professional, his military training clear in his calm demeanor.

Static filled the silence between transmissions. Todd waited thirty seconds before trying again, his patience a testament to his years of experience.

"Overlook Ridge testing. Over."

The speaker popped, and a gravelly voice cut through the white noise, surprising them both. "Reading you clear, Overlook. This is Lot 1. Haven't heard anyone on in days."

Todd and Jason exchanged glances, their eyebrows raised in surprise. The Lot 1 property sat at the entrance to their community, owned by a somewhat eccentric Italian man named George, who had lived there for decades.

"Good to hear your voice, George. How are things down there?" Todd asked, genuinely interested in the welfare of their distant neighbor.

"Oh...I don't know. Quiet for now, I guess. I'm holding up fine. Saw a vehicle pass through yesterday—looked like government or something, but no markings. Heading into the ranch. Haven't seen them come out, unless they snuck out last night." George's voice held a note of concern.

"Copy that. We spotted them too. You need anything?" Todd offered, always ready to lend a hand.

"Negative. Got the generator ready for when the power goes out and plenty of supplies. Got the garden in the greenhouse producing well. You?" George inquired, his voice steady.

"All good here. Jason and his family made it in from Texas. We'll keep this frequency open." Todd reassured him, glancing at Jason with a nod.

"Roger that. Good to know you've got help. Hey, I just want to let you know I'm going to blow the bridge on the road soon. I figure those who were coming would be here by now. Too many unknown vehicles coming off the highway. If you need to get out, you can still use the fire escape route. I'll check in same time tomorrow."

"Blow it. The fewer people we have wandering through the ranch, the better. Overlook out." Todd switched off the transmitter and leaned back in his chair, a sense of relief washing over him. "At least we're not completely cut off anymore."

"That's outstanding," Jason sounded off like it was the best news he'd heard in days. "If he blows the bridge, then we don't have to worry about unknown vehicles roaming around. Everyone else will be on foot, which makes the chances of them walking this far back less of an option. Now we just need to shut down that black SUV and see what that's all about."

"Yep," Todd replied as he leaned over to tie his shoes, his mind already thinking of the effect the bridge being blown would bring in the future. "It's going to take an effort to rebuild that bridge one day."

"True, He could probably just put a large culvert in and fill it in."

After a small dinner, Jason geared up and gave Bobbie a quick peck on the lips. "Be back in a little while, babe."

"Don't be doing anything stupid out there by yourself." Jason could hear the worry in her voice, but he offered her a reassuring smile.

"Me? Do something stupid? What would ever give you that idea?" He said with a playful wink, then walked out the door, leaving Bobbie with a mixture of concern and pride.

Jason double-checked his gear, ensuring everything was in place before mounting the ATV. "I should only be a few hours. If you hear gunshots, just stay away until and I'll call you on the walkie-talkie. If you hear gunfire and I don't radio you, give it a little and come looking for me. But let me call you, I don't want it giving my position away in the event someone is close."

"Roger that, buddy," Todd instructed as he cleaned his glasses, his voice firm but caring. "Make sure you identify what you're shooting at if you have to shoot. Don't need you killing our neighbors. Be careful!"

With that, Jason cranked the ATV and left down the road, the engine's hum fading into the distance as he ventured deeper down the road of the ranch.

Jason carefully maneuvered the four wheeler deep into the tree line as he approached the main intersection, methodically concealing it with a thick layer of pine branches and fallen foliage until it was nearly invisible to passing eyes. Slightly out of breath, he donned the ghillie suit, its fabric rustling softly as he adjusted the camouflaged material to break up his human silhouette. He meticulously double-checked his tactical gear, ensuring each piece was secured and easily accessible. A slight metallic sound of the bolt clicked as he chambered a round, the well-oiled mechanism sliding a 7mm Magnum round into place with satisfying precision. After securing the heavy sniper rifle across his back, he gripped the more maneuverable short-barreled carbine in his hands, its familiar weight providing a measure of comfort. Moving with deliberate stealth, he traversed the quarter-mile to the intersection, careful to minimize any noise from his boots against the rocky terrain. Upon reaching his destination, he identified an ideal observation point on elevated ground that offered clear sightlines down both converging roads, providing him with tactical superiority over anyone approaching the crossroads.

His brain kicked in as he settled into position, creating a small hollow in the scrub oak undergrowth that would conceal his presence while still allowing him to maintain watch. The late afternoon sun almost touching the top of the pine trees, which would work to his advantage by making his position even harder to detect. Jason adjusted his scope's elevation, accounting for the slight downward angle to the road, and pulled his hydration pack's drinking tube close for easy access. The weight of responsibility for protecting Overlook Ridge and everyone on it pressed heavily on his mind as he prepared himself for what could be a long vigil.

The Colorado sun touched the jagged mountains to the west, although it didn't seem to make a big difference in the already dim light. The day was already severely overcast, heavy clouds hanging low and threatening, causing the full day to be less than bright and casting an eerie pallor across the landscape. Jason passed the time by thinking of chess moves in his mind, mentally playing out strategies and counterstrategies as he'd learned through books and watching videos online. He had never spent so much time laying in the brush, and the stillness was both meditative and challenging. He noticed all sorts of interesting things as he lay there silently, his eye catching details he might have missed in motion. Deer walked within fifteen feet of him, their delicate hooves barely making a sound on the forest floor, while curious birds hopped closer, occasionally picking at his ghillie suit's artificial foliage. Nothing moved him from his watchful position, his discipline holding firm.

Just as he began to think about making his way back home because of the inactivity, the distinctive sound of an engine caught his attention, breaking the natural silence of the wilderness. The sound came from the right of the intersection, echoing off the hillsides. Jason felt his pulse beginning to surge, that familiar rush of adrenaline he knew so well from his combat days. He attempted to control his heart rate by breathing slowly into his nose and out of his mouth, just as he'd had learned in high school shooting competitions. After thirty seconds of mounting tension, a black SUV appeared through the tree line and decreased speed as it reached the crossroads, its tires crunching softly on the gravel. It came to a halt ten yards from the stalled out truck blocking the road, its engine idling ominously in the growing darkness.

Jason carefully studied the vehicle through his rifle scope, methodically scanning the tags, stickers, and any other identifying marks that might reveal if these were legitimate authorities. He searched for official government seals, military designations, or law enforcement markings that could explain their presence on the secluded ranch property. The passenger door creaked open with deliberate slowness, and Jason observed a pair of well-worn black tactical boots descend to the gravel, the kind favored by special operations units. He watched intently as a man moved with practiced precision toward the front of the black SUV, maintaining an unwavering focus on the abandoned truck ahead. Jason noted every detail of the man's equipment - from the professional-grade assault rifle, likely an M4 variant, to the heavily laden tactical vest festooned with magazine pouches and combat gear. As the first man approached the truck with his weapon shouldered in textbook formation, the driver's door swung open with a muted thud, and a second similarly equipped operator emerged, moving to support his companion. Both men positioned themselves in a tactical stance in front of their SUV's hood, their movements suggesting extensive military or law enforcement training.

Both men cautiously approached the vehicle in a synchronized sweep pattern, their rifles trained on potential threat points as they methodically cleared the old truck. They checked the interior through tinted windows, using tactical hand signals to coordinate their movements before thoroughly inspecting the truck bed and underneath the chassis for any hidden occupants. After being assured the truck was completely empty, they visibly relaxed their posture, lowering their rifles to a ready position across their chest rigs. Jason could hear fragments of their conversation carried on the mountain breeze, but the words were too muffled to decipher clearly. While the language was definitely English, he strained to detect any distinctive accent or regional dialect that might reveal their origins. These men were complete strangers to him, and the out-of-state license plates on their SUV confirmed they weren't local to the ranch or even Colorado. His mind raced through various tactical scenarios, weighing the risks and consequences of each potential course of action. The military training ingrained in him demanded absolute certainty before engaging. Taking a human life wasn't a decision to be made lightly, and he needed concrete proof of hostile intent before considering lethal force.

As the men stood and talked, Jason could hear a second vehicle approaching from the north headed to the intersection, its engine sound growing steadily louder against the backdrop of rustling pine needles. It would be only mere seconds before they came into view of the stalled truck and the black SUV blocking the crossroads, creating what Jason recognized as a perfect ambush scenario.

Just then, the men heard the approaching car as well, their heads snapping toward the sound in unison, and quickly raised their weapons and moved to a defensive position in front of the beat-up truck with practiced efficiency. Their boots crunched on loose gravel as they spread out in a tactical formation. Jason quickly moved his rifle to spot the approaching vehicle and quickly identified it as the neighbors from the brick house - the silver sedan he'd seen pass by countless times before. Just as the car came within view of the armed men, brake lights flared bright red as it slammed on the breaks, the tires skidding against dirt as the driver attempted to reverse out of the situation in a panic. The car swerved as it reversed, but it was too late - they'd driven straight into a trap.

Gun fire erupted violently from the two men as they dumped round after round into the car, which was desperately trying to steer backwards through the narrow road. The deafening crack of semi-automatic weapons filled the morning air as bullets peppered the silver sedan's hood and windshield. Jason knew he had to do something quick, his heart pounding against his ribcage as adrenaline surged through his system. His mind raced through multiple scenarios in a matter of seconds, weighing each option with the precision of his military training. His first thought was to fire his weapon close to the men, maybe causing them to cease fire and take a different position - but that could give away his location without guaranteeing their retreat. Jason's second thought was to shoot the black SUV to disable it, but then there would certainly be a shootout as they would not only be aware someone was targeting them, but their vehicle would be out of commission. The last choice in Jason's mind seemed like his only option, though it sat like lead in his stomach. Either hope the neighbors somehow make it out alive against the overwhelming odds, or take decisive action to stop the two men that were shooting without provocation on known ranch residents. The weight of the decision pressed down on him, but deep down, he knew exactly what he had to do. Years of combat experience had taught him that hesitation in moments like these only led to tragedy.

Jason put his crosshairs on the furthest man, adjusting slightly for the wind that rustled through the pines. He took a deep breath and started to release it slowly, his military training taking over with practiced precision. Halfway through his exhale, he held it and started a very soft squeeze on the trigger, feeling the familiar pressure build against his finger.

The rifle kicked hard into Jason's shoulder and the report was massive, echoing off the ridge walls like thunder. As Jason saw his target twist violently and fall to the ground, he had already chambered another round with fluid efficiency. The closest man immediately stopped firing at the car and ran to the other side of the SUV, panic evident in his hurried movements. Jason could see the man desperately dragging his wounded companion behind the vehicle for cover, leaving a dark trail in their wake. In the distance, Jason could hear the retreating car's engine roaring at near full throttle, tires sliding as it took corners back from where they came from. He knew at least the driver was still alive.

Training his rifle scope on the dark SUV, he could see an occasional movement from underneath the vehicle, shadows shifting against the dusty ground. Jason already knew the chances of the wounded man still being alive were extremely remote given the precision of his first shot and the amount of blood left behind. Jason knew it would only be a matter of minutes before the second man had to make his move - the mounting pressure of the situation would force his hand. The question cycling through Jason's mind was which desperate option the man would choose. Both choices - making a run for it or trying to reach the driver's seat - would likely end with his death, unless Jason somehow missed the shot, of course.

After a few tense minutes of absolute stillness, Jason noticed the weight of the vehicle distinctly dip to the passenger side, the suspension groaning under the sudden shift. This subtle movement was all he needed to see to understand that the man had entered the vehicle from the passenger side, likely crawling across the seats. Even though the windows were heavily tinted, making it impossible to see the figure inside, Jason knew exactly where his target was heading. The driver's seat. He adjusted his grip on his weapon, muscles taut with anticipation, knowing that the next few seconds would be critical. The SUV's dark exterior seemed to absorb the ambient light, creating an impenetrable barrier between hunter and prey, but Jason's military training had taught him to read a situation through more than just visual cues. The slight bounce of the chassis and the faint metallic sounds of movement inside the vehicle painted a clear picture in his mind.

As soon as the engine starter clicked, Jason squeezed off another calculated round, the bullet punching cleanly through the panel of the driver's door with deadly accuracy. The starter stopped before the engine cranked, indicating the pressure on the key had been released prior to the engine getting enough RPMs to start. All movement had ceased, leaving only the settling dust and deafening silence.

Jason sat motionless for another twenty minutes before slowly pulling his radio to his face.

"Brady to Papa Smurf. Brady to Papa Smurf. How do you read? Over," he said, barely above a whisper. Jason wasn't sure where he'd pulled those call signs from - Brady and Papa Smurf - but he slightly smiled as he said it, the unexpected moment of levity catching him off guard in the tense situation. His finger remained steady on the radio's transmit button, eyes never leaving the target vehicle.

"Go for Papa Smurf. Over." Came the clear measured reply from Overlook Ridge, Todd's voice carrying that familiar tone of controlled urgency.

"I have two suspects taking a dirt nap. I'm still observing, but no movements. Request assistance.

Road is clear between here and you. I'm a hundred yards west on the right side of the road. Stop at the turn and we'll approach together." Jason kept his voice low and professional, falling back on years of military communications training.

"Copy. I'll be there in a minute. Stay covered." Todd was already moving before he finished speaking, muscle memory taking over as he grabbed his tactical vest and sidearm, and rifle. Within seconds, he was striding purposefully toward his four-wheeler, the machine's keys already in the ignition. The familiar weight of his rifle across his back provided a grim comfort as he prepared to support his old friend.

Within a few minutes, Todd had made his way near the crossroads, carefully navigating his four-wheeler through the winding dirt path and slowing to look for Jason. The late evening shadows played tricks with his vision as he scanned the area. Todd could just make out the vehicles in the intersection around the scattered pine and juniper trees when Jason suddenly stood up from his concealed position, giving Todd an unexpected skip in the heart. The abrupt movement, even from his friend, made him jump.

Neither of them speaking, Jason approached Todd and sat sidesaddle on the four-wheeler with his AR-15 Carbine pointing forward, his practiced grip steady on the weapon. Todd slipped the ATV into gear and pressed forward slowly, the engine's low rumble barely audible in the crisp air as they crept toward the intersection. The ATV came to a complete stop about fifty yards from the blockade, and Todd killed the engine, leaving them in complete silence. Both men sat motionless, their heightened awareness evident in their faces as they methodically scanned the area for any sign of movement, paying particular attention to the driver's side of the SUV.

"How do you want to do this?" Todd whispered, his weathered hands already dismounting and raising his rifle to his shoulder in one fluid motion. His keen eyes never wavered from the vehicles, searching for any telltale glint of metal or shadow of movement behind the tinted windows. "I'll take left and you take right, and let's walk the road easy." His boots made no sound as he shifted his weight, positioning himself for optimal coverage of his chosen sector, the separation giving them a tactical advantage.

"Roger Wilco. One guy is on the ground on the other side, and I think the second guy is in the driver's seat. We need to be careful. He could be playing possum," Jason murmured. He was already advancing with precision, placing each boot deliberately in front of the other to minimize noise and maintain a perfect balance. His shoulders were squared, rifle held at the ready position as his experienced eyes continuously scanned between the driver's door and the vehicle's backseats. His past had taught him that assumptions could be deadly - either man could spring into action at any moment.

As Todd and Jason reached the vehicle, they instinctively spread further apart, falling into a combat formation. Approaching the vehicle simultaneously from the front and back, they moved like shadows across the ground, their boots barely making a whisper against the dirt. In almost pure silence, they positioned themselves perfectly to not only have a crossfire angle on any targets but also to cover each other's blind spots in the event the unexpected happened. Their rifles remained steady.

"Driver! Open the door," Jason yelled halfway through their approach, his sharp command startling Todd and shattering the tense atmosphere. The silence that followed was deafening, pressing against their ears like a physical weight. Jason repeated the command, his voice stronger and more authoritative, letting the loud presence fill his words. Still, no response followed, not even the slightest movement from within the vehicle.

"I'm going to open the door, cover me," Jason announced in a low, controlled voice, shifting his position to the side of the car while maintaining his tactical stance.

Todd moved wider to establish a better firing position, his boots crunching softly against the gravel as he shifted his weight, nodding his head in silent acknowledgment of the plan. His eyes scanned the surroundings, maintaining constant vigilance while Jason prepared to make his move. With one swift, practiced action, Jason reached out and grabbed the driver's door handle, pulling it hard while simultaneously retreating a few calculated steps backward, his movements fluid and precise.

As the door swung open with a metal on metal groan that seemed to echo in the still air, the man's lifeless body partially slumped out of the car, hanging grotesquely over the door frame like a broken marionette. The sickly sweet smell of blood wafted from the vehicle's interior. His hands were still rigidly clutching the keys in a death grip, knuckles white against the metal, frozen in what appeared to be his final desperate moments. A thin line of dried blood traced down from his nose, stark against his pallid skin.

Jason, seeing Todd had the seemingly dead person covered, swiftly moved to the rear of the

SUV and came around the passenger side with his weapon at the ready, scanning methodically for any additional threats. On the ground lay a man faced down in the dirt, arms limp at his side from being dragged across the rough road. After ensuring the immediate area was clear, Jason kicked the fallen weapon several feet away, watching it skid across the dusty ground, then used the toe of his tactical boot to turn the man's face over. Just as he expected - a clean neck shot, through and through with dried blood caked around the entry and exit wounds.

Todd maintained his defensive position, weapon trained steadily on the dead driver as Jason moved back around to the driver's side. Jason pressed two fingers firmly against the cold skin of the driver's neck, searching for any sign of life in the carotid artery.

"Nothing," Jason said as he looked at Todd with grim resolve. His expression carried the seriousness of the situation. "Other guy is dead as well. Now what?"

"Let's pull these guys out and see what information or identification we can find," Todd said as he shouldered his rifle with a swift motion, mentally preparing himself for the unpleasant but necessary task ahead. "We need to know who they were and what they were up to here."

As soon as Todd pulled the man out of the vehicle, his body falling out like a ton of bricks, he noticed something right away.

"Hey! This is the same guy I was telling you about. The one that came to the house acting weird. Huh!" Todd said as he knelt down over the body.

"No kidding. Well, I guess he won't be seeing you again as he thought."

"Yep, kinda makes sense now. He came scoping the place out. I'm sure it was only a matter of time before they came knocking again. I think the dogs might have kept them away since then. But I'm sure they would have made a run at us sooner or later." Todd stood, his face showing a sign of completeness.

Todd and Jason performed the grueling task of searching the bodies for identification or any other clue that might tell them who these individuals that just met their maker were. They methodically checked pockets, wallets, and clothing tags, their faces grim as they worked. The smell of dried blood still lingered in the air, mixing with more unpleasant odors that neither man cared to acknowledge. Todd's analytical mind cataloged each detail they discovered, while Jason kept a watchful eye on their surroundings, ever mindful of potential threats that might still lurk nearby. Their duty kicked in automatically, each man falling into what seemed like well-practiced roles - Todd documenting everything in his mental database with engineer-like precision, while Jason maintained a defensive posture, his hand never far from his weapon. They worked in practiced silence, communicating with subtle gestures and nods, as if they were ex-navy seals, which they were not. The grim task before them was made somewhat easier by their methodical approach, though the weight of what they were doing - searching through the belongings of the recently deceased - wasn't lost on either of them.

"I think I found something," Todd mentioned as he pulled a weathered piece of paper from the dead man's inner vest pocket, carefully unfolding it with his hands. "Looks like this guy is from New Mexico. Some kind of written directions or something. Not sure to where. Doesn't look familiar."

"Yeah, this guy had a driver's license from Raton," Jason confirmed, studying the plastic card he'd retrieved from another pocket, his expression grim. "Looks like maybe they were just taking advantage of the situation, opportunists who saw their chance when everything went south, they went north. The problem is, they've been around here for a few days - you can tell from the local dirt caked on their boots and how familiar they seemed with the area.

They must have been staying somewhere nearby." He paused, considering the implications. "My guess would be they invaded someone's home, or found an empty place with no food, so they had to go searching. Either way, we should probably check the surrounding properties when we can."

"Maybe. The important thing now is what to do with the bodies and should we report this to someone?" Todd said, already reaching into the vehicle to search for further clues. He rummaged through the center console, finding nothing but old receipts and a handful of loose change.

Jason stood quietly for a moment, chewing his lip while pondering their options. The darker side of his mind taking over was telling him the importance of handling situations like this with discretion, especially given the current state of things. His years of experience had taught him that sometimes the cleanest solution wasn't necessarily the most ethical one. "I think we should load the bodies up that old pickup truck, then use their truck to push it off the road. Won't be long before the animals figure out where free food is located." He glanced at the tree line, where shadows were already lengthening in the late afternoon light, knowing the local wildlife would make quick work of covering their tracks. Mountain lions, coyotes, and bears were always hungry this time of year, and nature had its own way of handling these matters. In times like these, the fewer traces left behind, the better. The thought made his stomach turn slightly, but survival meant making hard choices, and they couldn't afford to draw attention to themselves or the homestead.

"You don't say," Todd pondered. "Then we take their truck back to our place and strip it, drain the gas, and maybe bury it on the property somewhere," Todd suggested, his engineering mind already calculating the logistics. "I don't think we want people knowing what happened here. Not with everything going on."

"Agreed," Jason replied grimly, his tiredness starting to show in his movements.

And with that, Todd and Jason methodically loaded the dead men into the back of the old abandoned truck, being careful not to leave any evidence behind. Jason slipped into the driver's seat while Todd positioned the black SUV behind it, its powerful engine idling quietly. Slowly and deliberately, they pushed the old truck down the road from which it came until they reached a natural decline in the terrain. As it started to roll under its own weight, Jason smoothly exited the vehicle, watching as momentum took over. The truck continued straight for a few hundred yards, gathering speed, before departing the road in a gradual arc. Its momentum and considerable weight kept it rolling through the underbrush until it slammed into a sturdy pine tree fifty yards from the road, the impact partially obscured by the dense vegetation. The crash would look like just another abandoned vehicle to any passing stranger - exactly what they needed.

Satisfied with its position, Jason retreated to the black SUV where Todd quickly drove them to where Todd's four-wheeler sat waiting in the gathering dusk.

Jason opened the door and stepped out of the SUV, pausing to wipe beads of sweat from his furrowed brow with the back of his hand. "I'll drive your four-wheeler back and come back for mine tomorrow," he said decisively. "It's pretty well hidden behind that thicket of scrub oak. I don't think anyone is going to be roaming around after hearing all the gunfire - they'll steer clear of this entire area. Remind me to pick up my spent casings tomorrow as well."

The pair made their way back to Overlook Ridge, with Todd leading the way through the winding dirt road they knew by heart. The distant storm clouds where almost overhead now punctuated the recent events and their careful journey home. Once at the house, Todd pulled the SUV into an empty spot in the spacious four-car garage while Jason parked the four-wheeler alongside it and proceeded to shut the heavy garage door behind Todd with a metallic clang. The snow had just started, bringing with it the promise of several days of heavy weather. It would be a few days of staying put. The forced downtime would give them plenty of opportunity to go through the truck thoroughly and strip it of whatever useful resources they could find - gas, electronics, anything that might give them an edge in the increasingly dangerous world they now inhabited, and disposing of the truck once completed. Todd and Jason both knew they couldn't leave any evidence of their activities, so they'd need to be methodical in their approach, cataloging every item they salvaged and ensuring nothing of value went to waste. The storm would provide perfect cover for their work, keeping any unwanted visitors away while they dismantled the vehicle piece by piece in the shelter of the garage.

Chapter 9

TRAPPED BY SNOW

The winter storm hit Overlook Ridge with unexpected ferocity. Snow piled up against the windows in thick drifts while arctic winds howled through the pine trees, creating an endless moan across the property. Inside Todd's house, the wood stoves cranked out steady heat, keeping the interior warm despite the brutal conditions outside.

"That's been two feet since yesterday." Todd peered through his kitchen window at the measurement stick he'd planted in the garden. The marker was barely visible above the white expanse. "Haven't seen accumulation like this in several years."

Jason stood beside him, hands wrapped around a steaming mug of coffee. "The drifts against the garage must be six feet high. No way we're getting any vehicles out until this breaks."

In the living room, Bobbie had organized the kids into rotating shifts of board games and reading sessions. The sounds of laughter drifted through the house as Hyden celebrated another Monopoly victory over his siblings.

"At least we got everything closed up before this hit," Todd said. He checked the indoor temperature gauge - a comfortable 72 degrees thanks to the newly installed wood stoves. Bear and Buttercup lounged near the closest heat source, their fur collecting warmth.

"The greenhouse stoves are holding steady too." Jason tapped a small display, showing the remote temperature readings. "Your tomatoes will make it through just fine, Bobbie!"

"Thank goodness," Bobbie called back. "These kids need their vegetables."

The storm continued its assault, radio signals completely dead under the thick cloud cover. Outdoor electronic sensors flickered off and on, eventually failing altogether as ice built up on the devices. The family settled into a quiet routine, rationing their supplies and maintaining their shelter while nature raged outside. With the roads completely impassable and white-out conditions persisting for two days, Todd and Jason were able to let their guard down a little.

Todd and Jason huddled around the emergency radio in Todd's upstairs office, scanning frequencies through bursts of static. The small battery-powered device represented their solid connection to the outside world. Snow continued falling outside the window, creating an isolating blanket of white.

"Got something." Jason adjusted the dial carefully. A garbled voice emerged through the white noise.

"...widespread outages continue across the Eastern seaboard. Military forces have established control zones in major metropolitan areas. Civilian movement remains restricted..."

Todd jotted notes in his leather-bound journal, documenting each fragment of information they managed to catch. "Different from yesterday. They were still talking about 'temporary measures' then."

"Here's another." Jason shifted frequencies again.

"...refugee camps at capacity. FEMA resources stretched beyond limits. Citizens advised to shelter in place..."

The radio crackled, then fell silent. Jason fiddled with the controls but couldn't recover the signal.

"Check the emergency bands," Todd suggested.

They cycled through the frequencies designated for emergency services and civil defense. Most channels produced only static, but occasionally they caught snippets of local law enforcement communications - brief exchanges about blocked roads, stranded vehicles, and dwindling fuel supplies.

"Nothing from Pueblo for three days now." Todd flipped back through his notes. "Last transmission mentioned riots in the warehouse district."

"Colorado Springs has gone dark too." Jason set down the radio. "Even the military channels are quiet."

Bear and Buttercup lay at their feet, ears perking up at each new voice that emerged from the radio. The dogs had grown accustomed to these daily monitoring sessions, staying close as their humans pieced together the fragmentary news of a world in chaos.

Todd adjusted the ham radio's frequency while Jason logged their previous transmissions in a notebook. The equipment hummed in the warm office, a stark contrast to the howling storm outside.

"Radio check, this is Overlook Ridge. Anyone monitoring this frequency?" Todd's voice remained steady and professional. Static crackled through the speakers.

Jason leaned forward. "Try channel seven. There used to be folks on that one."

Todd switched frequencies. "Radio beck, calling any stations in the Blackhawk Ranch area. Come in."

A burst of static, then a voice broke through. "This is Mike. Reading you clear, Todd."

"Mike?" Todd recognized their neighbor from three miles down the valley. "How are conditions at your place?"

"Snowed in completely. Lost power two days ago. Running on generator, but fuel's getting low." Mike's transmission crackled. "Had some strangers trying to break into my barn yesterday."

Jason grabbed the mic. "Did you get a look at them?"

"Negative. Dogs scared them off. But found footprints in the snow - at least four people."

Todd marked the location on their property map. "Anyone else made contact?"

"The Williams family evacuated last week. Peterson's place is dark. No word from anyone past the gate." Mike paused. "Listen, I've got about three days of food left. My wife's insulin-"

The transmission cut out. Todd adjusted the dial but caught only static.

"Mike? Mike, do you copy?" Todd tried several times before setting down the microphone. He looked at Jason. "That's the third neighbor this week running low on supplies."

Bear and Buttercup sat alert by the door, their ears tracking sounds beyond human hearing. Through the window, the storm showed no signs of letting up, the white wall of snow obscuring everything beyond the first line of pine trees.

Jason marked another X on their map. "That's a five-mile radius with confirmed activity. No responses from anything further out."

The dogs' routine never wavered, even as the nights grew longer. Bear patrolled the perimeter of the house, her black fur blending into the shadows while Buttercup maintained her post in the middle of the driveway. Their breath formed small clouds in the frigid air as they moved through their practiced patterns.

Todd watched through the kitchen window as Bear investigated a noise in the tree line. The dog's posture shifted - head low, ears forward, muscles tense. But after a thorough check, she relaxed. Just another deer seeking shelter from the storm.

"Those two haven't missed a thing," Jason said, checking the door locks for the night. "Better than any security system."

Buttercup's ears twitched at every sound - the creak of the house settling, the wind whistling through gaps in the roof, the distant crack of snow-laden branches. She distinguished between familiar noises and potential threats, maintaining her vigilant watch without tiring.

During their wondering patrols, the dogs worked in tandem. Buttercup took the outer perimeter while Bear circled closer to the house. They communicated through subtle signals - a lifted paw, a tilted head, a soft whine. Their training showed in every movement, every reaction.

In the darkness, their keen senses extended far beyond the reach of the security lights. Bear's nose tracked scent trails through the snow, while Buttercup's ears caught sounds that traveled for miles in the crystal-clear mountain air. Together, they created an early warning system that no technology could match.

The dogs' presence alone deterred most threats. Their deep barks carried across the snow-covered landscape, announcing to any would-be intruders that the property was well-defended. But they remained silent unless necessary, understanding their role as guardians of the homestead.

The aroma of fresh-baked bread wafted through the house as Bobbie pulled another golden loaf from the oven. She'd discovered a way to stretch their flour supplies by mixing in ground nuts from last fall's harvest.

"Just like my grandmother used to make." Jason broke off a warm piece, savoring the nutty flavor.

At the kitchen table, Todd dealt another hand of canasta, almost certainly bluffing every hand.

"Your turn to deal." Jason slid the deck of cards toward the center. The kids were asleep upstairs, giving the adults a rare moment of peace.

Bear and Buttercup sprawled near the wood stove, their tails thumping against the floor as Bobbie shared bits of crust with them.

"Remember that time Dan came down and rode four wheelers around?" Jason arranged his cards. "When he hit that ditch and nearly killed himself?"

Todd laughed. "And we chased each other around the property playing cops and robbers?"

"That was a lot of fun," Bobbie added, settling into a chair with her own cards. "We did that in the middle of the night...."

The wind howled outside, but inside the house remained warm and bright. Todd had rigged solar-powered LED strips along the ceiling, creating a cozy atmosphere that felt almost normal.

"No red three's again!." Jason laid down his cards in disgust.

"Two in my pile." Bobbie swept the cards out of her hand and slammed them on the table to prove it. "You boys never could beat me at canasta."

Todd leaned back, watching his friends - no, his family now - enjoy the simple pleasure of a card game. Despite everything happening beyond their walls, these moments reminded him why they had prepared in the first place. Not just to survive, but to live.

"Anyone up for a movie after this hand?" Bobbie shuffled the deck with practiced ease.

"Only if Jason promises the Plex won't trip the breaker again," Todd said.

"No kidding. Might have to rig up the treadmill to provide more power to it," Jason protested, triggering another round of laughter.

Todd gathered the scattered cards, shuffling them back into order. These evening games had become their anchor, a touchstone of normalcy in their changed world. Around this table, they weren't survivors or preppers - they were simply family, sharing stories and laughter over hands of cards.

The night wrapped around Overlook Ridge like a frozen shroud, stars piercing through breaks in the cloud cover. Todd and Jason sat bundled in thick winter gear on the upper deck, their breath forming crystalline clouds in the frigid air. Below them, snow blanketed the property in pristine white, broken only by snow sliding off the roof onto the ground below.

"Remember when we thought this deck was just for summer stargazing?" Todd pulled his thermos from beneath layers of blankets, pouring steaming coffee into two metal cups.

Jason accepted the cup, letting the warmth seep into his gloved hands. "Feels like another lifetime. Back when our biggest worry was trying to figure out the zipline."

The security lights cast long shadows across the snow, creating a perimeter of visibility around the house. Beyond that boundary, darkness consumed the Colorado wilderness. The dogs' barks echoed from somewhere near the tree line, their routine checks continuing through the night.

"Thirty years in civil service." Todd's voice carried notes of disbelief. "All those contingency plans, emergency protocols. Not one scenario covered this."

"We planned for earthquakes, floods, even nuclear events." Jason traced patterns in the frost forming on his cup's rim. "But this slow collapse? The gradual unraveling of everything?"

Below them, Buttercup's white breath plumed in the security lights as she investigated something near the wood stumps. After a moment, she moved on, satisfied with her inspection.

"The kids are adapting better than I expected." Jason watched his coffee's steam disappear into the night air. "Yesterday, the older kids were teaching the little ones how to calculate supply rationing using their math workbooks."

"They're resilient. More than we give them credit for." Todd leaned further back in his chair, the cold seeping through despite the layers. "Bobbie's got them on a learning schedule that would put most schools to shame."

Silence settled between them, broken only by the wind's whistle through bare branches and the distant sound of ice cracking in the forest. The temperature had dropped another ten degrees since sunset.

"You know what's crazy to think?" Jason's words formed tight clouds. "Not the cold, not the isolation. It's knowing we might be some of the last people maintaining any sort of normal life."

Todd nodded, understanding deeper than words could express. "I built this place just in case. Now I'm really glad I did. Who would have thought.."

The security light near the garage flickered - a momentary reminder of their dependence on the systems they'd put in place. The solar arrays were holding up, but each equipment hiccup sparked fresh concerns about long-term sustainability.

"The radio's getting quieter each day." Jason pulled his coat tighter. "Fewer signals, fewer responses. Even the emergency bands are going dark."

"Makes you wonder about all those people who laughed at us." Todd's voice carried no satisfaction, only a heavy sadness. "Called us paranoid. Survivalist nuts."

"The ones who said you were wasting money on food storage and alternative power." Jason shook his head. "Wonder if they're still laughing? Dan!"

Bear's bark cut through the night - sharp, alert, but not alarmed. Both men tensed until Buttercup's responding bark signaled all-clear. Their dogs' language had become as familiar as their own.

"You ever second-guess bringing your family here?" Todd asked, refilling their cups.

Jason stared into the darkness beyond their lights. "Not one bit. I look at those refugee camp reports, the riots, the chaos in the cities..." He let the thought hang incomplete in the frozen air.

"We're not just surviving here." Todd's words carried the weight of conviction. "We're living. Growing food, educating the kids, keeping some piece of civilization alive."

The wind picked up, driving snow from the trees in glittering clouds. Both men sat in companionable silence, each lost in thoughts of the world they'd known and the one they now inhabited. Their preparations, once seen as excessive, had become the foundation of their continued existence.

"Clear sky to the south. A lot more stars are out now." Jason gestured toward the sky. "No more light pollution. No aircraft. Just the way they looked thousands of years ago."

"Nature's taking it all back, piece by piece." Todd watched as western clouds started to overtake the clear sky and snow flurries began to fall, erasing the day's tracks. "Maybe that's not such a bad thing."

Their coffee grew cold as they sat in the stillness, two friends who had become brothers in this transformed world. Below them, Bear and Buttercup had made their way back to the basement door, readily awaiting entry into the warmth of the house.

Chapter 10

First Real Threat

Todd wiped the grease from his hands with a shop rag, squinting at the carburetor parts spread across his workbench. Sunlight streamed through the garage windows, reflecting off patches of melting snow outside. The steady drip of water from the eaves created a peaceful rhythm.

"Where did that screw go? I just put it down right here?" Todd pointed to the brass component near Jason's elbow as he held a wrench.

Jason and Todd spent the next two minutes looking on the table, under the table, around where Todd was standing. Finally, Jason found the screw laying up against a half empty gas can and handed it to Todd.

"Now, where the hell did the wrench go?" Todd was certainly getting visibly frustrated at this point.

The warm garage filled with the scent of motor oil and gasoline as they worked. Todd had insisted on servicing the four-wheelers before spring arrived in full force. The machines would be essential for patrolling the property once the ground dried out.

"Remember that time we got stuck down in the valley trying to get up that hill on the fence line?" Jason adjusted the choke linkage with now practiced hands.

"At least we didn't have to walk back." Todd's weathered face crinkled with amusement. "That was a lot of fun. Found that Elk antler too. Good times.. good times."

A sharp bark cut through their conversation. Then another. The playful sounds shifted to urgent warning calls that echoed across the property.

Todd straightened, his expression hardening. Bear and Buttercup never barked like that without cause.

"Something's up." Jason was already moving toward the open garage door, wiping his hands.

The dogs' barking intensified, their deep voices carrying clearly from the direction of the main road. Todd grabbed his weapon from the workbench and stepped outside. The melting snow had turned the driveway into a muddy mess, but he could see both dogs standing alert halfway down the driveway, hackles raised.

"See anything?" Jason shielded his eyes against the glare.

Todd peering around the curve towards the road. "Movement by the tree line. Buttercup's got her attention fixed on something."

Bear paced back and forth along the driveway, her black coat gleaming in the sun. Buttercup remained statue-still, ears forward, focused on the woods beyond the driveway curve.

"Could be deer." Jason pulled out his pistol to ensure it was ready, just in case. "They've been moving around more since the storm passed."

Todd tracked the dogs' line of sight. A flash of movement caught his eye - something darker than the surrounding trees, moving with purpose rather than the casual meandering of wildlife.

"That's no deer." Todd retreated to the garage to retrieve his pistol, placing it behind his back. "There's people coming up the driveway."

The dogs' barking reached a fever pitch. Bear charged toward the group, then back to Buttercup's position, her agitation growing. Buttercup remained locked in place, a long series of barks and growling rumbling in her chest.

"I see them." Jason said, peering through the trees. "More than one. Maybe three or four, walking up the driveway." He had taken a few steps to his left to get a better angle.

Todd's mind raced through possibilities. The property was too far from town for casual wonderers. The mud would deter most vehicles. Anyone approaching on foot had a specific purpose.

"Bear! Buttercup! Hold!" Todd's command carried across the yard. Both dogs immediately stopped barking, but maintained their alert posture.

"Should we meet them halfway?" Jason's hand slipping his weapon behind his back, where Todd had placed his.

"Let's wait for a minute. The dogs will let us know if whoever is leaving the road." Todd glanced around to make sure they weren't getting flanked. "No sense showing our hand too early."

The shadows in the trees shifted again. Bear let out a single sharp bark, then fell silent at Todd's quick hand signal. Buttercup's ears swiveled, tracking a movement they couldn't yet see.

"How many you count?" Todd kept his voice low, though they were too far to be heard.

"At least three that I can see." Jason raised his head higher, trying to get a better view through the trees. "Let's hope its neighbors."

Bear's hackles rose higher, and she moved closer to Buttercup's position. The two dogs formed a unified front, their bodies tense and ready. Whatever was coming, they weren't about to let it pass unchallenged.

"Think we should move closer?" Jason's mind now thinking of options. "Get a better angle as they turn the corner?"

Todd considered their options as well. The garage offered a good vantage point, but distance meant limited response time if things went sideways. Yet approaching too quickly might provoke an unwanted confrontation.

The decision was made for them as the figures emerged from the last stretch of trees. Bear and Buttercup's posture shifted, their barking taking on a new urgency that demanded immediate attention.

"Hello!" the stranger called as he spotted Todd standing in front of the garage, his hands raised in what appeared to be a peaceful gesture.

"Stay where you are," Todd called back firmly as Jason silently slipped to his right unseen, using the shadows and garage to stay just out of sight of the stranger.

"Stay where you are or the dogs will be released," Todd commanded, his voice carrying the weight of authority. He gave a subtle whistle to Bear and Buttercup, signaling them to maintain their position, though their muscles remained coiled and ready. "What are you doing here?"

"We are looking for food." The words came out hesitant, almost apologetic. By this point, the rest of the clan had joined behind the man, their gaunt faces peering around him as they took in the well-maintained property with hungry eyes. Jason remained just out of view, pressed against the side of the garage with his pistol drawn and held low against his thigh, ready to act if the situation deteriorated. The afternoon sun getting lower on the range, adding to the tension of the moment.

"I'm sorry, I don't have any spare food. Where did you come from?" Todd asked, maintaining his position five yards from the garage door opening and thirty yards from the group of strangers. His hands remained loose at his sides, ready to move if needed.

"You mean to tell me you don't have anything you can spare?" the man exclaimed, gesturing with his hands at the property, his voice rising with each word. "Look at all this! We just need a little of food and we will leave. Just enough to feed our people."

"I'm sorry," Todd repeated firmly, his jaw set. "I don't have any spare food." The dogs continued their vigilant watch, their low growling creating an ominous undertone to the confrontation. Bear's black fur bristled along her spine while Buttercup's ears remained pinned back, both ready to spring into action.

Jason, peaking from around the side of the garage, was giving them a methodical assessment for any weapons or signs of hostile intent. So far, he hadn't spotted any obvious weapons, but the suspicious bulges on the men's hips under their jackets told him all he needed to know. His finger rested lightly against his pistol's trigger guard, ready to respond in an instant.

"Well, I find that hard to believe," the man spat, now sounding more upset and visibly agitated, his hands clenching into fists at his sides. His face reddened as he continued, "You think it's right to have all the supplies and not share it, huh? What are we supposed to do, just starve to death while you sit here hoarding all the food? Is that the kind of person you are?"

"I don't know what you think you know, but it's not my intent nor duty to feed every hand that comes down the road. I'm sorry, you'll have to seek food elsewhere." Todd's voice was firm and resolute, attempting to leave no room for argument. His stance remained steady, though his muscles tensed imperceptibly beneath his clothing as he watched the group's reaction.

"Fine! We'll just see about that," the man turned to the rest of his party in disgust, his boots scuffing against the dirt as he spun around. "Come on. Let's get out of here. We'll have to let the others know what we were told." His voice was deliberately loud enough for Todd to hear, carrying an unmistakable threat in its tone. The group began backing away, throwing dark glances over their shoulders as they retreated down the path they'd come from.

The group trudged down the driveway, their footsteps crunching on the gravel. Jason silently slipped up the hill from the garage, positioning himself behind thick foliage where he could maintain surveillance on them when they reached the road. To his surprise and growing unease, instead of turning right to head back up the road as expected, the group veered left toward the dead end. Meanwhile, Todd moved with deliberate casualness toward Bear and Buttercup, who were still alertly tracking the group's movements through their retreating sounds. He stroked their fur and spoke in low, soothing tones until their hackles lowered.

A few minutes later, Jason returned to the garage where Todd had retreated to, both men maintaining a watchful eye on the driveway tree line through the open bay door.

"You're not going to believe this," Jason said, keeping his voice barely above a whisper. "They turned left on the road."

Todd quickly snapped his head around and stared at Jason, his weathered features tightening. "Left did you say?"

"Left."

"Well, that's odd. There's nothing that way except a dead end. Did you hear him say 'tell the others'?"

"Sure did. That means they are probably camping somewhere down in the valley. We might have a problem on our hands. If there's more of them, they'll be back. Starvation could make people act irrational. I bet they make a run on us." The sound of concern resonated deeply in Jason's voice as he absently checked the weapon on his hip.

"I agree. They didn't see you, so they probably think I'm alone with the dogs. So I think we have the advantage." Todd's voice now matched Jason's concern as he stroked Buttercup's head thoughtfully. "We need to find that camp and see how many people we might be dealing with. The sooner the better."

The evening sun had long since dipped behind the mountains as Todd and Jason stepped out of the basement. Their breath formed clouds in the cold air while they clicked on their tactical flashlights.

Bear and Buttercup bounded ahead, their paws crunching in the thin layer of snow that blanketed the ground.

"Let's start with the greenhouse," Todd whispered, sweeping his light beam in wide arcs across the property. The dogs moved with practiced efficiency, noses to the ground as they led the way through the gathering darkness.

Jason kept his rifle slung but ready, matching Todd's pace as they approached the greenhouse. Their lights caught the glint of frost forming on the glass panels. The wood stove's chimney inside puffed steady streams of smoke into the night sky.

Bear's head snapped up, her ears perking forward. She moved toward the back corner of the greenhouse, her black form barely visible against the darkness. Buttercup followed close behind, her posture alert but not aggressive.

"Hold up," Todd raised his fist in a military style stop signal. Both men lowered their lights and crouched low, listening intently to the night sounds around them.

The dogs investigated something near the greenhouse foundation, their noses working overtime. Jason crept forward, keeping his profile low as he approached. His light beam revealed fresh footprints in the snow - prints that hadn't been there during their patrol last night.

"Someone's been scouting us," Jason breathed, tracing the prints with his light. The tracks led from the tree line to the greenhouse and back again, stopping at several points along the way as if someone had been studying the building's layout.

Bear and Buttercup continued following the scent trail, leading them around the exterior of the greenhouse. The prints showed the intruder had methodically circled the entire structure, likely looking for vulnerabilities. At the back side, they found where the person had scraped away snow to examine the vents.

Todd's flashlight beam caught something odd near the greenhouse's north wall. The freshly tilled soil showed several uniform depressions that didn't match their footprints or the dog's paw prints. He tapped Jason's shoulder and pointed to the disturbed earth.

"Check this out." Todd crouched down, keeping his voice low. The rectangular impressions formed a pattern in the dark soil, each about six inches long.

Jason knelt beside him, studying the marks while Bear and Buttercup continued their perimeter search. He brushed away some snow with his gloved hand to reveal more of the depressions.

"Those look deliberate." Jason traced the edge of one mark with his finger. "Too uniform to be random. Someone took measurements maybe."

Todd nodded, sweeping his light in a wider arc across the ground. Similar depressions appeared at regular intervals along the greenhouse foundation. "I don't understand what I'm looking at. Distance between support posts, maybe?"

Bear returned to Todd's side, her nose twitching as she investigated the marks. Buttercup stood on alert several yards away, her attention fixed on the tree line.

"I don't know either," Jason muttered, measuring the space between depressions with his hand span. "But I can tell you some animal did not make these looking for food."

The soil around each mark showed clean edges, as if someone had carefully pressed a tool into the ground rather than stumbling around in the dark. Todd recognized the methodical approach. - he racked his brain trying to figure out the reason, but just couldn't put two and two together. Jason had already given up on trying to figure it out about ten seconds after he thought about it.

Todd's flashlight beam caught something in the snow beyond the disturbed soil. He traced the light slowly across the ground, revealing multiple sets of boot prints that emerged from the darkness of the tree line. The tracks carved sharp, crisp edges in the fresh powder - they couldn't be more than a day old.

"Jason." Todd kept his voice low, gesturing with his light. "We've got company."

Jason crouched down to examine the prints while Bear and Buttercup worked on the scent trail. The tracks showed at least three different boot patterns, each leading from the trees toward the greenhouse windows. They stopped about ten feet short of the glass, as if the intruders had stood there studying the interior.

"At least size ten," Jason noted, comparing the distinct patterns. "Look at how they overlap - they came through multiple times, either at different hours or walked back and forth."

The dogs' behavior shifted as they reached the spot where the boots had lingered. Bear's hackles rose while Buttercup let out a low growl, her nose working overtime at something in the snow.

Todd swept his light across the ground again, counting the different tread patterns. "Three, maybe four sets. See how they spread out here?" He traced the way the prints fanned into a loose semi-circle facing the greenhouse. "They were checking sight lines through the windows."

The pristine edges of the prints stood out against the older, weather-worn snow around them. Some still showed the fine texture of the boot treads, preserved in the freezing temperatures. Jason brushed away a dusting of fresh powder, revealing the sharp detail underneath.

"These were made since yesterday's snow for sure," he said, studying the clear imprints. "During the night when we were working on the four-wheelers, or sleeping most likely."

Todd and Jason followed the boot prints back toward the tree line, their flashlight beams cutting through the darkness. Bear and Buttercup ranged ahead, their noses working the ground as they tracked the scent.

The prints led into a dense patch of pine trees, where broken branches and scattered needles marked the intruders' passage. Todd crouched to examine a snapped twig at chest height.

"Clean break, still sticky with sap," he noted, running his gloved finger along the jagged edge. "Recent."

Jason's light revealed more signs of disturbance - trampled undergrowth, scuffed bark on tree trunks, and displaced rocks along what appeared to be a makeshift path heading west. The dogs' interest intensified as they worked deeper into the trees.

"Look here." Jason pointed to where someone had cleared away pine needles, creating a small observation post with a clear view of the greenhouse.

They continued following the trail west, finding more evidence of recent human activity. Broken branches formed rough arrows, visible only to those who knew what to look for. The signs pointed toward the northwest where the desperate group had disappeared earlier that day.

Bear froze suddenly, her attention fixed on something ahead. Buttercup moved to flank her, both dogs' postures rigid with alertness. Todd and Jason immediately killed their lights and dropped into defensive positions.

Through gaps in the trees, they caught glimpses of artificial light - perhaps a campfire or lanterns - flickering somewhere in the distance. The dogs' reaction and the trail of evidence all pointed to the same conclusion: they'd found the direction of the strangers' camp.

Todd and Jason crept back toward the house, their boots silent in the fresh snow. The dogs maintained a protective formation - Bear ranging ahead while Buttercup brought up the rear, both alert for any movement in the darkness.

"We need to rethink the greenhouse security," Todd murmured as they approached the basement door. "Those measurements they took? That's pre-planning something."

Inside the warmth of the kitchen, they shed their snow-covered gear. Jason laid his rifle on the wooden table while Todd spread out a detailed property map he'd drawn years ago. Bear and Buttercup settled near the sliding glass doors, still watchful.

"Here's where we found the prints." Todd marked several X's on the map. "And their observation post was right about here." He tapped a spot in the tree line. "They've got clear sight lines to both entrance points."

Jason traced the potential approach routes with his finger. "That camp must be sitting about here." He pointed to several spots. "Just down in the valley behind the terrain. That's why we could see them from the greenhouse, but not the house at night."

They spent the next hour mapping out defensive improvements, Todd's engineering background emerging as they analyzed each vulnerability. Todd's prepper mindset had already anticipated many scenarios, but the methodical nature of their visitors required additional countermeasures.

"We need to consider that they've already mapped our routine," Jason said, reviewing their daily schedule. "They knew exactly when to scout the greenhouse - while we were distracted with maintenance work."

"Time to implement random patrol patterns." Todd marked several alternate routes on the map. "Vary our timing, change up the dogs' perimeter sweeps. Keep them guessing."

Bear's head lifted suddenly, her attention drawn to something outside. Buttercup moved to the window, a low growl rumbling in her throat. Both men instantly fell silent, moving to peer out the windows.

After several tense moments, the dogs relaxed. Todd peeked through the curtains, sweeping the darkness with keen eyes. "Probably deer. But that's another thing - we need better nighttime visibility. I really wish I would have invested in some good thermal binoculars."

"For sure! That would be a game changer." Jason made a mental note. "I tell what we should do. We should slip down into the woods and see what's going on at that camp. The older boys can keep watch, and if they see something, they can radio us to come back home. Then we'd probably have a real advantage of coming up from behind them. But seriously, we need to get down to that camp and gather some intel."

They refined their plans well into the night, drawing from years of knowing the terrain. Todd's basement workshop contained most of the materials they'd need - he'd stockpiled supplies precisely for situations like this.

"First light, we'll head down through the woods," Todd said, organizing their materials list. "I want to be back by noon."

"I'll take first watch tonight." Jason checked his rifle magazine. "We should assume they're already watching the house."

Todd nodded, reviewing their defensive diagram one last time. The bullish nature of their visitors' reconnaissance worried him - these weren't simple refugees looking for food, they were opportunistic raiders. They had taken the risk of coming onto the property and poking around the greenhouse.

Bear and Buttercup remained vigilant by the door as the men finalized their plan. Their instincts had proven reliable before, and their earlier reaction to the intruders' scent suggested these visitors posed a genuine threat.

"I don't think it's safe for the kids or Bobbie to be outside the house without us with them," Todd added, showing the dangers of leaving them alone. "They should stay inside, upstairs and make sure the doors are secured. Your older boys need to stay armed, or at least have a weapon close if it's needed, God forbid."

"Totally agree. I'll have a discussion with them." Jason sketched a quick note and stuck it on the pantry door for Bobbie to see first thing in the morning. "There, just in case she gets up early and wants to go to the greenhouse before I wake up or something."

They spent another hour sitting on the deck, thinking through the plan and making minor adjustments for the following day.

Chapter 11

THE CAMP RECON

The morning sun was just showing signs of dawn as Todd and Jason methodically packed their supplies. Their movements carried the practiced efficiency of men who'd been into these woods countless times before.

"Extra magazines?" Todd checked items off his list.

"Got three." Jason zipped up a tactical backpack. "Plus the spotting scope."

Todd's German Shepherds, Bear and Buttercup, lounged in the corner, their ears perking up at every sound from outside. The cold morning air carried the scent of dew-covered grass through the garage.

"How's Bobby handling all this?" Todd folded a topographical map of the area.

Jason paused, his hand hovering over a stack of energy bars. "She's worried, but she understands. Especially with what happened in the other day-"

A ground shaking rumble interrupted Jason as the ground beneath them shook like an earthquake.

The rumble was strong enough to rattle tools and the garage door. Bear and Buttercup leaped to their feet, barking frantically, trying to understand what they were sensing.

"What the heck was that?" Todd stepped outside the garage, pulling Jason with him.

They stood in motionless silence, waiting to see if anything else would happen.

"Do you know what that reminded me of?" Jason looking out at the horizon half expecting to see a smoke plum. "That sounded or felt just like the Abu Grab explosion in Iraq in '09."

Todd turned his head in a full scan of the area. "Hard to tell how far away that was. If I didn't know any better, it felt like an earthquake... like the ones I felt in California."

"Oh, I wonder if George blew the bridge?" Jason's face showing signs of wonder.

"Well, that would make sense. Let's see if we can reach him on the radio." Todd walked over to the ham radio and grabbed the microphone from the bench. "Overlook Ridge to George, do you copy?"

Todd and Jason waiting silently for a minute before Todd repeated the call.

"This is George. You guys hear that?" Jason now stepping closer to Todd. "I blew the bridge. You guys should have seen it. Wow!" George answered in a very noticeable tone of excitement and pride.

Todd looked over at Jason, who was smiling. "It shook the whole ground over here! Must have been a hell of a sight, over." Both Todd and Jason were already starting to relax, evident in their shoulders losing tension. Both were still smiling.

"Yeah, I should have warned you, but I didn't think it was going to be that big of an explosion. Wow," George was still excited about his accomplishment. "Well, I guess that's done. If you need to leave the ranch, use the fire escape road."

"Roger that. I will reach back out to you tonight and see how things are. Over." Todd used his hand and finger to circle his ear, showing that George was a little crazy.

"Ok, stay safe! Out here." And with that, Todd placed the microphone down and he and Jason both chuckled about how excited George had been. Both remarking they would have loved to see that explosion.

Todd and Jason loaded their gear onto the four-wheelers and strapped everything down tight. Bear and Buttercup bounded alongside as they started the engines, their paws kicking up small clouds of dust from the dry ground.

"Don't worry, they'll turn around once we reach the bottom," Todd called to Jason as he revved his engine.

The four-wheelers wound through the dense pine and scrub oak, following a path Todd had cleared years ago. Branches whipped past their shoulders as they navigated the rough terrain. The morning sun just starting to brighten the dawn through the canopy, throwing faded shadows across their path. The snow had just melted enough that the path was traveled with ease.

After fifteen minutes of riding, they reached the western edge of Overlook Ridge. Just as Todd had expected, Buttercup and Bear had stopped following about halfway and returned to the house. Todd cut his engine first, Jason following suit. The sudden silence amplified the natural sounds of the forest - birds calling, leaves rustling in the breeze.

"Now we walk," Todd whispered. Both men gathered their equipment and prepared for a half-mile hike into the Colorado expanse beyond Overlook Ridge.

They shouldered their packs and moved on foot, picking their way through the undergrowth. Their boots made a minimal noise on the forest floor, years of walking in these parts of the woods showing in their movements.

Jason tapped Todd's shoulder and pointed to a game trail cutting through the brush. They followed it, moving slower now, each step calculated. The slope gradually increased as they approached their chosen observation point.

At the crest of a small ridge, they dropped to their stomachs and crawled the final few yards. A natural depression in the rock formation provided cover while offering a clear view of the valley below.

Jason pulled out the spotting scope while Todd raised his binoculars. The camp spread out before them, a collection of a few travel trailers, mismatched tents and makeshift shelters scattered across a clearing.

"I count twenty-three," Jason whispered, adjusting the scope's focus. "No, twenty-four. Got another one behind that blue tarp."

Todd swept his binoculars across the scene. A group of men gathered around a smoking fire pit, while others moved between the tents. The camp had the disorganized look of a temporary settlement, but the number of people suggested something more permanent.

"They've got weapons." Todd focused on two men carrying rifles. "AR-15s, looks like. And that guy sitting by the first camper has a shotgun. Looks like the homeless encampment in the Springs."

Jason shifted the scope. "Got a couple of trucks and a couple of four wheelers next to the campers. Can't make out the plates from here. Looks like Colorado though."

A woman emerged from one of the larger tents, carrying what looked like a cooking pot. Children - Todd counted at least three - trailed behind her.

"Families," Todd muttered. "This isn't just some hunting party."

"Look at their setup," Jason responded. "Campers, a few generators, water collection system. They're planning to stay."

Todd lowered his binoculars and pulled out his notebook, sketching a rough map of the camp's layout. He marked the positions of the vehicles, weapons he'd spotted, and potential guard positions.

"They've got higher ground to the north," Jason continued his assessment. "But they left their southern approach wide open. Amateur move."

A man's voice carried up from the camp, sharp with authority. The group around the fire dispersed, moving with purpose toward various tasks.

"That's their leader," Todd marked the man's camper that he had emerged from on his sketch. "Gray jacket, baseball cap. Looks like the same guy that did the speaking at the house."

"Ex-Military you think?" Jason questioned. "Watch how the others defer to him."

They spent another thirty minutes observing, documenting movements and patterns. The camp operated with a loose structure - certainly not military order, but more like casual organized campers.

"We should head back," Todd tucked his notebook away. "Got what we need for now."

They backed away from the ridge with the same careful movements they'd used on approach. Once clear of the immediate area, they picked up their pace, retracing their steps to where they'd left the four-wheelers.

Bear and Buttercup waited exactly where Todd thought they'd be, their ears perking up at their masters' return. Todd gave them each a quick pat before dismounting his four-wheeler.

"What do you think?" Jason asked as they unloaded the gear and strapped it back down onto the four wheelers.

"I think we come up with a plan on how to deal with this. It's just a matter of time before things get serious. The footprints around the greenhouse, the small group that came asking for food. They know exactly where to get food when they are ready." Todd checked his watch. "We have the rest of the day. Let's secure everything down tighter and talk this over this afternoon."

"Agreed," Unloading his weapon and taking his tactical vest off, Jason was already thinking of what he would do. He realized it would take some convincing of Todd, however.

The aroma of Bobbie's beef stew lingered in the air as Todd and Jason stepped out onto the upper deck. The evening air carried a sharp bite - winter was in full swing in Colorado, but the front had moved on and slightly warmer temperatures were regaining a foothold for the time being. Stars started to pierce the darkness overhead, their light undiminished by the electrical grids only being used for emergencies in the North.

"Bobbie outdid herself tonight." Todd settled into one of the rocking deck chairs as he reached into his pocket and produced an electronic relaxer.

Jason nodded, taking the chair beside him. "Those garden vegetables made all the difference. She's got an entire list of things she's planning in the greenhouse. If it wasn't for her, we'd be eating Ramon noddles."

They sat in comfortable silence, both men processing what they'd observed at the camp earlier. The deck offered a clear view of the surrounding territory to the west, though now it showed only darkness broken by occasional starlight glinting off patches of remaining snow.

"Twenty-four people," Todd finally spoke. "That's a lot of mouths to feed."

"And they'll get desperate soon enough." Jason took a sip of his coffee. "Question is, do we wait for that to happen?"

"I know what you're thinking. A preemptive strike could backfire. We would be seen as the aggressors."

"True. But waiting gives them time to learn our routines, find our weak spots." Jason set his cup down. "They're already probing - those tracks around the greenhouse weren't just for wonder."

Todd leaned forward, elbows on his knees. "If we move first, we need to be surgical. Clean. No collateral damage with those families present. How do we do this without people getting hurt?"

"We could try to make contact first. Set boundaries." Jason's voice carried doubt even as he suggested it.

"They already crossed that line when they cased our property instead of approaching openly." Todd's finger traced the rim of his cup. "But a show of force might be enough to convince them to move on."

"Or it could push them to act sooner than they planned." Jason stood and walked to the deck railing, looking out into the darkness. "Either way, we need to decide soon. We probably only have a few days at best."

The men remained silent for several long minutes, each lost in their own strategic calculations, before Jason finally broke the uncomfortable quiet that had settled between them.

"What if we harass them enough to make them break camp and move somewhere else?" He sat back down in his chair and tapped the arm the armrest, the steady rhythm matching his racing thoughts.

Todd leaned back, squinting one eye as he considered the proposition, his weathered face creasing in concentration. The idea had merit, but the execution would be tricky.

"Maybe," Todd replied thoughtfully, maintaining his contemplative squint. "What would that look like? Can't strike their vehicles, cause then they couldn't move. Can't strike their remaining food supply, cause then they would come here faster-" His voice trailed off as he mentally cataloged the potential pitfalls of each option.

"I got it," Jason suddenly straightened, leaning back into his chair with renewed energy, his eyes bright with inspiration. "We burn them out."

Todd shifted his gaze over towards his friend, studying him with careful consideration. "Interesting. But how do we do that without burning our own place down?"

"The cold front just passed through, which means the winds will soon be shifting back west," Jason explained, gesturing with his hands to illustrate the weather pattern. "The winds should keep it moving west, away from us. Besides, they are in an open land with nothing but dry grass. Once that fire hits the tree line, I doubt it could advance with all the snow packed on the ground beneath the trees. The moisture content is too high."

Todd sat thinking, putting his calloused finger to his lips to ponder the implications. His eyes narrowed as he mentally mapped the terrain and wind patterns he'd observed over his years on the property. Jason waited patiently for Todd's reply and was still working out his own tactical details in his mind, drumming his fingers softly on the arm of his chair. After a minute of careful consideration, Todd started nodding his head with growing conviction.

"I like it. I think that might actually work," he said, leaning forward in his chair. "If they catch it in time, they'll move their vehicles as fast as they can to save them. They must have come from the west because there's no access from the east - nothing but wilderness that way. Which means they would naturally retreat further west. Even if we only manage to move them a mile further west, that gives us a much greater buffer zone." Todd's voice grew stronger, more confident in the developing strategy. "If they persist in harassing us after that warning shot, well, then we'll just have to take it up a notch. Show them we mean business."

"The next step would be something like we start picking off men in the raiding parties. If several men go out and don't come back... they'll be forced to do something different. I would hate to take away fathers from children. They are just trying to survive. Not sure I would have even walked down the driveway." Jason was now standing again, his nervous energy making it impossible to stay seated. His fingers drummed against his thigh as he paced the composite wooden planks of the deck.

"I don't want to kill anybody unless it's in self-defense," Todd added solemnly, his weathered face creased with concern. "Those kids down there won't survive with their fathers. We'd be creating orphans in an already desperate situation."

Jason knew he was right, but the way Todd had stated the situation hit him like a punch to the gut. He agreed with Todd - they needed a solution that wouldn't tear families apart.

"Agreed." Jason's mind wandered, reflecting on how his previous statement would have sounded to any sane person before everything had changed so dramatically. The very idea of discussing tactical elimination of other human beings would have been unthinkable or be seen as a joke.

The men finished their soothing coffee in contemplative silence, watching the steam rise into the frosty night air before retreating into the warmth of the house. The plan continued to formulate options in their thoughts as they processed the gravity of their situation.

Once settled inside, Todd decided to sleep on the back deck with Bear to oversee the greenhouse, setting up a makeshift bed with thermal blankets and his old camping pad. If any visitors arrived in the middle of the night, the dog's keen senses would alert him instantly, and he could flood the area with the powerful back flood lights he'd installed last summer. The elevated back deck offered a perfect tactical view of both the greenhouse and the dense woods surrounding the locations where they'd found signs of activity from the tree line. He settled in for what he hoped would be an uneventful night watch.

Todd and Jason gathered their supplies in the pre-dawn darkness. They loaded the ATVs with jerry cans of gasoline, road flares, and accelerant-soaked rags wrapped around arrows. Bear and Buttercup watched from the deck, their ears perked forward as their masters prepared for the mission.

"We'll need to set multiple ignition points," Todd said, securing the last container. "The wind's picking up from the east, just like you predicted. I just hope it dies out before it does any real damage."

Jason checked his rifle, then slung it across his back. "If we time this right, they'll have no choice but to move west. The fire will create a natural barrier between us."

They drove their ATVs through the woods with their lights off, using only the moonlight to navigate. They took a circuitous route to avoid detection. The frozen ground crackled beneath their tires as they approached their chosen position. Dawn was still an hour away when they reached the elevated ridge overlooking the camp.

"Look there." Todd pointed to several vehicles parked in a clearing. "They've got at least four trucks, so they should be good to move the children and women out quickly.. They'll have no choice but to move west if the fire reaches them. Let's hope it does."

Jason pulled out his binoculars. "I count, maybe four guys in the open right now. Must be the night watch party or something. We'll need to create a wide enough arc of fire to force them further west. Let's split up like we discussed."

They split up, moving through the scrub oak to place their incendiary devices. Todd poured gasoline in strategic lines, creating paths for the fire to follow. Jason set up the road flares in a long line, spacing them evenly to ensure maximum coverage.

The sky began to brighten in the east as they finished their preparations. The wind had picked up, blowing steadily from behind them - perfect conditions for their plan. They took positions on opposite ends of their planned fire line, waiting for the optimal moment to strike.

"Ready?" Todd's voice crackled softly over the radio.

"Ready," Jason confirmed. "On your mark."

Todd lit the first flare, and the brush caught immediately. The flames spread along the gasoline trail, creating a bright orange line in the dim morning light. Across the clearing, Jason's flares ignited in sequence, their chemical fire catching the accelerant-soaked ground.

The wind carried embers and smoke westward, exactly as planned. The fire grew rapidly, consuming the drought-stricken vegetation. Smoke billowed into the sky, creating a thick curtain that drifted toward the camp.

They sprinted back to their observation point, keeping low and moving fast through the undergrowth. The crackling of burning wood filled the air as they pulled their binoculars and spotting scoop out to observe.

From their vantage point, they watched the orange glow spread. The fire line formed a perfect arc, pushing west with the wind. Black smoke rose in thick columns against the lightening sky.

"Look," Jason pointed toward movement in the camp below. Figures darted between tents and vehicles. Shouts carried up to their position as the group below realized the danger approaching them.

Todd peered through his binoculars. The camp erupted into frantic activity. People poured from tents, grabbing what they could carry. Vehicle engines roared to life, positioning themselves to link up their campers.

The fire continued its steady march westward, consuming everything in its path. The heat was visible now, distorting the air above the flames. Just as they'd planned, the only clear escape route lay to the west, away from Outlook Ridge.

The camp below descended into chaos as the fire line grew closer to the camp. Through the thickening smoke, Todd tracked the group's hasty evacuation. Tents collapsed, supplies scattered across the ground as people rushed to load the vehicles.

"They're moving faster than expected," Jason said, adjusting his position behind a large boulder. "Look at how dis-organized that loading operation is. They're freaking out," he chuckled.

A man's voice carried up from below, barking orders through the smoke. The evacuation proceeded with chaos - vehicles moving for quick departure, leaving chairs, cooking equipment, and other minor supplies behind.

Todd shifted his focus to the fire line. The flames had grown into a towering wall, driven by the steady wind. Thick smoke rolled westward, forcing the camp's occupants to cover their faces as they worked.

"They better work faster," Todd said, packing away his observation gear. "That fire's picking up speed."

The camp's vehicles began pulling out one by one, heading west along the only clear route from which they came. Through gaps in the smoke, Todd counted four trucks towing campers, plus two SUVs - all loaded with people and supplies.

Todd and Jason made their way back to the ATVs. "Mission accomplished. They're moving out exactly as planned. That couldn't have gone any better."

The convoy disappeared into the morning haze, leaving behind only trampled ground and scattered debris. The fire continued its controlled burn, creating exactly the barrier they'd intended between their property and the former camp location.

"That fire will probably run another mile before it does out. At least I hope. Otherwise, we might have just burnt half of southern Colorado." The worry was evident in Todd's voice.

"Na, it will be fine. Once it hits the tree line on the other side, it will burn out. I think. Maybe. Hopefully." Jason responded with a noticeable doubt but hopeful tone.

Todd and Jason guided their ATVs back through the winding forest paths toward Outlook Ridge. The morning sun now filtered through the trees, a slight fog coming off the frozen ground. Smoke from their controlled burn was still being carried west by the persistent wind.

They pulled up to Todd's garage, where Bear and Buttercup bounded down from the deck and out the basement door to greet them. The dogs circled the vehicles, tails wagging as their masters dismounted.

"Those jerry cans are sure lighter coming back empty," Todd grunted, lifting the metal containers from the ATV's rack. He stacked them near the workshop door for cleaning.

Jason unstrapped the rifle cases and tactical gear. "At least we didn't need these." He carried the weapons inside to return them to the gun rack.

The unused road flares and accelerant-soaked arrows went back into their designated storage containers. Todd marked off the used supplies in his inventory notebook, making notes to replenish what they'd consumed.

"Some gas spilt out on the ride back. We should clean these ATVs before any gas residue corrodes something," Todd said, pulling out a water hose. Bear settled nearby, watching as he sprayed down the metal surfaces. Jason disappeared into the house.

A few minutes later, he emerged from the house with two steaming mugs of coffee. "Bobbie's got breakfast going. Says we earned it." He handed a mug to Todd and helped wipe down the second ATV.

They worked in comfortable silence, methodically returning each piece of gear to its proper place. The morning's operation had gone smoothly - no need for words to complicate that satisfaction.

Chapter 12

NORMAL PACE

Life settled into a cautious routine over the following weeks. Todd spent his mornings checking the perimeter fences, Bear and Buttercup trotting faithfully at his heels. The German Shepherds' ears perked at every rustle in the undergrowth, but the threats they investigated turned out to be nothing more sinister than squirrels and rabbits.

"Another quiet day, girls." Todd scratched behind Bear's ears as they completed their rounds. The dog leaned into his touch, tail wagging.

Jason had established a network of trail cameras throughout the surrounding forest, positioning them at strategic points along likely approach routes. Each evening, the two men would review the footage over coffee at Todd's kitchen table.

"Nothing but deer, elk, and a few cougars again." Jason clicked through the images on his laptop. "Still think we should rotate the cameras weekly, keep our coverage fresh."

"Agreed." Todd topped off their mugs from the French press. "Better to stay sharp even when nothing's happening. That's the hardest part. Not to get lazy when times are easy."

They maintained their shooting practice, heading out to the range Todd had set up with a natural backstop behind the house. The crack of their rifles echoed through the hills twice a week, keeping their skills honed.

"Your groupings tightened up," Todd observed one afternoon as they inspected their targets.

"Bobby's been giving me grief about burning through so much ammo." Jason reloaded his magazine. "Told her it's cheaper than a gym membership."

They took turns staying up for night watch, four-hour shifts that left them bleary-eyed but satisfied they weren't leaving themselves vulnerable. Todd used the quiet hours to tinker in his workshop, the familiar rhythms of engineering problems keeping his mind sharp.

The vegetable garden flourished under Bobbie's attention. Todd had expanded it by another thirty square feet, the fresh rows as neat and precise as any military formation. Root vegetables and hardy greens filled the beds - practical crops that would store well.

"Getting to be time to put up the tomatoes." Jason helped Todd harvest another basket of ripe fruit one morning. "Bobby's got her mother's canning recipe. I'm not a big canning fan, but I've noticed I've become a lot less picky these days."

"As long as it's not a casserole." Todd wiped sweat from his forehead. "Or anything that looks like a casserole." Jason chuckled, never understanding Todd's distaste for anything that even remotely resembled a casserole.

They maintained radio contact with their like-minded neighbors, checking in during scheduled windows using the same channels. The conversations were casual on the surface - weather reports, garden updates, local gossip - but underlying each exchange was the silent understanding that if something went wrong, they'd know who to call.

Todd kept his bug-out bags packed and ready, one by the bed and one in his truck. He rotated the supplies monthly, checking expiration dates and updating the charts, and changing out the seasonal gear. The routine was so ingrained he could have done it in his sleep.

"Do you feel like we are overreacting to the situation?" Jason asked one evening as they sat on Todd's upper deck, watching the sun sink behind the hills.

"Rather be paranoid than dead." Todd sipped his bottled coke. "Besides, most of what we're doing is just good sense. Garden's feeding us, shooting practice is a solid hobby, and the dogs need the exercise of working the perimeter."

Bear and Buttercup lay at their feet, alert even in rest. A twig snapped in the forest and both dogs' heads came up, ears forward, before relaxing again.

They'd hardened the property's infrastructure too, installing solar backup systems and reinforcing doors with braces from the inside. Todd had made metal window covers that could be installed from the inside to ensure bullets wouldn't penetrate to the inside of the house. Todd had always been prepared, but now every system had redundancies, every weakness addressed. He had at least three of every tool, unfortunately half were either miss placed of missing all together. Jason wondered how a man that is so meticulous could misplace so many tools.

"Thinking about putting in that plastic covered greenhouse I have in the garage," Todd mentioned as they checked the backup generator's fuel levels. "Get a jump on the growing some things that don't require so much attention. Like herbs and such Like a spice garden."

"Makes sense. Just need to either find some half way level ground, or use the tracker to do some work." Jason glancing over at the old backhoe sitting lonely on the edge of the clearing. "Might as well be productive while we're playing sentinel."

The weather turned warmer as spring approached, bringing longer days and shorter nights. They adjusted their patrol schedules accordingly, even adding fishing string trip wires down the driveway that would set off noise makers.

"Bears are getting active again," Todd noted one morning, reviewing camera footage that showed a large black bear ambling through the frame. "Need to make sure they don't tear down a wall to get food."

"And keep the dogs close after dark." Jason zoomed in on an image of a mountain lion. "That's a healthy-sized male."

Despite the circumstances that brought them together, the Glose family's presence had transformed Todd's house into something warmer than it had been in years. Laughter echoed through rooms that had known only silence, and the kitchen buzzed with activity as Bobbie worked her culinary magic.

"These biscuits are incredible," Todd said, reaching for his third one at breakfast. "Having fresh food is such a big deal."

"Bobbie's famous recipe," Jason grinned, drowning his portion in honey. "I could eat these every day. I'm just happy she figured out a way to stop burning bread. Back home, it became a running joke of how many times she would burn bread in the oven."

The kids had found their rhythms too. They took turns helping Bobbie in the garden, learning which plants needed what care. Even Bear had warmed up to them, especially when they snuck her bits of bacon under the table. To her, they were family now.

During evenings, they gathered in the living room. Card games became fierce competitions, with Todd teaching the younger ones poker or showing them card tricks he barely remembered. Buttercup would curl up by the stove, tail thumping against the floor whenever someone celebrated a winning hand.

"Full house!" Rose laid down her cards triumphantly. "Pay up, Uncle Todd."

"That's my girl." Jason beamed as Todd pushed his pile of chips toward her. "Taking after her old man's poker face."

They'd set up a projector in the front bedroom, screening movies from Todd's extensive collection on Friday nights. Bobbie would make popcorn the old-fashioned way, in a pot on the stove, and they'd all pile onto couches and sleeping bags spread across the floor.

"I haven't felt this relaxed in months," Todd admitted to Jason one evening as they watched the kids squirt water guns at each other in the yard. The spring air was sweet with pine, and somewhere in the distance, a hawk called.

"Never thought I'd say this about the end of civilization," Jason replied, "but there's something to be said for slowing down, being with family."

The dogs romped with the children, their barks mixing with squeals of delight. Even their security patrols had taken on a lighter tone, with Jason and Todd swapping stories and jokes as they made their rounds.

All in all, life had settled into a comfortable pattern at Overlook Ridge. The two men had found a natural rhythm working together, their different skills complementing each other perfectly.

They'd found peace in their isolation, purpose in their daily routines. The world beyond their mountain might have changed, but on Overlook Ridge, they'd built something that worked. Something that felt right.

"You know," Todd said, watching Bobbie hang laundry on the line while humming to herself, "for all the chaos that brought us here, we've landed on our feet."

Jason smiled, clinking his mug against Todd's. "That we have, old friend. Thanks to you."

Chapter 13

POWER FAILURE

The mountain air carried the sweet scent of blooming wildflowers through Overlook Ridge. Bobbie and the kids were in bed as Todd sat at his kitchen counter, scanning through maintenance logs when the overhead lights flickered. His German Shepherds, Bear and Buttercup, raised their heads from their beds in the corner.

The lights dimmed again, longer this time, before plunging the house into darkness. Todd's fingers froze over the paperwork.

"Jason, you see that?" Todd called out to his friend, who was tinkering in the adjacent room.

"See what? I can't see anything, the power just went out." Jason's boots thudded against the tile as he entered the kitchen. "Grid issue?"

Todd pulled a flashlight from under the counter. "Let's check the breakers first."

The beam cut through the darkness as they made their way to the electrical panel in the basement.

Bear and Buttercup followed close behind, their nails clicking against the floor.

"Everything looks normal here." Todd ran his hand over the breaker switches. "Nothing tripped."

Jason turned his flashlight on. "You wanna check the main breakers outside?"

"I guess." Todd's mind raced through possibilities. "If it's the grid, then we'll fire up the generator and check the radio."

They headed to the breaker panel behind the garage where Todd had installed an overly equipment electrical panel and generator backups. The generator hummed to life with a push of a button, and Todd and Jason made their way to the garage and settled into chairs at the radio station.

"Breaker, breaker, anyone copy?" Todd adjusted the frequency dial.

Static crackled before a voice broke through. "Randy here from Lot 47."

"Randy, we've lost power up here on Overlook Ridge. What's your status?"

"Same here, Todd. Been dark for about five minutes now."

Jason leaned closer to the microphone. "See any lights off in the distance?"

"Negative. Everything's down. Looks dark up north as well."

Todd switched frequencies. "Any Blackhawk residents, please respond."

More voices filtered through, each reporting the same situation. No power across all of Blackhawk Ranch.

"Martha from lot 92 reporting complete blackout."

"Jim here, lot 156, same situation."

"Carlos from Lot 23. Power's been out for ten minutes now."

Jason pulled up a chair. "That's reports from all corners of the ranch. No lights up north, it's probably widespread."

Todd grabbed his logbook and started noting down times and locations. "Check the emergency scanner. See if there's any chatter from emergency services."

Jason flipped through frequencies on the second radio. Nothing but static filled the room.

"Dead air." Jason's face tightened. "But that's pretty typical now days."

Bear whined at Todd's feet while Buttercup paced near the garage entrance.

"Anyone have contact with Trinidad or Walsenburg?"

Silence answered back before Randy's voice crackled through again. "Negative. Tried reaching my daughter in Trinidad. Nothing getting through."

Todd switched to the CB radio, scanning through channels. Hearing more voices filtered through, all reporting the same situation across the region.

Todd marked each location on the map. "This is too widespread to be equipment failure."

"Could be an EMP." Jason's voice remained steady, but his fingers drummed against the desk.

"Do you think we'd be talking on the radio if it was an EMP?" Todd looked over to Jason with an 'are you stupid' look. "We need to see if it's wider spread."

They spent the next twenty minutes coordinating with other ham operators across the ranch, establishing a communication network, and gathering information. The dogs settled near the doors, their ears perked at every new voice through the radio.

"We should check the batteries on the solar system," Todd said, reviewing his notes. "Make sure our backup power is solid. I really don't like that generator running too much. It's noisy. Probably here it for several miles. We don't want to be attracting the less desirables."

Jason nodded. "I'm on it. Hey, if this power outage is state-wide or something, there could be a whole new influx for people looking for help. It's like starting the disaster all over again."

The generator's hum filled the silence as Todd and Jason exchanged looks. Years of preparation had readied them for this scenario, but the reality of it settling in across their mountain community brought a weight to the air that even the dogs seemed to sense.

"Who would have thought? " Todd said as they secured the garage doors and walked back to the house in near pitch dark. Each thinking of the next steps.

Back in the house, Todd and Jason moved through each room with methodical precision to identify the non-critical systems.

"Killing the water heater." Todd called as he pulled the breaker. "We'll heat water as we need to. No sense in keeping it 120 degrees all the time."

Jason disconnected other non-essential equipment and several kitchen appliances. "What we should do is unplug everything or turn everything off, then bring up important stuff one at a time, and someone can watch the load. That would tell us the threshold of how much each item is costing us in a power draw."

"Brilliant," Todd stomping his way back up the stairs. "At night, we won't need much. Just typical

LED lights. I'm betting we have more power than we can use, but we should keep the draw as low as possible so we don't overwork or burnout the equipment."

Bobbie appeared in the kitchen doorway, wrapping her robe tighter. "The kids are all awake now. They heard the generator."

"Good timing." Todd gestured her to the dining room table. "We need to go over some changes."

The three adults gathered around the table while Bear and Buttercup kept watch near the windows. Todd spread out a diagram of the house's electrical system.

"Number one priority is security." Todd circled specific areas on the blueprint. "Motion sensors and cameras stay powered. Everything else gets rationed."

Bobbie leaned forward. "What about the greenhouse?"

"Automated systems are off. We'll handle watering manually." Jason traced the power lines with his finger. "Heating will run on minimal power during critical hours."

"The kids need to understand - no electronics unless they ask." Todd pulled out a fresh sheet of paper. "We're establishing a usage time from sunset to sunrise."

Bobbie nodded. "I'll work out a schedule for laundry and cooking during peak solar hours."

"The generator stays off unless there's an emergency." Jason marked zones on the blueprint. "Too much noise attracts attention."

Todd sketched out a daily timeline. "Two hours of power in the morning, four hours mid-day, two hours in the evening. Everything else runs on solar, which won't carry the entire house but everything we need."

"What about heating?" Bobbie asked.

"Wood stove becomes primary. Electric heat only kicks in if temperature drops below freezing." Todd made another note. "We'll move everyone to the second floor at night. Easier to heat, better defensive position anyway."

Jason stood. "I'll check the solar battery levels. We need exact numbers to plan consumption."

"I'll let the kids know." Bobbie pushed back from the table. "They need to understand these changes."

Minutes later, the full family gathered in the living room. Sleepy eyes and half awake kids slummed on the couches. Todd laid out the new protocols while Jason drew up schedules on a whiteboard.

"Each person gets one battery-powered light." Todd distributed LED lanterns. "These stay in your rooms. Use them only when necessary."

"Don't be leaving them on while you sleep." Jason pointed to the house layout. "No playing with electronic stuff between 10pm and dawn unless absolutely necessary." Jason checked his watch. "It's late. Let's finish the critical shutdowns and get some rest. Tomorrow we'll fine-tune the schedules."

They moved through the house, powering down systems. The internet router, entertainment centers, and all non-essential appliances went dark. Only security systems and minimal lighting remained active.

Todd stood at the kitchen window, watching the darkness beyond. The usual distant glow of distant cities was absent, leaving only stars to illuminate the landscape. Bear and Buttercup flanked him, their ears perked toward the night sounds.

"We'll need to adjust the dogs' routines, too." Jason joined him at the window.

Bobbie finished noting down the new protocols. "I'll post these in the older kids' room. No excuses for forgetting."

"Remember," Todd turned to face them, "this isn't just about saving power. Every light, every sound carries for miles up here. We need to be invisible after dark now. Like Jason said, this might cause a whole new wave of people coming looking for people who have power."

The house settled into its new rhythm as systems powered down one by one. The familiar hum of modern life faded into mountain silence, broken only by the occasional creak of the house and the soft padding of dog paws on tiled floors.

Jason whispered as he slipped into bed next to Bobbie. "It's so quiet now. I guess that means no-"

"Go to sleep, Jas!" Bobbie cut him off with a voice that left no room for rebuttal.

Chapter 14

MAKING IT STRONG

✳ Sunlight streamed through the glass panels, casting diamond patterns across the earthen floor. Bobbie wiped beads of sweat from her forehead as she knelt beside the wooden planter boxes. The greenhouse air hung thick with the scent of damp soil and green things pushing through dark earth. The power failure of recent demanded adjustments, but the greenhouse had grown into an almost self sustaining environment. With the heat of spring, less and less external heat needed to be applied.

"Bruce, honey, hand me those tomato markers." She reached toward her second oldest, who dug through a box of wooden stakes.

"These?" Bruce held up a handful of weathered markers, their tips stained with last season's dirt.

"Perfect." Bobbie pressed them into the soil beside the tiny sprouts. Their leaves, no bigger than her polished pinky nail, reached toward the warming rays above. "Jack, how are those peas coming along?"

Her middle son crouched at the far end of the greenhouse, carefully untangling tendrils from their metal support. "They're getting all twisted up again. Don't know how they do it overnight."

"Plants are sneaky that way." Bobbie shuffled over to help, her knees leaving impressions in the soft ground. "See here? You've got to be gentle when you wrap them. They're still learning which way to grow."

Rose pressed her face against the glass wall, leaving small fingerprints. "Mama, the butterflies are back! Can we plant more flowers for them?"

"Already ahead of you, sweetie." Bobbie pointed to the neat rows of marigold and zinnia seedlings pushing through the soil near the door. "Those'll bring plenty of butterflies once they bloom."

Hyden, her eldest, hauled in a fresh bag of potting soil. "Where do you want this, Mom?"

"By the cucumber starts. We'll need it when we thin them out next week." She watched him set down the heavy bag, noting how big he'd grown over the last few years. Soon he'd be looking down at her.

Juliet walked between the rows, a watering can clutched in her hands. Water sloshed over the sides with each step.

"Careful there, Jules." Bobbie steadied the can. "Remember what we talked about? Just a little drink for each plant."

"Like this?" Juliet tipped the can with exaggerated care over a row of lettuce sprouts.

"That's my girl."

The morning light grew stronger, and Bobbie opened the ventilation panels to let in the fresh spring breeze. She'd waited all winter for days like this, when the world seemed to wake up again. Her children moved between the rows with practiced care, each knowing their tasks from months of helping in the greenhouse.

"Look how strong these pepper plants are getting." Bruce ran his finger along a sturdy stem. "Better than the last batch."

"That's because we started them earlier." Bobbie checked her planting calendar pinned to the wall. "The timing makes all the difference."

Jack untangled the last rebellious pea vine. "Can we plant the squash seeds today?"

"Not quite yet. Ground's still too cool." She pressed her hand into a tray of soil, testing its warmth. "Another week should do it."

Juliet had moved on to organizing seed packets, arranging them by their planting date. "Mom, we're almost out of carrot seeds."

"Put it on the list, honey. We'll need to see if Uncle Todd has any more ready." Bobbie surveyed their morning's work - neat rows of green life reaching skyward, each plant tagged and tended with care. The greenhouse had transformed from its winter sleep into a nursery of possibility.

Hyden wiped his hands on his jeans. "Should we set up the irrigation system?"

"Good thinking. The days are getting longer - they'll need regular watering soon." Bobbie checked the collection of rain barrels against the back wall. "Let's test the lines first. Make sure nothing cracked over winter."

Rose had settled into a sunny corner, arranging pebbles around a cluster of herb seedlings. "Pretty garden," she declared, patting the soil with tiny hands.

The morning stretched on, filled with the quiet sounds of growth - leaves unfurling, stems stretching, roots pushing deeper into welcoming earth. Bobbie moved between her children, guiding hands and sharing knowledge passed down through seasons of nurturing green things toward the sun.

Outside the main greenhouse, Todd and Jason unloaded sections of PVC pipe from Todd's garage. The spring breeze carried the scent of sage grass and smoke from the smoker on the deck.

"Hand me that T-joint." Todd knelt beside the partially assembled irrigation system. "We'll want the pressure consistent across all the beds."

Jason passed him the fitting. "Bobbie's got quite the operation going in there. Those kids are learning more about agriculture than I did in four years of college. Oh wait, I didn't go to college."

Through the greenhouse panels, they watched as Bobbie demonstrated the proper transplanting technique to Bruce and Jack. Her hands moved with practiced efficiency, separating delicate roots without breaking a single strand.

"Speaking of which." Todd connected another section of pipe. "That new herb greenhouse we talked about - I pulled it out of the garage this morning. Figure we can get it assembled before dinner."

"Perfect timing. Bobbie's been wanting to expand her medicinal garden." Jason sorted through a box of sprinkler heads. "The mint already taking over half the main beds, it seems."

Inside the greenhouse, Juliet pressed a tomato seed into a pot of fresh soil. "Like this, Mama?"

"Just right, sweetheart." Bobbie guided her daughter's hand to cover the seed with a thin layer of earth. "Not too deep, or it'll have trouble reaching the sun."

Hyden emerged from between rows of climbing peas, carrying a clipboard. "Mom, I've mapped out where we can put the new herb beds once the other greenhouse is up."

"Let's see what you've got." Bobbie studied his careful drawings. "Smart thinking, putting the lavender where it'll get the most sun."

Todd connected the last section of the main line. "Jason, hit the valve. Let's test for leaks."

Water coursed through the pipes, emerging in fine spray from the carefully spaced heads. The mist caught the sunlight, creating tiny rainbows above the plants.

"Pressure looks good." Jason adjusted a connector. "Though we might want to reduce flow to the seedling area."

Rose squealed with delight as the water sparkled overhead. "Look, Mama! Rainbow rain!"

"That's your Uncle Todd's engineering at work." Bobbie smiled at her youngest. "He knows exactly how much water each plant needs."

Bruce helped Todd secure the last support bracket. "Can you teach me how this system works?"

"Sure thing, kid." Todd pointed to the main control panel. "See these timers? They'll make sure every bed gets watered on schedule. Your mom can program different zones for different plants."

Jack emerged from the supply shed carrying boxes of herb seedlings. "Where should I put these until the new greenhouse is ready?"

"Let's set up a temporary spot in the shade." Bobbie cleared space on a wooden worktable. "Hyden, grab that shade cloth from the back, please."

Todd and Jason began assembling the framework for the smaller greenhouse. The aluminum struts clicked together with satisfying precision.

"Juliet, want to help me sort these herbs?" Bobbie opened the first box of seedlings. "We need to group them by watering needs."

"I remember!" Juliet carefully lifted out a tray of thyme. "These like it dry, like the lavender."

"That's right." Bobbie beamed at her daughter. "And what about these?"

"Mint and lemon balm - they're thirsty plants!" Juliet set them in a separate group.

The new greenhouse took shape under Todd and Jason's experienced hands. Its peaked roof would provide perfect ventilation for the herbs that preferred drier conditions.

"Looking good." Jason stepped back to check the alignment. "Bobbie, what do you think about adding some built-in drying racks along the back wall?"

"Perfect." She nodded approvingly. "We can hang bundles right after harvest."

Bruce helped Todd install the last of the polycarbonate panels. "Uncle Todd, how come these are different from the big greenhouse?"

"These filter UV rays differently." Todd tapped the translucent material. "Helps prevent leaf burn on sensitive herbs. Plus, they're better insulators for temperature control."

Rose wandered between the rows of sorted seedlings, pointing to each one. "This is mint for tea, and this is sage for chicken, and this is..."

"Oregano." Bobbie gently corrected. "Remember how it smells like pizza?"

Rose crushed a leaf between her fingers and giggled at the familiar scent.

The irrigation system hummed quietly, delivering precise amounts of water to each bed. New sprouts stretched toward the filtered sunlight, their leaves unfurling with promise. In the fresh-built herb greenhouse, empty shelves waited to be filled with fragrant life.

The metal door of the shipping container groaned as Todd pulled it open, revealing rows of shelving packed with supplies. Afternoon sunlight streamed in, catching the dust that danced through the air. The familiar smell of cardboard and plastic containers filled his nostrils. A very unique smell.

"Let's start with the liquor inventory." Todd grabbed his clipboard and pen. "We need exact counts."

Jason moved deeper into the container, running his fingers across the bottle labels. "Got thirty bottles of Jack Daniels on this shelf alone. Premium trading currency right here."

"Mark those down as Grade A trade items." Todd made a neat column on his paper. "Whiskey and vodka will be worth their weight in gold when things get rough."

"Speaking of vodka..." Jason shifted to the next shelf. "Twenty-five Smirnoff, fifteen Grey Goose. Plus those cases of craft bourbon you picked up last year."

Todd scratched numbers onto his list. "We should assign point values to everything. Make it easier to negotiate fair trades later."

"What's your thinking on that?"

"Take a bottle of Jack - that could be worth ten points. Then we measure everything else against that baseline." Todd moved to a different section. "A pack of batteries might be five points, ammunition could be fifteen to twenty depending on caliber."

Jason pulled out his pen and notepad to calculate. "So that shelf of whiskey alone is worth three hundred points in trade value."

"Exactly. We need a standardized system." Todd pointed to some boxes on the lower shelves. "Those medical supplies - bandages, antibiotics, painkillers - they'll be worth even more than booze."

"Twenty points per bottle of antibiotics?"

"At least. Maybe more, depending on availability." Todd flipped to a fresh page. "Let's categorize everything by essential value. Medical supplies and ammo at the top, then alcohol, then food and water."

Jason nodded as he counted bottles. "Tools and building supplies should be high value too. Can't repair anything without them."

"Good point." Todd created a new column. "Hand tools, power tools when we have electricity, nails, screws, lumber. All crucial for rebuilding."

"Don't forget skills as currency." Jason tapped his temple. "Your engineering knowledge, my uncanny ability to measure once and cut twice - that's worth points too."

"True. We should factor in labor exchange rates." Todd jotted more notes. "One day of skilled labor could equal fifty points of goods."

They worked methodically through the container, counting and categorizing. The shelves held everything from canned goods to a few extra solar panels, each item carefully considered for its future worth.

"Here's something to think about," Jason said, holding up a bottle of hundred-dollar scotch. "Luxury items. They'll have different values for different people."

"Good call. We'll need subcategories for non-essential goods." Todd created another column. "Premium liquor, chocolates, coffee - comfort items people will trade high for when they're desperate for normalcy."

"Coffee's definitely going in the premium category. People get crazy without their morning fix."

"We should have stocked up on dirty magazines?" Todd chuckled. "It's like the old west. It was alcohol, sex, and bullets."

"Well, we got two out of three." Jason shook his head. "Now we just need bullets." They both laughed.

Todd moved to the back of the container, where several large sealed water barrels stood. "Water purification supplies need their own category. Filters, tablets, bleach for sterilizing."

"Those iodine tablets you stocked up on - they'll be worth their weight in gold." Jason picked up a box of water filters. "Ten points each?"

"At least. Clean water is everything." Todd marked down the numbers.

"Need to watch for inflation too." Jason stacked some boxes more neatly. "If everyone starts using alcohol as currency, the value could drop."

"That's why diversity in supplies matters." Todd gestured around the container. "We've got options for any scenario. Multiple types of trade goods."

The afternoon light had shifted, casting longer shadows through the container doors. They'd filled several pages with neat columns of numbers and categories, creating a complete economic system from the stored supplies.

"One more shelf." Jason pointed to the top row. "The rare stuff - those bottles of Pappy Van Winkle you've been hoarding."

"Those don't even get point values." Todd grinned. "Those are ours. I figure if things go terrible, we can just drink ourselves into the afterlife."

A low rumble cut through their inventory discussion. Todd's head snapped up, his pen freezing mid-stroke on the clipboard.

"You hear that?" Jason stepped toward the container's entrance.

The distinctive drone of aircraft engines grew louder, echoing across the Colorado countryside. Todd clicked his pen closed and tucked it into his shirt pocket.

"Military transport from the sound of it." Todd secured the clipboard under his arm and followed Jason outside.

The afternoon sun hit their faces as they emerged from the cool darkness of the container. Jason shielded his eyes, scanning the sky. A massive grey C-130 appeared over the ridge, banking in a wide arc that brought it directly over Todd's property.

"That's a Hercules." Jason tracked the plane's movement. "Flying awful low for these parts."

The aircraft's four propellers churned the air as it descended to under two thousand feet above ground. Its shadow raced across the ground, and for a split second, darkening the shipping container and surrounding field.

"No markings I can make out." Todd squinted upward. "At least none that I could see."

The C-130 banked again, beginning another circle. Its engines changed pitch, the deep throb resonating in their chests.

"They're slowing up for another pass." Jason reached for his glasses he rarely used and put them on. "They definitely saw us."

Todd watched the plane complete its second pass. "I haven't seen an airplane since this whole thing started, especially any military aircraft."

"I don't know if this is a sign of things getting better, or worse." Jason held up his hand to block the sunlight from the west. "Maybe they are doing some type of survey."

The aircraft maintained its circle pattern, each circuit bringing it closer to the ground.

"Could be National Guard." Todd didn't sound convinced.

"Wrong paint scheme." Jason's expression hardened. "Guard birds have distinct markings. This one's definitely Air Force."

The C-130's cargo ramp hung partially open, a detail that caught Jason's eye. He grabbed Todd's arm and pointed.

"Look at the tail section. There's a few people on the back ramp?"

Todd nodded slowly. "Yep. They're looking for something."

"Or someone." Jason took his glasses off and tucked them into his shirt pocket. "You think it's a warning that someone is coming?"

The plane's shadow passed over them a third time. Todd felt the hair on his neck rise as he watched the giant aircraft lumber through the sky. Years of living on the property with just his dogs, Todd had learned to trust his gut. Right now, it screamed danger.

After a third pass, the C-130 leveled out and had throttled back up, clear in the propeller's sound pitch.

"Heading due east now." Todd tracked it as it maintained altitude.

"They were scouting." Jason's jaw clenched. "Getting a sense of population, maybe? Getting lay of the land?"

"Question is - why here?" Todd looked around the sky in a three hundred and sixty degree sweep. "Why just this property?"

The C-130's engine noise faded gradually until only the dogs' anxious whining broke the silence.

Todd stared at the greenhouse's glass panels glinting in the late afternoon sun. The structure stood out like a beacon against the landscape - too visible, too obvious.

"That plane could've spotted this from twenty miles away." Todd walked towards the perimeter of the greenhouse. "We need better coverage."

Jason crouched near the foundation, examining the current thought. "How do we hide it when it needs sunlight?"

"We can make some sort of material that we can cover it with quickly." Todd gestured toward the outbuilding. "We can create a canopy system."

"Yeah." Jason pulled out his notepad. "Then if we hear an aircraft approach, we can just pull ropes of something and cover it quickly."

After discussing the logistics of what to use and how to make it work, they retrieved the tarps and began planning the new concealment system. Todd sketched a basic framework while Jason laid out the materials.

"See, if we run support cables here and here-" Todd pointed to opposite corners. "We can create a peaked cover that won't snag on anything."

"What about these gaps?" Jason pointed at the spaces between panels. "Even with the tarps, you'll see geometric patterns from above."

"We layer it." Todd grabbed a stick and drew in the dirt. "Or we make it solid material like a tarp. It may not make the structure invisible, but it would hide it from being a greenhouse."

Jason nodded as the plan took shape. "Those pine logs we cleared last month would work perfect for poles. They're long enough to get the cover above the roof line."

They worked steadily, stringing cable that was once used as a zipline between posts to support the new cover. Todd climbed a ladder to secure the prime points while Jason handled the ground-level attachments.

"This cover will probably come in handy for multiple things." Jason wiped sweat from his forehead. "During the summer months, we might could pull the cover to provide shade when we are working in there."

"Agreed." Todd descended the ladder. "I just like the thought of someone like the government figuring out where food is."

"No kidding." Jason chimed in, sharing his concern. "Last thing we need is the government robbing Peter to pay Paul."

"Yep. It would be a good idea to monitor all frequencies if we see another aircraft fly over." Todd moved to the next support post. "CB, shortwave, police bands. Listen for any chatter."

They continued working as they refined their procedures, adding pulleys to the top of the poles. The greenhouse's distinct shape gradually disappeared under the cover.

"Wonder what it looks like from the air?" Jason asked. "Probably would just look like a big tent or make shift barn."

"Maybe, just don't need anyone to recognize it as a greenhouse." Todd secured another tarp section. "That would be a dead giveaway for having food. All activity freezes when aircraft are spotted," Todd dictated. "Everybody needs to stay out of sight until it leaves."

"Sounds like a plan?" Jason answering in the affirmative.

"Once the sound is gone, we should be clear." Todd paced as he thought. "We'll have to see if they start making regular flights over, or if this was just a onetime fluke."

"Well, I kind of hope it wasn't a fluke." Jason wiping dirt from his jeans. "If it was, we just need a lot of work for no reason. I guess it's better to be safe than sorry."

Todd nodded. "Yeah, I have a feeling it won't be the last time we get a fly over."

As the sun had dropped below the western mountain range. The greenhouse now had a cover that could be pulled into place by a system of pulleys in under a minute. The structure would then be hidden from peering eyes from the sky.

Static crackled through the small emergency radio on Todd's kitchen counter. He adjusted the antenna, his weathered fingers finding the sweet spot that brought the signal in clearer. Jason leaned against the small granite countertop, arms crossed over his chest.

"I heard parts of a transmission coming in from Colorado Springs saying the power was out across the entire state," the radio announcer's voice cut through the white noise. "Emergency services have ceased due to lack of personnel. Marshal Law is still in effect. Nighttime curfew is still ongoing. Citizens are advised to stay in their homes."

Todd's German Shepherds paced near the back door, their nails clicking against the tile floor. Bear's ears perked up at every burst of static.

"Same story in Pueblo?" Jason pushed himself off the counter and walked to the window. "I found a site on the internet before it went dead. Said all the grocery stores were emptied."

The radio signal strengthened for a brief burst. "Staff shortages have forced the closure of all emergency departments. National Guard are establishing a perimeter-" The transmission cut out.

Todd twisted the dial, searching for the frequency again. "Lost it. But that's all the major cities gone to hell in a handbasket."

"Imagine being in the cities at this point." Jason pulled back the curtain, scanning the hill to the south. "All the major cities have probably have lost control and turned lawless. There's no way any police officers and firefighters are staying on the job while their families are in harm's way. I know I wouldn't."

Buttercup whined and pressed her nose against Jason's leg. He scratched behind her ears without taking his eyes off the window.

"I'm sure the Nation Guard has been called up to try to take control of the population." Todd switched to another frequency, catching fragments of chatter. "I bet half of them couldn't never even showed up once the collapse started."

Jason let the curtain fall back into place. "I think all of this is going to get worse before it gets better. I would have thought that most of the bad stuff was over during the winter. Perhaps they had enough food to last the winter, but now that the power grid is out, it put a whole new level of emergency on people."

"Agreed." Todd pulled a notebook from his back pocket, flipping through pages of inventory lists. "We are running low on dog food. We might have to start giving them more scraps... or eat 'em," Todd joked.

The radio squawked back to life, repeating the emergency adversary to shelter in place, marshal law being declared and listing the curfew times.

The transmission died again in a burst of static. Todd switched it off.

"I guess all hell has broken loose from here on out in the cities." Jason pulled his phone from his pocket, but quickly returned it once he had realized he did it out of habit. "I sure am glad we are out of the way of all that."

Todd walked to the refrigerator to retrieve a water bottle. "Let's gear up and walk the property line before it gets dark."

"Like old times, riding the fence line. " Jason's mouth curved into a half-smile.

"Just like the old west, almost." Todd snapped his holster to his belt. "Except we're not riding horses."

Bear and Buttercup watched as Todd and Jason made their way to the stairs. The dogs' instinct kicked in - they knew the movement down the stairs meant going outside.

Todd and Jason moved through the dense pine forest that bordered Overlook Ridge, their boots crunching on fallen needles. Bear and Buttercup ranged ahead, noses to the ground, zigzagging between trees as they tracked scents invisible to human senses.

The late afternoon sun filtered through the canopy, and longer shadows covered their path. Todd adjusted his tactical vest. The weight of extra magazines and supplies giving a sense of comfort against the growing chaos in the wider world.

"Everything looks good here." Todd ran his hand along the barbed wire. They'd reinforced it last summer, adding an extra wire to prevent anything from going through without causing pain. Todd had also energized the top wire along the fence that ran between the top of the property to where the tree line got thick with the solar batteries in the garage. "No signs of tampering."

"Your solar setup is still running strong." Jason swept his head in a slow arc, checking their surroundings.

"We just need to keep the panels clean. The batteries are holding charge. It would keep the electric fence hot for months if we needed it to."

Buttercup froze, her body rigid. Her ears swiveled forward and her nose twitched. Bear mimicked her stance, both dogs laser-focused on something ahead.

Jason raised his hand in the universal 'stop' signal. They crouched behind a patch of scrub oak, weapons pulled to the ready. The dogs remained motionless, waiting for commands.

Through a break in the trees, a massive mule deer stepped into view. The buck's antlers spread wide, at least a five-by-five, his coat still carrying the gray of winter. The animal paused, ears flicking, testing the wind.

Jason brought his rifle up, smooth and silent. The scope found the deer's vitals. His breath slowed, matching his heartbeat.

The buck's head snapped up, nostrils flaring. But it was too late.

Jason's finger squeezed. The rifle cracked. The sound echoed off the mountainside as the deer dropped, its legs folding beneath it.

"Nice shot." Todd held the dogs next to his position, trembling with excitement. "That's about four hundred pounds of meat right there."

"Clean through the heart, I guess." Jason clicked the safety forward before reaching down and retrieving the spent cartridge. "It didn't even take a step."

They approached the fallen deer. Todd kept watch while Jason checked to make sure it was dead. The dogs stayed at heel, though Bear's tail wagged with barely contained enthusiasm.

"We need to get this dressed and hung quickly. We don't want that meat to get tainted." Todd pulled a length of paracord from his vest. "I'll go back and get the four wheeler."

"This'll feed us for months." Jason unsheathed his knife. "Assuming the freezers keep running."

"Solar's good. Plus, I've got that smoke house we built last fall." Todd tied off the deer's legs. "Between smoking, jerky, and the freezer, we won't waste an ounce."

As Todd left to retrieve a four wheeler, Jason worked with practiced efficiency, field dressing the deer where it fell. The dogs sat at attention, knowing they'd get their share of the organs once the humans finished. Todd quickly returned just as the setting sun fell behind the peaks to the west. They loaded the cleaned carcass onto the back of the ATV and made their way back to the house.

"I'm so glad we don't have to carry this back to the house." Jason wiped his blade clean on a patch of grass.

"Better than carrying it for sure." Todd checked his watch. "We've got about an hour of good light left. We should have this thing cleaned and stored by dark."

They started the trek home, taking turns and maneuvering the ATV through the trails, trying to avoid as many bumps as they could while all the while watching their surroundings. The dogs ranged ahead and behind, alert for any threat. The weight of the deer made the journey slow, but the meat would be worth every struggle.

"Remember when we used to have to get tags and licenses for this?" Jason adjusted the sling on his rifle.

"Different world now." Todd powered over a large bump between the trees. "Game laws mean little when people are in survival mode."

The ATV wheels caught on a rock. Jason helped lift it over, careful not to spill their precious cargo. Buttercup's head snapped around, focusing on something in the forest. After a moment, she relaxed, continuing her patrol.

"Probably a rabbit." Todd watched the dog work. "She'll let us know if it's anything we need to worry about."

They pushed on through the bumpy trail system; the ATV leaving twin tracks in the soft earth behind them. The deer's weight seemed to make the four wheeler back tires nearly flat, but neither man was going to stop and worry about it. In times like these, meat walking into your sights was a blessing not to be wasted.

Chapter 15

THE SURPRISE VISITOR

The late spring wind whipped across the ridge as Todd and Jason worked on repairing a section of barbed wire fence at the top of the property line. Metal posts clanked against their tools while they secured the loose strands that had become slack with the warming weather.

"Hand me that wire cutter." Todd wiped sweat from his brow despite the moderate air. His boots dug into the rocky soil as he braced himself against the fence post.

Jason reached into their toolbox and passed the cutters. "Think this'll hold through the next winter? The last winter really did a number up here."

"Should do fine once we—" Todd froze mid-sentence, his eyes fixed on something in the distance. Along the north road, a figure stumbled forward, weaving back and forth across the gravel path.

Jason followed Todd's gaze. Through the morning haze, a woman in tattered clothes dragged herself toward the property. Her dark hair hung in front of her face.

"Is she a neighbor, you think?" Jason's hand instinctively moved toward his hip where he carried, though he was only minimally armed for fence work.

Todd shook his head. "I don't think so. She must have walked in from the fire escape road."

The woman's unsteady gait brought her closer. Her clothes were slightly torn around the midsection, with dirt and what looked like dried blood on one sleeve. Every few steps, she glanced over her shoulder as if checking whether something followed her.

"She needs help." Jason took a step forward, but Todd's arm shot out to block his path.

"Hold up. Something's not right. Look at how she's moving—like she's running from something." Todd's eyes narrowed as he scanned the tree line behind her. "I'm wondering if there's more than just her."

The woman spotted them and raised an arm in their direction. "Please! Help!" Her voice carried on the wind, cracking with desperation.

Jason shifted his weight. "We can't just ignore her now."

"No, but we're not rushing in blind either." Todd picked up his binoculars from their tool bag and studied the road behind her. "No vehicle as far as I can see. She either walked a long way or..."

"Or what?"

"Or someone dropped her off." Todd lowered the binoculars. "Let's spread out a little, just in case."

Jason pulled out his pistol but kept in down to his side. "If something goes sideways, I'll go right."

The woman slowly fell to her knees on the gravel road in visible exhaustion. She pushed herself back up, her movements jerky and panicked. Blood had soaked through her sleeve, dark against the white fabric.

"I think she's injured." Jason noticing the woman looked honestly desperate.

Todd grabbed his shoulder again. "Wait. Let me go first. You circle wide, keep an eye on the tree line and road behind her. Anyone else shows up, you signal me and we both back off. Okay?"

"Roger, roger." Jason nodded, though his jaw clenched with tension.

Todd made his way over the fence and slowly approached the woman, while Jason quietly moved along the fence line to the right, maintaining distance but keeping both Todd and the woman in view. The morning sun was behind her, lighting up the woman in full sunlight.

"Ma'am?" Todd called out when he was within thirty yards. "Are you alright?"

The woman's head snapped up at his voice. Her face was streaked with dirt and tears. "Please... he'll find me." Her words came between gasping breaths.

"Who'll find you?" Todd kept his distance, studying her movements.

"I can't... please, I just need to hide." She took another stumbling step forward.

Jason watched from his position near the tree line, every muscle tense. Something about the woman's desperation felt genuine, but Todd was right—it may not be what it seemed.

"Ma'am, you're hurt. Can you stay where you are?" Todd's voice remained steady, calming.

The woman's eyes found Jason in the tree line. They darted between Todd and Jason, then back to the road behind her. Her hands shook as she hugged herself, blood seeping through her fingers where she gripped her injured arm.

"Please. I need some help." Her voice dropped to a whisper carried on the wind.

Todd and Jason exchanged glances. Years of friendship had taught them to read each other's concerns without words. The woman clearly needed medical attention, but her fear of being found raised red flags they couldn't ignore.

The wind picked up, carrying the scent of rain. Thunder rolled in the distance as dark clouds gathered to the east. The woman swayed on her feet, exhaustion evident in every movement.

Todd inched closer while keeping a defensive stance. The woman's eyes were wide with fear, but clear - no signs of drug use or confusion that might indicate she was dangerous or unstable.

"What's your name?" Todd kept his voice firm but gentle.

"Sarah." She winced as she shifted her injured arm. "Sarah Miller."

Jason maintained his position, scanning the tree line in a methodical sweep. No movement caught his eye, no sounds beyond the rustle of leaves in the wind. Still, he knew that threats weren't always obvious.

"Sarah, who did this to you?" Todd gestured to her bloody sleeve.

Her breathing quickened. "My boyfriend... ex-boyfriend. He's gone crazy! We ran out of gas on the highway and he told me to stay with the car until he gets another one." She swallowed hard. "I told him I was leaving, and he attacked me and tied me up in the car. I managed to free myself and got away, but I'm sure he's looking for me."

Todd glanced at Jason, who gave a subtle nod - her story matched her genuine fear and the fresh injury.

"How'd you get up here?" Todd kept his distance and continued to look beyond her for more people.

"I ran... through the woods. Saw this road and started walking." Sarah's legs trembled. "I have no idea where I am. I've been walking for hours."

Jason circled wider, checking the view of the road. No tire tracks, no signs of pursuit. The gravel showed only her stumbling footprints leading up from the lower switchback.

"Todd." Jason's voice carried across the distance. "Road's clear. No vehicles."

Sarah's knees buckled. Todd rushed forward to catch her before she hit the ground, years of instinct overriding caution. As he grabbed her shoulders, he noticed the wounds on her hands - broken nails, scrapes consistent with running through the various thorns that adorned Blackhawk Ranch.

"Jason, get the first aid kit from the four wheeler." Todd helped Sarah sit on a nearby boulder. "Ma'am, I need to check that arm."

Sarah nodded weakly. Todd carefully rolled up her sleeve, revealing a deep gash that might would need stitches. The wound pattern matched her story - rope or zippy ties had left large red circles around her wrists.

Jason returned with the kit, his eyes still scanning their surroundings. "I think we should get off the road and back inside the fence line. We are wide open here."

"I have medical supplies." Todd cleaned Sarah's wound with a tiny bottle of antiseptic. "But before we go there, I need you to be straight with us. Is there anything else we should know?"

Sarah met his gaze. "He's dangerous. He was a Marine. If he tracked me here... I saw him shoot a man and take his car. Then it ran out of gas. He was going to do it again. So I tried to stop him." Her voice cracked.

"Jason." Todd's tone shifted to one of practiced precision. "Let's get her back to the house. We'll figure the rest out there."

Jason nodded and helped them over the fence and back onto the property. They reached the four wheeler and Sarah climbed onto the back.

"Sarah, we'll help you, but you need to tell me everything." Todd mounted the ATV and cranked it. "What's his name? What kind of vehicle? Any weapons?"

"Mark Reeves. We were in a black Ford pickup until it ran out of gas." Sarah's words came faster now. "He has a pistol."

Her descriptions were specific - not the vague answers of someone making up a story. The defensive wounds matched the attack pattern she described. Her timeline tracked with the scraps and bruising along with the dirt on her clothes.

Jason walked in reverse behind the ATV. "Clear behind us. Let's move."

Thunder rolled closer now. The wind carried the first drops of rain.

"Yep, we need to move." Todd pressed the throttle harder and made his way down the bumpy trail towards the house.

Todd titled his head sideways so Sarah could hear him over the engine noise. "Sarah, we're going to help you. But we do this our way. You stay quiet. Don't touch anything. You do what we ask. Do you understand?"

"Yes." Sarah's voice steadied slightly. "Thank you."

"Jason, run ahead and make sure the dogs stay on the deck." Todd driving at a walking speed. "We'll get you inside, bandage you up, then we'll figure out what we do."

Rain began falling in earnest, drumming against the tree leaves. The weather would make tracking harder - both for them and for any potential pursuit. Both Todd and Jason were already thinking of having to deal with a potential threat if the man showed up.

The four-wheeler rumbled into Todd's garage, its tires splashing through puddles forming on the gravel driveway. Jason jogged ahead to secure the dogs while Todd helped Sarah dismount, her movements stiff from the cold rain and injury.

"Let's take a look at that arm." Todd helped her off the four wheeler and sat her down in a metal chair. Rain drummed against the metal roof as he flipped on the fluorescent lights, illuminating his workspace.

Sarah's teeth chattered as she sank onto a metal shop stool. Blood had soaked through the makeshift bandage on her arm, mixing with rainwater to create pink rivulets down her skin.

"Here." Todd pulled a clean shop towel from his workbench and handed it to her. He retrieved his advanced first aid kit from a cabinet while Jason returned from the house.

"Dogs are secure." Jason positioned himself near the garage door, maintaining watch. "I let Bobbie know we have a visitor," his mind quickly shifting to thoughts of security. "With this rain, someone could walk up on us and we'd never hear them."

Todd laid out his medical supplies on a clean workbench. "This'll sting, but we need to clean it properly." He soaked gauze in an antiseptic solution. "Sarah, how long ago did this happen?"

"Maybe four or five hours?" She winced as Todd began cleaning the wound. "We were on the highway when the truck ran out of gas."

"That's about ten miles from here." Jason crossed his arms. "Long way to walk."

"I stuck to the dirt road at first, then cut through when I thought I heard a vehicle." Sarah's fingers curled around the edge of the stool. "Adrenaline, I guess."

Todd examined the gash more closely under the bright shop lights. "You'll need stitches, but I think we can butterfly it for now. We need to get this really clean. The last thing you need is an infection out here."

The basement door opened, and Bobbie stepped out, carrying a stack of clean towels and fresh clothes. Her eyes widened at Sarah's condition.

"I heard what happened." Bobbie set the items down and approached slowly. "I'm Bobbie, Jason's wife. Let me get you some water."

Sarah's shoulders relaxed slightly at Bobbie's presence. "Thank you. I'm Sarah."

"Hold still." Todd applied butterfly bandages with precision. "Bobbie makes the best food you've ever tasted."

"Let me look at those scrapes on your face, too." Bobbie dampened a clean cloth and gently cleaned the dirt from Sarah's cheeks. Her touch was smooth and careful.

Sarah's eyes welled with tears. "I'm sorry to bring trouble to your door. I just didn't know where else to go."

"It will be ok." Bobbie placed a hand on her shoulder. "No one should be alone out here, especially when it's nigh time."

Jason moved to the workbench, lowering his voice. "Todd, we'll need to be on our toes tonight. If someone is looking for her, this is the last stop on the road."

"Agreed." Todd finished wrapping Sarah's arm. "But first, let's get her warm and fed. I think shock is setting in. Then we'll come up with a plan."

Bobbie helped Sarah stand. "I have clothes you can change into. Let's go to the house. You can get cleaned up while I heat some soup."

Sarah clutched the fresh clothes to her chest. "Thank you. All of you." Her voice cracked. "I know this is crazy, just showing up like this."

"Sometimes crazy finds us whether we're looking for it or not." Todd packed away his medical supplies. "The important thing is, you're safe for now."

Bobbie led Sarah toward the house while Jason and Todd exchanged glances. Years of friendship had taught them to read volumes in a simple look. This situation could escalate quickly if Sarah's ex-boyfriend tracked her to the property.

"I'll re-electrify the fence." Jason walked purposefully to the weathered gray breaker box mounted on the wall and flipped a heavy black breaker switch with practiced efficiency. "Make sure we don't have any uninvited guests. It's not foolproof, but it's something." He knew the electrical current wouldn't stop a determined intruder, but the warning signs and potential shock might make someone think twice about climbing over. The goal is to make them approach down the driveway.

Todd nodded, wiping blood from his hands with a clean shop towel. "Keep an eye on that south hill, too. If he's military like she says, he might try to get to higher ground, then come the back way."

The garage fell quiet except for the steady drum of rain on the roof. Through the open door, gray clouds hung low over the valley, reducing visibility across the property. Perfect weather for someone trying to approach unseen.

"You thinking what I'm thinking?" Jason's hand rested near his hip.

"That this isn't over?" Todd locked his medical cabinet with a firm click, double-checking the latch. "Yeah. But right now, let's focus on getting her stable and calmed down. See if we can get more of the story out of her when she's feeling safer. In the meantime, I'll put Buttercup and Bear outside. They'll let us know if someone is approaching - their noses work better than any security system I could install. One problem at a time."

They stepped out of the garage into the steady drizzle, securing the heavy door behind them with a single pull of the door. The house lights glowed warm and inviting through the weather, making the wet ground shine. Through the upper deck glass door, they could see Bobbie moving purposefully around the kitchen, already preparing food for their unexpected guest. Steam rose from pots on the stove, carrying the promise of something hearty and comforting.

Todd paced in front of Jason in the basement utility room, where they stopped to talk. Jason stood against the wooden worktable with tools spread all over hell and gone, his fingers drumming against the front edge.

"We can't just put her out there again," Todd said, pausing to look through the small basement door window at the darkening landscape. "The math just doesn't add up to let a woman wonder in the dark to death."

Jason leaned forward. "What about our own security? We don't know anything about her."

"Except that she's alone and desperate." Todd's voice carried the weight of decades of experience. "Remember when I first showed you this place? Told you it was meant to be a sanctuary?"

"Yeah, but that was different. We all knew each other."

Todd turned to face his friend. "Different times call for different measures. Sarah might have some skills, she looks fit. She could be invaluable in helping us out."

"Or she could be lying." Jason stood up, joining Todd at the window. "Everything you've built here, all the preparations-"

"Mean nothing if we lose our humanity in the process." Todd's eyes fixed on the distant tree line. "My father used to say character shows itself in how you treat others when you have nothing to gain."

Jason crossed his arms and stared at the ground before replying. "Did your father really say that?"

"No, but he would have if he'd had thought of it. He told me stories about growing up, communities coming together, sharing what little they had." Todd moved to the table, pulling out a worn notebook from his back pocket. "Look at our inventory. We've got enough supplies for at least six months, even with an extra mouth to feed."

"It's not just about supplies, Todd. It's about trust. I think we should waterboard her first."

Todd chuckled at the comment. "Which is why we'll be smart about it. Set up boundaries, clear rules. But we can't turn our backs on someone who needs help, not when we have the means to provide it."

Jason ran a hand through his thinning hair on the back of his head, exhaling slowly. "I agree with you, just trying to play devil's advocate. She might not be the last one coming down the road."

"Then we'll deal with each situation as it comes." Todd replied evenly.

Todd and Jason made their way upstairs to the kitchen, where Bobbie was serving a bowl of soup to Sarah. Todd noticed how different she looked from when they found her. He couldn't help but notice her attractiveness. His mind temporarily running wild with thoughts.

"We've made a decision." Todd exchanged a look with Jason, who gave a subtle nod. "We'd like to offer you shelter here at Overlook Ridge. There will be conditions, but you'll have a warm place to sleep and food in your belly."

The silence that followed seemed to stretch for an eternity. When Sarah's voice came back, it was thick with emotion. "I... I don't know what to say."

"Say you'll follow our rules and pull your weight. That's all we ask."

"Of course. Yes. Thank you." The relief in her voice was palpable. "I won't let you down."

Todd and Jason made their way out of the kitchen. Todd turned to Jason. "Well, that's done."

"Hope we're doing the right thing." Jason moved toward the second-floor bedroom. "I'll start clearing out the east room."

"Sometimes the hardest decisions are the ones that remind us of who we are." Todd followed his friend. "And right now, being human might be the most valuable survival skill we have."

The two men worked in companionable silence, preparing space for their new guest.

Jason smirked before speaking. "Maybe she'll warm up to you." Emphasizing the word 'warm'.

"Well, I'll do my part for humanity if I must," Todd replied with a little laugh. "She might be a complete nut job for all we know. Time will tell.

The sun fell below the mountains to the west, casting darkness across Overlook Ridge, where a small act of kindness had just changed the dynamics of their carefully planned sanctuary.

Steam rose from the ceramic bowl as Sarah spooned another mouthful of vegetable soup. A single lamp on the wooden table casting a soft light over the room where she sat with Bobbie.

"This soup is amazing." Sarah dabbed her mouth with a napkin. "I haven't had actual food in a week or two. The veggies are really good."

"Most of them came straight from the garden." Bobbie rested her elbows on the table, her own bowl untouched. "I grow everything I can out here. Have to make the most of what we've got."

Sarah's spoon clinked against the bowl. "You're lucky to have all this space. Back in Trinidad, my apartment barely had room for a window box to grow."

"Trinidad?" Bobbie leaned forward. "What brought you to Trinidad?"

"Life, I guess. I'm originally from Santa Fe until I moved to Trinidad a few years ago." Sarah stared into her soup. "I used to run an aerobics studio there. Sunrise Fitness on Common Street. Had about fifty regular clients."

"An aerobics instructor, huh?"

"Different lifetime now." Sarah's fingers traced the rim of her water glass. "The studio was everything I'd worked for. Started teaching classes right out of high school, saved every penny. Took me eight years to get my own place."

"Must have been rough, having to leave it."

"Very. I had no choice. The town was falling apart. Riots, people blocking off roads, the police were nowhere to be found. It was getting pretty danger-ous." Sarah shook her head. "My ex-boyfriend asked me to go with him. I should have known better, but at that point, he was my only way out of the city."

Bobbie reached across the table, her hand stop-ping short of touching Sarah's arm. "Life has a way of throwing curveballs."

"More like fastballs straight to the face." Sarah pushed her half-finished soup away. "Sorry, I don't mean to dump all this on you. The soup really is delicious."

"No need to apologize. We've all got our stories." Bobbie stood and walked to the kitchen window. Beyond the glass, pine trees swayed in the moon-light. "Sometimes sharing them makes the load a little lighter."

"I used to dream about having a place like this." Sarah joined Bobbie at the window. "Away from everything, the quiet. Back when I had the studio, I'd planned these fitness retreats. Take clients up into the mountains for weekend workshops. Never got around to it."

"Hopefully, things will settle down out there, and we all can get a second chance at normal life."

"Maybe." Sarah's reflection ghosted against the window glass. "Though I've learned not to count on maybes anymore."

The curtains of the open kitchen window blew inward, knocking the dish soap from the window seal as it did at least three times a day. Bobbie pulled the window closed.

"Thank you. For the soup, and for listening." Sarah turned from the window. "Been a while since anyone asked about... me."

"I'm sure we'll have many more talks, especially if you're going to be here for a while. There' are a few things I could use your help on." Bobbie gathered their bowls from the table. "You'll meet the kids in the morning."

Todd hunched over the keyboard in his upstairs office, the blue glow of the monitor casting shadows across his weathered face. Jason stood behind him, arms crossed, watching the loading icon spin.

"Come on, come on." Todd's fingers drummed against the desk.

The Starlink connection bar flickered green. Web pages started loading for the first time in weeks.

"Holy crap, it's up." Jason pulled up a chair. "Quick, check the major news sites before we lose it."

Jason's fingers flew across the keys. "CNN's down. Fox News too." He typed another URL. "Wait, got something. Reuters is up."

Headlines splashed across the screen. Market closures. Food shortages. Military deployments.

"Look at the date stamp." Todd pointed at the corner of the screen. "These are from ten days ago. First real news we've had since the blackout."

"Scroll down." Todd leaned closer. "There. Supply chain collapse across the Pacific. Chinese ports shut down. Australian wheat exports stopped."

"Save everything you can." Todd grabbed a notebook from the desk drawer. "We might not get another chance at this."

Jason clicked through tabs, downloading PDFs and screenshots while Todd scribbled notes. The connection meter dipped to yellow, then red.

"Losing it." Todd's clicked faster. "One more page."

The screen went blank with the click of the next link. Todd smacked the desk. "Dammit."

"Hey, we got something at least." Jason still trying to refresh webpages. "More than we've had in weeks."

"True." Todd leaned back in his chair, rubbing his eyes. "At least now we know it's not just us. The entire world's systems have broken down."

"Question is, what do we do with this information?"

"Share it with the neighbors, for one." Todd stood and stretched. "People need to know what we're up against. This is going to be a long emergency."

The Starlink router on the window sill blinked red, its brief window of connectivity closed. Jason began printing what he had saved.

Todd spread the printed pages across his desk while Jason paced behind him, doing almost small circles in the room. The full moonlight filtered through the office window, placing a silver light in the valley below.

"Look at this." Todd's finger traced across a headline. "Ninety-five percent of trucking companies ceased operations last week. No fuel deliveries. Refineries shut down."

Jason stopped pacing. "That explains why we haven't seen many vehicles going up and down the highway anymore."

"It gets worse." Todd shuffled through another page. "Military's mobilized in all fifty states. Not for peacekeeping - they're trying to maintain basic infrastructure. Power plants, water treatment, hospitals."

"Hold up." Jason leaned over Todd's shoulder, squinting at a paragraph. "Says here the strategic petroleum reserve is depleted. Government's been lying about the levels for months."

Todd cleaned his glasses. "Where'd you see that?"

"Third paragraph down. Some government insider is quoted." Jason tapped the paper. "No wonder diesel prices were shooting through the roof even before the chaos."

"Cross reference that with this." Todd slid another printout forward. "Food reserves. Depleted in all major urban centers. Farming equipment's idle without fuel."

Jason dropped into the spare chair. "No food? If that is just in America, imagine other countries? That can't be right."

"Reuters wouldn't write that just to write it." Todd pulled up another document. "Look at the embedded photos. Ports are all ghost towns. Container ships anchored offshore with nowhere to dock. Probably no crews to unload them. There either stuck at sea, or staying away from the chaos."

"What about the West Coast?"

"Same story, different reason." Todd spread out a map covered in red marks. "Military tried to step in, but they're spread too thin. Ports are burned out shells."

Jason folded his arms and rubbed his growing beard. "This is way beyond what anyone was thinking. It seems no one in charge thought it could happen."

"Most folks thought this was temporary." Todd shuffled through more papers. "But look at this report on the market. All the banks have closed their doors. There's been a run on every bank."

"Speaking of banks." Jason pulled up a saved file. "Found this the last time the internet was up. Federal Reserve's been running the money printers at triple capacity. Trying to paper over the cracks."

Todd adjusted his glasses. "Where'd that come from?"

"Cached page from CNBC just before the power outage hit." Jason scrolled. "Said the dollar's worth about twenty percent of what it was last year, but they're hiding it with price controls. That means inflation is out of control and the dollar is basically worthless."

Todd circled several passages in red ink. "Power grid is the real nightmare. None of this will come back until power is widely restored, and you can't restore power without the right people. Military has no clue how to run a power station. Besides, without fuel and such-" Todd's voice tricking off at the thought of how complex the situation was.

"What about the military?"

"That's another punch to the gut." Todd flipped to another page. "Everyone flocked to the military bases for food or security. They're overloaded. Factories are closed. Says here the processing plants are at a standstill and have been looted. No food, no manufacturing, no batteries, no nothing."

Jason turned from the window. "Those factories aren't coming back online with the ports closed and the people gone."

"And Asia and Europe have their own problems." Todd held up a printed article. "See this? Whole countries are dark. No power, no fuel, which for Europe means no heat."

"Todd." Jason's voice dropped. "Things might never return the way it was. At least not for a very long time."

"True, no one was ready for this. It was a perfect storm. I've been saying it!" Todd gathered the papers into neat piles. "Hell, I'm not sure I'm ready for this, and I've been prepping for years."

"Best we can hope for is for all the bad people to die off so we can get back to some sort of normal community." Jason picked up one of the printed websites. "No telling how many people have died. Guess this takes care of the over-population problem. Can you imagine India and China?"

"Agreed. It's depressing to think about. Let's go check on Bobbie and Sarah and tell them we learned some news." Worry showing on Todd's face.

Chapter 16

A Bite Of Bitterness

The mountain air carried a crisp autumn chill as Todd and Jason sat in deck chairs, their conversation drifting between topics under a blanket of stars. Bear sprawled near Todd's feet, her black form barely visible in the darkness, while Buttercup maintained her usual vigilant position by the deck railing.

"Can't beat these Colorado nights," Jason said, taking a sip from his coffee mug. "Makes me miss living up here."

Todd stretched his legs. "You should move back permanently. Plenty of room for-"

A low growl from Bear cut through the peaceful evening. Buttercup's ears perked up, her body tensing as she joined in with a deeper, more threatening rumble.

"What's got into them?" Jason straightened in his chair.

Todd leaned forward, scanning the darkness. A beam of light swayed back and forth, growing larger as it moved up the winding driveway through the trees.

"We have a visitor!" Jason's hand instinctively moved to his empty holster.

"I bet you it's Sarah's ex-boyfriend." Todd pushed himself up. "Come on."

They rushed through the sliding glass door into the house. Todd flipped off the deck lights while Jason headed straight for the gun in the living room.

"What're you thinking?" Jason pulled out his preferred Colt 10mm.

Todd grabbed his AR-15 from the corner of the room. "Could be a lost hiker, but..." He checked the magazine and racked the charging handle. "Better safe than sorry."

They made their way down to the basement door and cracked it open. Buttercup's barking echoed loudly in the basement as she and Bear attempted to exit the house, sharp and aggressive. Bear's deeper woofs joined in, creating a chorus of warning.

"Quiet down, girls." Todd's command carried over their barks. The dogs reduced their barking to low growls.

Jason moved out the door, staying in the shadows. "Single light source. Can't make out how many people."

"Take the left." Todd gestured toward a tree fifteen feet directly in front of the door. "I'll cover the front. Dogs, with me."

The two men moved into position, years of knowing the property clear in their careful movements. Bear and Buttercup flanked Todd, their bodies rigid with tension.

The visitor rounded the last curve of the driveway and was almost in full view of Todd and Jason. The flashlight beam swept across the front of the house. Gravel crunched under the approaching footsteps.

Todd positioned himself behind the solid wood post that held the deck up, AR-15 at the ready. "Buttercup, come."

The German Shepherd moved silently to her assigned position, her dark eyes fixed on the source of the flashlight.

From behind the tree, Jason kept his eyes trained on the side approach, using the tree as cover. Sweat beaded on his forehead despite the cool air breeze in his face. His heart beating faster.

The footsteps stopped. The flashlight inspecting the surrounding area.

"Sarah!" A male voice called out. "You in there?"

Todd's grip on the rifle tightened. He exchanged glances with Jason.

"Who's asking?" Todd's voice boomed from underneath the first floor deck.

"I'm looking for my girlfriend, Sarah. Our car broke down on the highway. I think she walked this way."

Bear's growl deepened. Todd placed a steadying hand on her head.

"Sarah who?" Todd called out. "Don't recognize the name."

A pause. "I know she's here," the man now talking at full throat. "I know you're here Sarah! Let's go!"

Todd shook his head grimly at Jason, his weathered features tightening with concern. This was exactly what Todd had feared would happen - the very scenario that had nagged at him since they'd first encountered the woman. A serious threat now loomed over Overlook Ridge, all because of the simple act of charity they'd shown to Sarah. His mind was already calculating the potential outcomes, none of them particularly promising.

"Stay where you are," Todd commanded. "Keep your hands visible."

"I don't want no trouble. I'm here for Sarah."

Jason looked over to Todd, keeping his weapon at the ready. "That's a double negative... so does that mean he wants trouble?" he whispered, grinning. "Either way, I think he's going to get it."

Buttercup's hackles raised, her teeth bared in a silent snarl. The man continued to use his flashlight beam to dart between windows, probing for a view inside.

"Sir," Todd's voice carried an edge of steel, "You need to leave the property. If you don't, I will release my dogs."

"I ain't going nowhere until I talk to Sarah."

"This is my property," Todd called out, keeping his rifle trained on the shadowy figure. "I'm giving you one last chance to leave peacefully."

The beam of light swung toward Todd's voice, but the thick post shielded him from direct illumination. Sarah's ex-boyfriend Mark took two steps forward, his boots crunching on the gravel.

"Listen here, old man. I know Sarah's in there. She's my girlfriend, and she's coming with me." Mark's voice rose, taking on a ragged edge. "Sarah! Get your ass out here now!"

Todd watched Mark's free hand clench and unclench, his stance widening as if preparing for confrontation. The man's shoulders hunched forward, predatory, while his flashlight beam jerked erratically between the house and Todd's position.

"You don't get to make demands on my property." Todd's voice remained steady, measured. "Turn around and walk away."

"The hell I will!" Mark kicked a rock, sending it skittering across the driveway. "You hiding her? I'm the one who saved her. She comes with me."

Bear's growl deepened at the man's rising aggression. Mark swung the flashlight toward the sound, revealing a glimpse of Bear's face - teeth bared in a snarl.

"I've dealt with her type before," Mark spat the words. "Playing the victim, wrapping men around her finger. Well, I ain't leaving without her."

His free hand moved toward his waistband, and Jason shifted his position slightly for a better angle.

Todd kept his voice level, projecting authority without aggression. "This is private property. You're trespassing. Leave now, or I'll have no choice but to defend my home."

Mark's flashlight beam slashed through the darkness, searching for the source of Todd's voice. "You don't understand. That woman owes me."

"Whatever's between you and Sarah, this isn't the way to handle it." Todd shifted his weight, maintaining his cover behind the post. "Walk away before this gets worse."

The beam of light dropped, and in the dim glow, Mark's hand emerged from his waistband clutching a chrome-plated pistol. The weapon caught the moonlight as he raised it.

"I tried being nice." Mark's voice cracked with barely contained rage. "Now you're gonna tell me where she is, or things are gonna get real ugly."

Jason caught Todd's eye, giving a slight nod toward Mark's left flank. Todd responded with an almost imperceptible shake of his head - not yet. They needed to maintain the advantage of their concealed positions.

Bear's growl deepened into something primal, and Buttercup's muscles coiled tight as a spring. Todd kept one hand on Bear's collar, knowing the Belgian Malinois protective instincts could trigger at any moment.

"You're making a mistake," Todd said. "Pointing a weapon at someone on their own property - that's a felony in Colorado."

"Shut up!" Mark swung the gun toward the sound of Todd's voice. "I know she's here. Sarah! Get out here now!"

Jason eased to his right, using the shadows to gain a better angle. His boots made no sound on the gravel as he moved, keeping the tree between himself and Mark.

"Last warning." Todd's finger rested outside the trigger guard of his AR-15. "Lower your weapon and leave."

"Or what?" Mark's laugh held an edge of hysteria. "You gonna shoot me, old man? Over some whore?"

Todd caught Jason's eye again. This time, he gave a slight nod. Jason responded by tapping his chest twice - ready.

Mark took another step forward, sweeping his gun between the deck and the house windows. "I'm coming up there. And if I find her-"

The sharp crack of a branch in the darkness made Mark spin toward the sound. His flashlight beam caught Jason's movement, and Mark's gun started to swing in that direction.

"Drop it!" Todd's command thundered across the yard as he stepped clear of the post, his AR-15 aimed center mass. "Now!"

Mark froze, caught between two armed men. His head whipped back and forth, the flashlight beam jerking erratically as he tried to track both threats.

"You don't want to do this," Jason said, his 10mm trained steadily on Mark. "Put it down."

Sweat gleamed on Mark's pale face, his eyes wide. His gun hand trembled, moving between the two men as his breathing grew ragged.

"Both of you back off!" Mark's voice rose to a shout. "This ain't about you!"

Bear and Buttercup's growls grew louder, more threatening. Todd could feel the tension radiating from both dogs, their bodies rigid with protective fury.

"You've got three seconds," Todd said. "One."

Mark's gun settled on Todd. "Don't try me, old man!"

"Two."

Jason moved closer, using Mark's fixation on Todd to close the distance.

"This is your last chance," Todd said. "Thr-"

The muzzle flash lit up the darkness as Mark's pistol barked. The round cracked past Todd's head, splintering a wood post behind him. Todd dropped to one knee, bringing his AR-15 up in a smooth motion. Bear and Buttercup scattered, not sure what was going on.

Jason squeezed off two quick shots from his position. Mark returned fire wildly, his flashlight beam swinging in erratic arcs as he backpedaled.

Todd's rifle reported once, the sound echoing off the mountainside. Mark screamed, his leg buckling beneath him. The flashlight tumbled from his grip, spinning across the gravel.

"Ahhh!" Mark's voice was thick with pain and rage. He fired again, the rounds going high and wide.

Todd and Jason both responded, their weapons filling the night with thunder. Mark half-crawled, half-stumbling as he back peddled, disappearing into the tree line. His ragged breathing and occasional curses faded into the bushes.

The echo of gunfire died away, leaving only the sound of ringing in their ears, and the dogs continued barking.

Todd and Jason moved cautiously from their positions, weapons still at the ready. Bear and Buttercup circled the area, their noses working the ground as they tracked recent scents.

"Clear left. You good?" Jason called out as he powered on his flashlight, sweeping it across the tree line.

"I'm good." Todd kept his AR-15 shouldered while scanning the darkness. "Buttercup, come."

The German Shepherd trotted to Todd's side while Bear continued sniffing near where Mark had fallen. Jason carefully approached the spot, his boot scuffing through loose gravel.

"Got blood here." Jason crouched down, examining dark spots on the stones. "Good amount of it, and it's dark. I think we got an artery or a gut shot."

Todd joined him, directing his light at the ground. A trail of crimson pools of blood led toward the woods, clearly visible on the pale gravel. Bear followed the scent, her black form disappearing into the shadows before Todd whistled her back.

"He's hurt bad enough to leave a trail," Jason said, "but not bad enough to stop him."

"Might have caught him in the leg." Todd checked his magazine. "How many rounds you got left?"

Jason ejected his magazine, counted quickly. "Seven. Plus one in the chamber."

They followed the blood trail to the tree line, where it disappeared into thick underbrush. Todd pulled out his radio and tossed it to Jason.

"Need to let Bobbie know what's happening," Todd said. "Have her lock down the house, get everyone to the top floor."

Jason nodded. "So, we have two options, basically. We can go search now, or wait until morning. Guy's wounded, angry, and armed - bad combination."

"Agreed. I don't want him patching himself up, then coming back in the middle of the night. We need to know for certain where he is." Todd switched to a new clip on his weapon. "Let's just give him a few more minutes. We need to be real careful about an ambush."

"Take the dogs?" Jason asked.

"I don't think so. We've got enough moonlight, and he's leaving an obvious trail." Todd checked his watch. "Let's move before the blood dries."

Moonlight filtered through the pine branches as Todd and Jason followed the blood trail down the slope. Their boots crushed pine needles underfoot, each step deliberate. The scent of the damp ground hung in the air, growing stronger as they descended.

"Trail's getting wider," Todd whispered, sweeping his rifle barrel across the tree line. "He's losing more blood."

Jason kept his distance, scanning their six o'clock position. A branch snapped somewhere in the darkness, and both men froze. Nothing followed except the whisper of wind through the trees.

"Down there." Todd pointed with his chin toward a fallen log. Dark spatters marked where Mark had presumably stopped to rest. "He's heading towards the clearing to the west. Downhill."

They moved forward, using the trees for cover. The blood trail wound between scrub oak and juniper, leading deeper into the property. Todd paused at a log that had fallen across the path from the last winter storm, examining the ground.

"He sat here." Todd's finger traced a larger blood-stain. "Tried to bind the wound - look at the torn fabric."

Jason crouched next to him. "That's a lot of blood, Todd. If we caught the femoral..."

"He's still mobile." Todd stood, scanning the darkness ahead. "But I'm sure he's getting weaker. No way you can lose this much blood and not slow down."

The trail continued down the slope, becoming more erratic. Mark's footprints showed where he'd stumbled, catching himself against trees. Broken branches and disturbed ground marked his passage.

A sound echoed up from below - metal striking stone. Todd and Jason dropped to one knee, weapons ready. The noise came again, followed by cursing.

"Sounds like he ran into the rock outcropping," Jason whispered. "Bottom of the property's just beyond that."

Todd nodded. "He's trapped himself. Nothing but heavy scrub oak from there."

They advanced slowly, using the terrain for cover. The blood trail led straight toward the outcropping - a natural barrier of thorns and bushes that marked the property's edge. Mark's ragged breathing carried clearly in the still night air.

"You bleeding out down there?" Todd called out, his voice carrying across the darkness. "Need medical attention. We can help."

"Stay back!" Mark's voice cracked with pain and desperation. "I'll shoot!"

Jason moved to Todd's right, establishing a cross-fire position. "You're leaving a blood trail a blind man could follow. Let us help before you bleed out."

A shot rang out, the bullet whining off a tree well above their heads. Todd and Jason pressed against trees, weapons trained on the source of the muzzle flash.

"That's four rounds he's fired," Jason said. "Most carry six in those cheap revolvers."

Todd kept his AR-15 steady. "You've got two choices," he shouted. "Surrender now and we get you medical help, or bleed out against those rocks. Your call."

Harsh laughter echoed up the slope. "You don't get it. This is going to be my last stand and I'm taking-" His voice dissolved into wet coughing.

The moon emerged from behind clouds, illuminating the rocky ground ahead. Dark smears marked Mark's path across the granite. He'd backed himself into a corner, hemmed in by natural barriers.

"Running out of time," Todd called out. "And blood. Make your choice."

Another shot cracked through the night, going wide. Mark's curse echoed off the rocks, followed by the distinct click of an empty chamber.

"That's five," Jason said, moving forward in a crouch.

Todd advanced down the left flank, keeping to the shadows. "It's over. Toss out the gun."

They could see Mark now, slumped against the rock face. His right leg was soaked with blood, and he clutched the revolver in a shaking hand. Moonlight revealed his face - pale, drawn with pain and fury.

"Stay back!" Mark tried to stand, using the rocks for support. "I swear, I'll-"

His leg gave out, and he slid down the granite, leaving a red streak. The revolver clattered against the stone but stayed in his grip.

Todd and Jason moved closer, weapons trained center mass. Mark's chest heaved with labored breaths, his eyes wild in the darkness.

"Drop it," Todd commanded. "Now."

Mark's fingers tightened on the grip. Blood pooled beneath his leg, black in the moonlight. His gaze darted between the two men, then to the empty darkness beyond the property line.

"I ruined everything," he gasped. "I... I should ha ve..."

"Last chance," Jason said. "Drop the gun."

Mark's grip on the revolver loosened. His eyes rolled back, and he slumped forward onto the rocky ground with a dull thud. The weapon clattered against the stone, spinning away into the darkness.

Todd kept his AR-15 trained on Mark while Jason approached from the side, his 10mm still ready. Their movements were purposeful as they cleared the area.

"Cover me," Jason said, crouching beside the fallen man.

Todd kept his rifle trained on Mark while Jason pressed two fingers against his neck. Blood had spread in a wide pool beneath Mark's leg, soaking into the loose soil and staining the granite.

"No pulse." Jason pulled his hand back and wiped it on his jeans. "Femoral artery, just like we thought. He bled out fast."

Todd lowered his rifle and joined Jason beside the body. Mark's face was ghost-white in the moonlight, frozen in a mask of rage and pain. His leg wound had soaked his pants leg even though a makeshift tourniquet was applied.

"What a waste," Todd said, checking Mark's pockets. He pulled out a wallet and cell phone. "All this over a woman who clearly wanted nothing to do with him."

Jason stood, holstering his pistol. "We need to decide what to do with him. Can't leave him here."

"Agreed." Todd leafed through the wallet. "Mark Davidson. Colorado driver's license. No family photos, just some cash and cards."

"There's really not a way to report this. Just like the other two guys." Jason scratched the back of his head. "I'm sure those other two dudes have already been reclaimed by the animals and nature."

Todd placed his wallet and phone back into his jacket pocket. "She came to us for protection. Last thing she needs is to know we just killed him. We'll just tell her he ran away."

"So we bury him?" Jason surveyed the surrounding area. "Ground's too rocky here. Need somewhere with softer soil."

Todd nodded toward the western edge of the property. "That clearing past the Pine grove. The ground's easier to dig there, and the undergrowth will keep the bigger animals away."

"What about the blood trail?"

"Rain's coming tomorrow. Should wash most of it away." Todd checked his watch. "We'll need the ATV and shovels. Some tarps too."

Jason pulled out his radio. "I'll tell Bobbie we're handling it. She'll keep everyone in the house." He stepped away to make the radio call.

For the next hour, they worked quickly and efficiently. The ATV's headlights cut through the darkness as they transported Mark's body to the clearing. A cool mountain breeze carried the scent of pine and approaching rain.

"Here." Todd killed the engine near a cluster of young pines. "Soil's deeper, and these trees will grow faster with the extra nutrients."

"Circle of life. Damn him for making it end like this," Jason said as he grabbed a hand full of Mark and drug him off the ATV.

They unloaded their tools and wrapped Mark's body in a heavy blue tarp. The sound of shovels biting into earth filled the night as they dug, trading positions when the other was tired. Neither man spoke much - the gravity of their task reflected in their grim expressions.

"That's deep enough," Todd said after an hour of digging. Sweat soaked through their shirts despite the chill. "Need to make sure it stays buried."

They rolled Mark's body into the grave, then carefully arranged fallen leaves and branches in layers as they refilled the hole. Todd scattered pine needles over the disturbed ground while Jason gathered rocks to place naturally around the site.

"What about his car?" Jason asked, tamping down the last of the soil.

"We'll search around for it tomorrow. I have the feeling he walked like she did. If we find it, we'll push it off one of the old mining roads." Todd surveyed their work with a critical eye. "Make it look like he ran off the road after getting shot or something. There's going to be a ton of abandoned cars."

Jason nodded, leaning on his shovel. "And Sarah?"

"She doesn't need to know. We'll tell her he ran off and we doubt he'll be back. I think she is fitting in nicely. Besides, I like having her around." Todd gathered their tools. "Gives me something to look at." They both chuckled at his honest remark.

"What... I don't do it for you?" Jason responded with a fake jealous voice.

They loaded the ATV in silence, each lost in their own thoughts. The eastern sky had begun to lighten, turning the sky a dark shade of blue.

"You good with this?" Todd asked as they prepared to head back.

Jason looked at the fresh grave, now nearly invisible under its cover of forest debris. "Had to be done. Guy made his choice when he pulled that trigger."

"Still." Todd started the ATV's engine. "Taking a life always leaves a mark."

"Well, not my first, and may not be the last." Jason climbed on behind Todd. "Or your last if things don't turn around. Right now, it's like the old west out here. Who would have thought we'd have to do things like this?"

They rode back through the pre-dawn darkness, the ATV's headlight illuminating the trail. Behind them, the clearing returned to its natural silence, keeping its new secret beneath layers of earth and leaves.

Todd killed the ATV's engine inside the garage, the sudden silence broken only by their boots on gravel. The pre-dawn air carried a sharp chill as they unloaded their shovels and unused tarp.

Jason wiped down the tools with an old rag, removing traces of dirt before hanging them in their designated spots. Todd folded the tarp with mechanical precision, tucking it away with the others on a top shelf.

The house stood dark and quiet when they entered through the basement door. Their boots made soft thuds on the stairs as they made their way to the kitchen. Bear and Buttercup lay curled up in their beds, raising their heads briefly to acknowledge their return.

"I'll talk to Bobbie," Jason said, his voice low. He found her in their bedroom, sitting up in bed with a book.

Bobbie set the book aside. "I wasn't able to go back to sleep. Everything okay?"

Jason closed the door behind him and sat on the edge of the bed. "It's done. He won't be coming back. Ever."

Her hand found his, squeezing gently. "You guys had no choice."

"I know." Jason's shoulders sagged with exhaustion. "We buried him out past the pine grove. Better if Sarah doesn't know the details."

Bobbie nodded, understanding in her eyes. "Get some sleep. You look worn out."

Todd had already retreated to his room on the third floor, exhausted from the night's events, while Jason made his way to bed on heavy feet. The house creaked and settled around them in the pre-dawn silence. Both men fell into an uneasy sleep as the first light of dawn crept over the eastern hills, brightening the Colorado sky in streaks of gold. Their troubled dreams were filled with shadows of how things played out hours before, even as the world outside awoke.

The following morning, the sun rose across Overlook Ridge as Todd and Jason set out with the dogs. The birds chirped in the crisp mountain air. Todd adjusted his hoodie against the morning chill while Jason walked beside him, both men watching the dogs explore ahead of them.

"These morning walks keep getting earlier." Jason rubbed his eyes. "But I guess that's what happens when you have two energetic dogs."

"Bear's not exactly energetic." Todd chuckled as he watched the black malamute waddle along the trail. "More like enthusiastically food-motivated."

Buttercup ranged ahead, her black and tan coat gleaming as she moved with the fluid grace of a working dog. She paused occasionally, nose twitching as she picked up various scents, before continuing her patrol of the property perimeter.

"She takes her job seriously," Todd pointed at Buttercup's alert posture.

"Unlike some other dog we know." Jason gestured toward Bear, who had stopped to scratch her back against a pine tree, tongue lolling out in pure contentment.

The trail wound through stands of juniper and pine before opening into an area thick with scrub oak. The dense, twisted branches formed natural corridors and hideaways. Buttercup's ears perked up, and she trotted toward a particularly dense thicket. Bear, noticing her companion's interest, abandoned her tree-scratching and followed.

"What've you found, girls?" Todd called out as both dogs disappeared into the bushes.

The rustling of branches and occasional snaps of twigs marked the dogs' progress through the undergrowth. Jason stepped closer to the thicket's edge, trying to keep sight of them.

"Should we call them back?" Jason's hand rested on the sidearm he always carried.

"Give them a minute. Buttercup probably caught the scent of a rabbit or something." Todd crossed his arms, watching the bushes sway with the dogs' movement.

The morning quiet broke with a sharp yelp. Buttercup burst from the scrub oak, her usual confident stride replaced by a scrambling retreat and her tail tucked low. She bolted straight to Todd, pressing against his legs with her fur bristling and licking her lips.

"Whoa, girl. What's wrong?" Todd reached down to steady his normally unflappable shepherd. Her muscles trembled beneath his touch.

"Bear? Where's Bear?" Jason stepped toward the thicket, his voice rising with concern.

Crashing sounds emerged from the scrub oak as Bear backed out, her black coat covered in leaves and twigs. Unlike Buttercup's panic, Bear seemed more confused than scared. Her head tilted to one side as she stared back into the thicket.

"Both dogs are out now." Todd kept one hand on Buttercup's head, feeling her continued tremors. "But I've never seen Buttercup spooked like this."

Jason moved closer to the scrub oak, but Buttercup let out a low whine. Todd felt her tension increase.

"Hold up," Todd called to Jason. "Something's got her seriously worked up. She doesn't seem right."

Bear ambled over to them, still appearing puzzled rather than frightened. She sat down heavily, scratching at her ear as if the whole incident meant nothing to her.

"Should we check it out?" Jason already had his pistol out. The morning sun made it easy to spot anything unusual.

Buttercup's whine deepened, and she shifted to place herself between Todd and the thicket.

"I've never seen her act like this," Todd frowned, studying his German Shepherd's behavior. "Even when we've run into bears or mountain lions, she stands her ground. This is different."

The scrub oak stood silent now, its twisted branches revealing nothing of what had frightened Buttercup. The morning breeze rustled through the leaves, carrying no unusual sounds or scents that the men could detect.

"Maybe we should come back with some better equipment, like a machete," Jason suggested, his hand still clutching the pistol at his side.

Todd knelt beside Buttercup, running his hands through her fur to check for injuries. His fingers brushed something wet above her right eye. He parted the fur, revealing a two small gashes that oozed blood.

"That's not from thorns." Todd's stomach tightened as he examined the wound pattern. "This is a bite mark."

Buttercup flinched as he probed the area. The punctures formed a distinct pattern - too precise for random scratches from branches.

"How bad?" Jason kept his eyes on the scrub oak while maintaining his grip on the pistol.

"Clean cut. I don't know." Todd pulled a handkerchief from his pocket and pressed it against the wound. "Bear, come here."

The black malamute plodded over, still showing no signs of distress. Todd checked her over but found no injuries beneath her thick coat.

"Bear's fine. Probably too thick-headed to notice any danger." Todd shook his head at the dog's perpetual state of contentment.

Jason edged toward the thicket. Dry leaves crunched under his boots as he approached the dense tangle of branches. The morning sun starting to provide deep shadows through the twisted limbs, creating pockets of darkness perfect for hiding.

"Jason, wait-" Todd started to call out.

The distinctive buzz cut through the morning air. Jason froze mid-step, the sound sending ice through his veins. The rattle grew louder, echoing from somewhere in the shadows ahead.

"Rattler." Jason's voice dropped to barely above a whisper. He took a slow step backward, keeping his movements smooth.

The buzzing intensified. Branches rustled as something moved through the undergrowth, tracking Jason's retreat.

"That's odd." Todd stood, keeping pressure on Buttercup's wound. "Rattlers aren't typically this high in altitude. Makes perfect sense now. She's been bitten."

Jason continued his careful withdrawal. The rattling was still loud, accompanied by the sound of leaves crunching beneath his boots as he backtracked out of the thicket.

"Yep. I see it, I think. Not too big, but certainly pissed.." Jason's hands tightened on his pistol. "Dad gum. Makes you wonder how many more are out here."

Buttercup's whine deepened into a cry. She tried to move forward, but Todd held her back, feeling the tremors still running through her body. Even Bear seemed to finally sense the wrongness of the situation, her usual dopey expression replaced by focused attention on the scrub oak.

The rattling stopped. Silence fell over the thicket, broken only by the whisper of wind through the leaves. Jason took another step back, his boot scraping against a rock.

Todd moved forward, his boots silent on the rocky ground, leaving Buttercup sitting and wincing her right eye. He drew his own pistol as he approached, the weight familiar in his hand.

"Where exactly?" Todd kept his voice low as he joined Jason.

Jason pointed with his free hand. "Right there, under that twisted branch. See the pattern?"

The snake's scales created a diamond pattern against the leaf litter, its triangular head raised and ready. The rattle buzzed again, a warning that sent shivers down Todd's spine.

"Got it." Todd raised his pistol, squinting down the sights. The snake's head provided a clear target against the darker ground. He squeezed the trigger.

The shot cracked through the morning air. Pine needles rained down as birds took flight. The snake's body thrashed once, then lay still, its head obliterated by the hollow point round.

"Clean shot." Jason kept his weapon trained on the area. "But we should check for others."

Todd turned back to Buttercup. The German Shepherd's breathing had grown labored, her muscles twitching beneath her coat. Bear pressed against her companion, whining softly.

"We need to get her back. Now." Todd tucked his pistol away and scooped up Buttercup. The shepherd weighed close to seventy pounds, but adrenaline made the load manageable. "The garage has better light."

Jason led the way, now watching the surroundings as they backtracked along the trail. Bear stuck close to Todd's heels, her usual meandering forgotten as she followed.

The garage's metal door groaned as Jason yanked it open. Sunlight streamed through the windows, illuminating the workspace. Todd laid Buttercup on the concrete floor, her body trembling against the cool surface.

"Get the first aid kit from the cabinet." Todd pointed as he inspected the wound more closely. The punctures had swollen, angry red circles forming around each fang mark. "And grab that bottle of peroxide."

Jason retrieved the supplies, setting them beside Todd. "How bad?"

"Bad enough." Todd cleaned away the blood, revealing the full extent of the bite. "Rattler venom spreads fast. She's already showing symptoms."

Buttercup whimpered as Todd dabbed peroxide on the wound. Bear settled beside her, pressing her bulk against Buttercup's side in an uncharacteristic display of awareness.

"Should we try to suck out the venom?" Jason knelt beside them, his face tight with worry.

"That's an old wives' tale." Todd shook his head as he applied antibiotic ointment. "Makes it worse, actually. We need anti-venom, but we don't have any of that. It thought about getting some, but it's like thousands of dollars and doesn't store for long."

Buttercup's breathing grew more labored. Her eyes, usually bright and alert, had taken on a glassy sheen. Her face beginning to swell large. Todd stroked her head, feeling the heat radiating from her skin.

"What can we do?" Jason hovered over them, wishing he could do something. "Let me get her some water."

Todd kept pressure on Buttercup's wound with gauze, his movements gentle. "It's ok girl. Let's get her inside the house."

He lifted her again, muscles straining. Bear followed as Todd moved toward the basement door, his typical gait replaced by careful steps.

"Stay here, Bear." Todd commanded as Jason Todd pick the heavy dog up and into his arms like a baby. "Guard the house."

The black malamute sat, watching as Todd carried Buttercup inside. Her head tilted at the unfamiliar, serious tone in his voice.

"I'll run ahead and get a spot ready." Jason ran ahead, opening the basement door and leaving it open for Todd.

"Go. I got her." Todd cradled Buttercup, feeling each labored breath. Her face swelling larger and her right eye beginning to close.

Todd carried Buttercup through the basement door, her weight growing heavier with each step. The German Shepherd's breathing came in shallow pants, her chest rising and falling in an irregular rhythm. The swelling around her face had spread, distorting her usually noble features.

Jason darted ahead, clearing a path to Buttercup's bed in the corner of the kitchen. The padding provided comfort instead of laying on the tile floor. Now it would serve a different purpose.

"Easy, girl." Todd lowered Buttercup onto her bed. Her muscles trembled beneath his hands as he arranged her into a comfortable position. The gauze around her wound had already begun to show spots of red seeping through.

Jason returned with a large bowl of water, setting it within easy reach of Buttercup's muzzle. "Should we try to get her to drink?"

"Maybe. I don't think she'll drink right now." Todd stroked Buttercup's head, careful to avoid the swollen area around the bite. Her fur felt hot and damp beneath his palm. "Let her rest for a minute. See if you can find out anything about what to do from any field manuals we have."

Footsteps creaked on the floor above them. Bobbie and Sarah appeared in the doorway, their morning routine interrupted by the commotion. They wore workout clothes, suggesting she'd been in the middle of exercising on the back deck.

"What's going on?" Boobie's eyes widened as she took in the scene - Todd kneeling beside Buttercup's bed, Jason hovering anxiously nearby, and the German Shepherd's labored breathing filling the room's air.

"Rattlesnake got her." Jason crossed to his wife, his voice tight with concern. "Over by the shooting range, in the scrub oak. Never seen one up here before."

Bobbie pressed a hand to her mouth. "Oh no. Poor Buttercup." She moved closer, kneeling beside Todd to examine the shepherd. "The swelling's pretty bad already. She looks like a hound dog."

"It's spreading fast." Todd dabbed at Buttercup's face with a cool cloth. The shepherd's right eye had swollen completely shut, and the left was beginning to close. Her breath wheezed through her throat, each inhalation a struggle.

"The kids are still asleep." Bobbie touched Buttercup's flank gently. "Should I keep them upstairs when they wake up? Rose will be so sad if she sees Buttercup like this."

Jason nodded. "It's ok, they just need to stay quiet for a while if they're down here. Also, they don't need to be going out into the woods anymore. Not until we sweep the area good for more. If there is one, there's probably more. This could be a deadly situation for anyone who gets bitten out here." He paced the kitchen floor, his boots scuffing against the tile. "There has to be something else we can do."

Buttercup shifted on her bed, a whimper escaping as she tried to find a more comfortable position. Todd steadied her, murmuring soft words of comfort. The shepherd's good eye fixed on him, clouded with pain but still trusting.

"The venom's really taking hold now." Todd checked the bandage again. The swelling had spread down her neck, making the collar tight around her neck. "I think I need to take her collar off, and I guess just let the wound weep."

Bobbie retrieved the first aid kit they'd brought in. "Here, let me help." She worked with Todd to carefully pull the bandage off, revealing the angry red flesh beneath. The puncture wounds stood out starkly against Buttercup's skin, surrounded by tissue that had turned an alarming shade of purple.

"Well, this thing is useless for things like this." Jason stopped pacing to peer at a field medical book he found on Todd's living room shelf. "Doesn't look like there's anything we can do. Says here she needs to drink water. If she doesn't drink, it's not a good sign."

"Moving her might make it worse, so let's hope she will drink on her own." Todd shook his head as he applied fresh gauze, dabbing it softly on the wound. "And the nearest emergency vet is over an hour away."

Buttercup's breathing grew more labored. Each breath seemed to require more effort than the last, her chest heaving with the exertion. She tried to lift her head toward the water bowl, but the movement proved too much.

"Here, girl." Bobbie cupped her hand in the water, bringing it to Buttercup's muzzle. The shepherd lapped weakly at the offered moisture, most of it dribbling down her swollen face.

"At least she's trying to drink." Todd sat back on his heels, feeling helpless as he watched his loyal companion struggle. "That's something."

Jason resumed his pacing, the rhythm of his boots matching Buttercup's strained breathing. "Maybe I should get on the radio, see if anyone has anti-venom. There might be someone who keeps it on hand."

"By the time you got back..." Todd's voice trailed off as Buttercup let out a particularly painful wheeze. He stroked her head, trying to provide what comfort he could.

"The swelling's still spreading." Bobbie pointed to Buttercup's neck, where the angry inflammation continued its advance. "Should we try a cold compress?"

"At this point, it's been fifteen minutes. I think we'll know for certain in the next hour if she's going to make it or not." Todd said, sitting next to Buttercup on the ground.

Time crawled by as Todd sat beside Buttercup, the shepherd's labored breathing marking each passing minute. The swelling had stabilized, no longer advancing down her neck, but her face remained distorted and puffy. Her good eye drifted open and closed, focusing on Todd whenever consciousness returned.

Bobbie moved quietly through the kitchen, preparing lunch while keeping a watchful eye on the situation. The smell of fresh bread filled the air, mixing with the antiseptic scent of the medical supplies scattered around Buttercup's bed.

"Try to rest, girl." Todd's hand never left Buttercup's side, monitoring her breathing and temperature. The initial fever seemed to have broken, her fur no longer radiating intense heat.

Jason alternated between checking his watch and flipping through the field manual, searching for any information they might have missed. The book's pages rustled with each frustrated turn. Although he wasn't finding anything concerning a dog being bitten by a rattlesnake, he was intrigued by all the information in the book.

Sunlight crept across the kitchen floor as morning stretched toward afternoon. Buttercup's breathing, while still strained, had settled into a more regular pattern. She managed several small drinks when Bobbie refreshed the water bowl, though most dribbled from her swollen muzzle.

"The kids are getting restless," Bobbie whispered as she passed Jason. "Rose keeps asking when they can go outside."

"Tell them Buttercup's not feeling well and they need to stay quiet. Let them go downstairs or to the greenhouse. They can take Bear outside with them." Jason closed the manual, setting it aside. "The older ones probably have some chores to do out there, anyway."

Todd's legs had gone numb from sitting on the hard floor, but he maintained his vigil. Every twitch or whimper from Buttercup drew his immediate attention, though the violent tremors from earlier had subsided.

The kitchen clock ticked past another quarter hour. Buttercup shifted position slightly, her movements more controlled than the earlier thrashing. Her good eye half opened, tracking Todd's face with more awareness than before.

Finally, after what felt like days, Todd's joints protested too loudly to ignore. He rose stiffly, muscles cramping from the prolonged stillness. The couch beckoned, offering a slightly better vantage point to watch over Buttercup.

Jason checked his watch again, marking the time since the bite. He crossed to where Todd sat, his expression thoughtful.

"It's been a while now." Jason's voice carried a note of cautious optimism. "The book said the worst usually hits within the first thirty minutes for humans. I think she's going to pull through."

Todd rubbed his face, exhaustion settling in as the adrenaline faded. "Yeah, maybe you're right." He glanced at Buttercup, who had managed to lift her head slightly. "The swelling's stopped spreading, at least."

"And she's more alert." Jason settled into a chair across from Todd. "Plus, she's drinking when Bobbie offers water. Those are good signs. She looks like a hound dog in the face."

"Still worried though." Todd couldn't shake the image of Buttercup's panic in the scrub oak, so unlike her usual confident demeanor. "Never seen a western rattler up this high in altitude before. Makes me wonder what else might be changing around here."

Buttercup's tail thumped weakly against her bed, responding to their voices. The sound, however faint, brought a slight smile to Todd's tired face.

"That's my girl." Todd leaned forward, maintaining eye contact with his loyal companion. "Keep fighting."

Bobbie appeared with sandwiches and a coffee for Jason and a coke for Todd, setting them on the table between the men. "You both need to eat something. It's been a long morning."

The aroma of Jason's fresh coffee filled the kitchen, mixing with the lingering scent of baked bread. Outside, Bear's occasional bark reminded them that life continued beyond their vigil.

"Thanks, babe." Jason accepted a sandwich, though his attention remained fixed on Buttercup. "At least we know what happened now. Those puncture wounds were pretty distinctive once we got a good look at them."

Todd nodded, cradling the sandwich between his hands. "Just glad we found that snake. Would've driven me crazy if it got away."

Buttercup's breathing had eased further, the harsh wheezing softened to a more natural rhythm. Her swollen face prevented any real expression, but her good eye remained bright and focused, tracking their movements around the kitchen.

Buttercup remained largely inactive for the next few days, her usual energetic patrols of Overlook Ridge temporarily suspended. Only moving when absolutely necessary, she would slowly make her way to her water bowl or trudge outside to relieve herself, each movement deliberate and careful. As the days passed, the angry swelling gradually retreated from her neck and face, and her characteristic shepherd alertness began to return. Her good eye grew brighter, and she started showing more interest in her surroundings, even managing to thump her tail when Todd or Jason approached. To the immense relief of the family, who had spent a few days monitoring her recovery, everyone was deeply grateful that Buttercup had pulled through the hardship of the snake encounter with her fighting spirit intact.

Chapter 17

A Glimmer of Hope

The morning rose across Overlook Ridge as Todd traced his finger down a yellowed inventory sheet. Numbers and checkmarks filled the precisely ruled columns - detailed ammunition counts, categorized food stores, and meticulously tracked medical supplies. His methodical mind cataloged each item with practiced efficiency.

Jason crouched beside a stack of sturdy wooden crates in the climate-controlled storage room, methodically prying one open with a well-worn crowbar. The lid popped free with a satisfying crack, releasing the scent of sealed packaging. "Here's another case of those premium freeze-dried meals you ordered last year. Still sealed tight, not a spot of moisture damage."

"Mark it down - twenty-four units. Let's just hope these packages are not filled with sawdust." Todd made a careful notation in his precise handwriting. "That puts us at... six months of emergency rations, not counting Bobbie's impressive greenhouse output. Not to mention we still have a bunch of deer meat we haven't even touched yet. Better than I projected. It think we are actually gaining in food supplies."

"Speaking of which..." Jason stood and stretched his back, working out the kinks from crouching. "Have you seen what she's done with that place lately? It's like a perfectly organized jungle in there. She's developed a genuine gift. She's got Sarah up to speed as well."

Through a narrow, reinforced window, the greenhouse's double-paned glass glinted brilliantly in the morning light. Inside, Bobbie and the children moved with purpose between the carefully spaced rows of thriving plants, her practiced hands checking leaves and stems for signs of health or distress. The spring seedlings she'd tenderly nurtured had exploded into robust, productive growth.

"Let's take a break and check it out." Todd set down his clipboard on a nearby shelf. "These inventory sheets aren't going anywhere, and I want to see her latest improvements."

They stepped out into the warm mountain air, inhaling deeply. The transition from spring to summer had painted the ridge in vibrant greens, from the swaying pines to the hardy scrub oak. Todd's loyal dogs bounded eagerly ahead of them, tails wagging joyfully as they approached the gleaming greenhouse.

Bobbie looked up as they entered, her capable hands deep in the rich, custom-mixed soil. "Just in time - help me harvest these heirloom tomatoes. They're at peak ripeness."

"Already?" Jason picked up a sturdy collection basket. "Seems early in the season."

"The new soil mixture we developed is working absolute wonders." Bobbie proudly pointed to vines heavily laden with perfectly red fruit. "And wait until you see the specialty peppers I've been cultivating."

Todd ran his hand along a robust tomato vine. "Engineering the perfect growing medium took some serious trial and error, but looks like we finally got the mineral balance exactly right."

"More than right." Bobbie skillfully pulled a fat, unblemished tomato free and placed it gently in Jason's basket. "Between the greenhouse and the terraced outdoor gardens, we're producing more than we can possibly eat fresh. Time to preserve for winter using those canning supplies."

"Add that to our inventory surplus." Jason grinned knowingly at Todd. "Remember when we worried about having enough supplies cached away?"

"Planning and preparation, that's always been the key." Todd plucked another perfectly ripe tomato. "Though I'll admit, Bobbie's exceptional green thumb has exceeded even my most optimistic calculations."

Bobbie brushed dark soil from her hands. "Come see the expanded herb section. I've got medicinal plants really thriving now too - organic echinacea, wild-strain yarrow, and potent calendula. It's becoming quite the natural pharmacy in the making."

They followed her down the meticulously maintained row, ducking under hanging cucumber vines heavy with fruit. The air was thick with the heady smell of growth and fertility. Carefully introduced beneficial insects buzzed industriously between the abundant blooms.

"The bees are clearly happy." Todd watched an industrious bumblebee methodically work its way through bright marigold flowers. "That new ventilated hive box design is really paying off better than expected. Ol' Bruce is really doing a fantastic job with the bees."

"Everything's paying off." Jason picked a fresh sprig of Genovese basil, crushing a leaf between his fingers to release its intense scent. "We've got food production completely dialed in, redundant security systems in place, solar power grid running smooth as silk..."

"Don't forget the integrated water collection and filtration system." Todd pointed to the carefully engineered ceiling, where condensation dripped in a precisely calculated pattern. "Engineering that multi-stage system was quite a challenge, but now we're catching and recycling every precious drop."

Bobbie moved purposefully to a well-organized shelf of promising seedlings. "Next phase is expanding the medicinal garden section. I've been extensively studying traditional herbal remedies from your books, thinking smartly about what we might need long term."

"What about cannabis?" Jason affectionately squeezed her shoulder. "Though at this rate, we'll need to build another greenhouse before winter sets in."

"Already drafted the detailed plans." Todd pulled a carefully folded paper from his pocket. "Thought we could modify this southeastern corner of the property, maybe add an efficient aquaponics system for year-round fish protein..."

"Of course you have." Jason laughed warmly. "Can't help yourself, can you? You always thinking three steps ahead."

"That's exactly why this works so well." Bobbie gestured proudly around their thriving domain. "Todd plans everything meticulously. Jason helps build it strong. I make it grow and flourish. We each bring something essential to the table."

They continued through the humid greenhouse, sturdy baskets filling steadily with the morning's bountiful harvest. Bobbie enthusiastically pointed out promising new growth, Todd discussed potential infrastructure improvements, and Jason made mental notes of minor repairs needed. The contented dogs lounged peacefully in sunny spots between the productive rows, completely at ease in the well-ordered routine they'd carefully built together on their mountain sanctuary.

As evening fell across Overlook Ridge, Todd adjusted the dials on his ham radio setup. The equipment hummed softly in the cozy radio room, its warm glow casting a yellow light across the polished wooden desk. Jason settled into the adjacent chair, headphones at the ready for their nightly check-in with the local network.

"Overlook Ridge, checking in for evening net." Todd's voice carried the practiced cadence of an experienced operator.

The radio crackled with Steve Morton's response from his property three miles down the valley. "Todd, glad you're on. We've got a situation developing in town."

Jason leaned forward, catching the edge in Steve's normally steady voice.

"What kind of situation?" Todd keyed the mic, exchanging a quick glance with Jason.

"Gang's moved in. About thirty of them. Took over the sheriff's office this morning. Deputies pulled out yesterday - got orders to support riot control in the larger cities."

"The entire department?" Jason grabbed the spare mic.

"Every person who they had. Military's spread thin across all the major cities. Left us hanging out here with nothing but a martial law declaration and no one to enforce it but ourselves."

Another voice cut through - Bill Henderson from the east side of the ranch community. "They've already shut down everything. Taking 'protection fees' to anyone that wants to stay in town."

Todd pulled out his notebook, writing rapidly in a handwriting style that only he could read. "Any violence?"

"Not yet," Steve replied. "But one fellow got roughed up when he tried to stand up to them.

They're carrying serious hardware - military-grade stuff."

"They are organized," Bill added. "I don't think they are from around here. Somehow, they knew exactly when law enforcement pulled out."

Jason rubbed his jaw, mind racing through tactical scenarios. "They'll push south once they've stripped the town bare. Ranch country's their next logical target."

"Already seeing their scouts." Another neighbor joined the frequency. "Two pickup trucks cruising the north access road this afternoon. Just watching with binoculars."

Todd's pencil moved faster across the page, mapping out threat vectors and defensive considerations. "Everyone, check your supplies. How are you looking for immediate needs?"

A chorus of responses filtered through the radio - most neighbors had decent stores, but several voiced concerns about medical supplies and ammunition.

"We need to coordinate." Jason's mind kicked into high gear. "Set up communication protocols, establish watch rotations. They'll eventually come to the Ranch."

"Agreed." Todd keyed the mic once again. "Steve, Bill - We need to be ready if they come onto the

Blackhawk. If we make a good defense, they might leave us alone."

"Copy that." Steve's transmission carried the weight of grim determination.

Todd sketched a rough map of the ranch roads, marking potential choke points and defensive positions, and showed Jason. "If they come from town, we will be the last stop."

The responses painted a sobering picture - it was clear to Todd that the worst wasn't over. The hard winter hadn't taken enough bad guys out of the picture.

"We've got geography on our side," Jason pointed out. "One road in, steep terrain everywhere else. We can work with that."

"If we coordinate," Todd agreed. "But we need to be smart about it. It might be time to get up to the house on the ridge and do some shooting practice from that distance."

"That's a good idea. We can use the long gun to keep them away from the house. It really just depends on how many there are. There's only a few of us." Jason sounding more worried than usual.

"If they decide to attack, we should hear the noise before they get to us," Todd added. "If we catch it in time, we can go support."

The check-in continued as darkness settled over the ridge. Each transmission added another piece to the troubling puzzle. Todd finally signed off, setting down his headphones with careful precision. The map before him told a clear story - their peaceful mountain community had become the front line of a very different kind of battle.

"We should brief Bobbie and Sarah," Jason said quietly. "They'll need to adjust to new security protocols."

"Already thinking about that." Todd's mind was running through multiple scenarios. "We'll need to move some of our cached supplies, create redundant storage locations."

The radio fell silent except for the soft hum of equipment. Outside, coyotes called in the darkness - wild voices that carried new menace in light of the evening's revelations. The peaceful sanctuary they'd built was about to be tested in ways they'd hoped to avoid but had always known might come.

Chapter 18

REFLECTIONS ON THE PAST

The mountain air carried a crisp bite as Todd settled into his weathered Adirondack chair on the deck of his Overlook Ridge home. The late afternoon sun shining bright across the valley below, flooding the landscape in amber. Jason lounged in the chair beside him, both men nursing cups of coffee - a luxury they'd learned to savor since the collapse.

"Remember when we used to carpool to work every morning and stop for hotdogs at seven in the morning?" Todd traced the rim of his cup with his finger. "Damn, I miss those hotdogs."

"The old Choke and Puke." Jason took a slow sip. "Then we'd go to work and do absolutely nothing except wait for lunch."

"Funny how something so simple became such a treasure." Todd watched as his two dogs played in the yard below, their paws kicking up dust in the driveway as they chased each other. "Back then,

I worried about project deadlines and retirement accounts."

"And I spent my days learning how to fly and trade stocks. I miss those flying days." Jason stretched his legs. "I remember when we got out of work, then flew to Kansas to gamble all night? We returned the next morning just in time to go back to work."

The wind rustled through the pine trees, carrying with it the sweet scent of wild sage. Todd's mind couldn't help but note the solar panels needed adjusting - another task for tomorrow's endless list.

"Your family's done well here, Jas. They seem to really enjoy it."

"Because of you." Jason set his cup down. "This place - having somewhere to go when everything fell apart. We wouldn't have made it without you and Overlook Ridge."

Todd shook his head. "I bought this land half thinking I was paranoid. All those years of prepping, stockpiling. My colleagues used to joke about it."

"Not joking now, are they?"

"Wouldn't know. Probably all dead."

A comfortable silence fell between them, broken only by the occasional bark from the dogs. The sunset showing the clouds in brilliant strokes of purple and orange, nature's reminder that some things remained unchanged.

"Miss flying?" Todd glanced at his friend.

Jason ran a hand through his stubbled beard. "Every day. But it was never the same once I moved away from you. I remember when I didn't even have my license, and I flew into that small airstrip and picked you up? I still can't believe you went flying with someone that only had about five hours of flight time. Wish we could go back and do it all over again."

"Life had other plans." Todd leaned forward, his voice dropping. "You know what I miss most? The simplicity. Walking into a store, buying whatever you needed. Not having to think three steps ahead about every little thing."

"Or checking the news without wondering if it's the last time we'll have internet access."

Todd's dogs trotted to the basement door and were let in by one of the children. They quickly made their way up to the upper deck where Todd and Jason sat, their presence a constant comfort in this new world. Todd reached down to scratch behind their ears. "These two don't seem to mind the changes. As long as they've got food and someone to chase squirrels with."

"Dogs adapt better than humans." Jason watched as the larger of the two flopped at Todd's feet. "Sometimes I wonder what my co-workers would think if they saw me now. Trading technology for gardening skills."

"Speaking of gardens," Todd gestured toward the greenhouse they'd built last spring, "your wife's tomatoes are thriving again. Never thought I'd get so excited about vegetables."

"Bobbie's got a gift. Though she still complains about trading in her gym for a root cellar. Glad her and Sarah get along so great. They're like best friends."

The temperature dropped as the sun dipped below the horizon. Todd pulled his jacket tighter, remembering the work clothes that had once hung in his closet. Now his wardrobe consisted of whatever would last the longest, keep him warmest.

"You ever regret it?" Jason's question hung in the cooling air. "Choosing this life before it chose us?"

Todd watched as the first stars appeared in the darkening sky. "Regret being prepared? No. Regret not convincing more people to prepare? Every day."

"Well, we told them something was going to happen sooner or later. Who would have thought?"

"We did." Todd stood, his joints protesting the movement. "And we're still doing it. One day at a time."

The dogs perked up at his movement, ready for their evening routine. Security checks, perimeter walk, counting supplies - the new normal that had replaced evening news and microwave dinners.

Jason rose too, collecting their cups. "Remember when we used to spend hours debating politics, religion, and market trends?"

"Now we debate water filtration systems and ammunition storage." Todd cracked a smile. "But you know what? I wouldn't trade this - any of it. Having purpose, having family." He looked at his friend. "Having someone who understands-"

Jason smiled, showing that he felt the same. "Good times. Good times."

Chapter 19

HOLDING THE LINE

The afternoon sun filtered through the open door of Todd's garage, casting a near blinding light across the workbench where he and Jason hunched over their latest project. Metal parts scattered across the surface gleamed in the light while the radio crackled softly in the background, its occasional background chatter of neighbors communicating a familiar comfort.

Jason wiped sweat from his brow with the back of his hand. "Pass me that wrench, if you can find it."

Todd was searching the table when the radio's steady hum erupted into frantic words.

"...anyone listening? We need help!" The voice crackled through the speaker, thick with panic. "They're coming through our fence-"

Todd dropped the wrench with a clang and lunged for the radio. "This is Todd at Overlook. What's your situation?"

Jason's shoulders tensed as he moved closer to the radio, his eyes fixed on the speaker.

"Todd? Thank God!" The voice belonged to Mike Peterson, their neighbor a about a mile down the road. "We've got multiple people breaching our perimeter. They're armed-" A burst of gunfire cut through his words.

"Mike, how many?" Todd's fingers tightened around the radio. "What direction are they coming from?"

Static crackled across the channel. More gunfire erupted in the background, closer this time.

"Can't tell... maybe twelve... they're-" Mike's voice disappeared into a burst of static.

"Mike? Mike, do you copy?" Todd's knuckles whitened around the radio. Nothing but dead air answered.

Jason grabbed his jacket from the workbench. "We need to move."

Todd's dogs started barking outside as they heard the gunshots faintly echoing off the ridges surrounding the homestead, their deep growls echoing through the garage walls. He crossed to the gun rack in three quick strides, spinning on his heels as he grabbed his assault rifle.

"Might be nothing," Todd muttered, but his actions betrayed his words as he pulled out his AR-15 and began loading magazines.

Jason checked his pistol, muscle memory taking over as he verified the chamber. "Mike doesn't spook easy. You heard those shots. The question is, should we go find out, or do we setup an over-watch and wait to see if they come this far back?"

The radio remained silent, its dead channel a reminder of their neighbor's cut-off cry for help. Todd distributed ammunition between them, his movements sharp and focused.

"I don't know. Could be raiders," Todd said, his engineering mind already calculating distances and response times. "Or worse."

"Whatever it is, Mike needs help." Jason grabbed extra magazines, stuffing them into his cargo pockets. "But if they hit his place-"

"We could be next." Todd finished the thought, already moving toward the garage door. His dogs' barking intensified, setting his teeth on edge.

Jason paused at the doorway, scanning the tree line. "How do you want to play this?"

"We need eyes on the road first." Todd shouldered his rifle, checking the scope. "But we do this smart. It's probably too late for Mike. By the time we get there, we'll be fighting on unfamiliar ground. I think we need to defend here."

"I'll take up the sniper position at the house on the hill overlooking the road. You could post up at the edge of the property and hold whoever comes down the road I missed. I'll get Hyden and Bruce to circle around through the back of the ridge to watch our backs and re-enforce if we need it. But I don't want them engaging unless it's life or death," Jason suggested, his knowledge of the terrain showing through. "Gives us cover and high ground."

Todd nodded, his mind mapping out the route. The dogs fell silent suddenly, causing both men to freeze.

"Buttercup? Bear?" Todd called out. The German Shepherds came to his side.

Jason pressed against the doorframe, his weapon ready. "We need to get setup quickly. I'm going to go get Hyden and Bruce and tell them the plan." Jason disappeared in a flash to the house.

The garage fell silent except for Todd's measured breathing and the soft tick of cooling metal from their abandoned project. Whatever was happening at Mike's place, it had reached their doorstep faster than expected.

Within a minute, Jason emerged from the house with Hyden and Bruce in tow. All three were armed to the teeth. Jason slung his sniper rifle across his back as he laid out the plan to his older boys.

"You boys are to back us up from a distance. You are not to advance on anyone under any circumstances," Jason commanded, his voice carrying the weight tactical experience. "No shooting unless you know exactly who you're shooting at - positive target identification only. If they start targeting your position, you are to move back to the house immediately and lock it up tight. They won't reach me on the high ground unless they have a rocket launcher." He checked his rifle magazine one last time as he spoke. "If we get overrun, Todd will meet you back here and I will follow when I can. Keep your radios on channel three and call out all your movements," Jason continued, not mincing words as he was already moving out of the garage. He walked backward toward the tree line, his eyes locked on his sons' faces to ensure they understood the gravity of his orders. "Be safe! Remember, no heroics! I mean it - we stick to the plan!"

More gunfire echoed in the distance, closer than Mike's property. The sound bounced off the ridge, making it impossible to pinpoint the exact location.

"Time's up," Todd muttered, his expression hardening as he checked his weapon one final time.

Hyden and Bruce moved towards the trail system. Todd started his trek to the top of the property, all four moving in what seemed like practiced synchronization, their movements translating into wordless communication. Todd's logical mind complemented Jason's cunning instincts as they prepared to defend the homestead.

Todd crouched behind a fallen pine tree at the property's edge, his rifle trained on the winding dirt road. Through his scope, he tracked Jason's progress up the steep incline to the ridge house. The afternoon sun only had a few hours before touching the mountains. Todd listened intently for any sound or movement coming from the east.

After a few minutes, his radio crackled. "In position," Jason's voice came through, barely above a whisper. "I've got a clear line of sight for about a thousand yards down the main road."

Todd clicked his radio twice to acknowledge, keeping his eyes fixed on the approach. The wind shifted, carrying the acrid scent of smoke from the direction of Mike's property. More gunfire echoed off the ridges, but the sound seemed to come from multiple directions now.

"We are in position to the north of you, dad," Hyden's voice whispered through the radio. "No movement. Mr. Todd, your dogs are with us."

Todd was relieved that the dogs were with the boys. He had been worried they had run ahead to comfort any strangers. Another double click of his radio to acknowledge the communication. He adjusted his position behind the log, finding better cover while maintaining his view of the road.

The radio crackled again. "Movement," Jason's voice cut through. "Twelve people walking fast up the main road. All men, no children, no women. They look like they know where they are going."

Todd pressed himself lower against the earth, his finger resting beside the trigger guard. Through his scope, he could see the group briefly through the trees, though they hadn't yet rounded the bend in the road to come into clear view.

"Hyden, visual confirmation on the road," Jason reported. "Hold the dogs until Todd tells you to release them."

As the group got closer, their voices grew louder. Jason steadied his breathing, years of shooting practice taking over as he prepared for whatever was about to happen. The familiar feel of his sniper rifle pressed against his shoulder, its scope offering a clear view of the stretch of road where there would be almost no hiding.

"Todd, they are almost in range. If I shoot, they will probably scatter into the woods. Then we'll lose sight of them and they could flank us. Let's wait until you can see them, then we give them the whole nine yards. How copy?" Jason said, never blinking as he peered through his scope.

"Roger that. Standby, I can hear them coming." Todd's heart starting to race as he knew all hell was about to break loose.

As Jason trained his crosshairs on the man carrying the heaviest fire power - what appeared to be a modified AR-15 with a drum magazine - he began controlling his breathing, waiting for the call from Todd. His finger rested lightly against the trigger guard, muscles relaxed but ready. As the group approached the corner, moving in a loose formation that suggested more enthusiasm than training, they came into full view of Todd's position. He methodically scanned the raiding party for any children or teenagers, his experienced eyes taking in every detail of their appearance and gear. Confirming there were only middle-aged men, most wearing mismatched tactical gear and carrying an assortment of weapons. He clicked the radio button to make the radio call, his thumb steady despite the gravity of what was about to unfold.

"On my shot, open fire," he said rather calmly as he clicked the safety off.

Todd selected his target, studying the lead man, who appeared to be the one in charge. The man's face was clearly visible through his scope - a dark, unkempt beard framing weathered features, his manly bearing betrayed by an obvious beer gut straining against his black shirt and camouflage pants. The sight triggered memories of militia photos from Idaho that Todd had studied in preparation for exactly this scenario. He closed his left eye while he peered through the scope. He tried to regulate his breathing while slowly applying steady pressure to the trigger until the familiar recoil caught him mid-exhale. Todd's eyes instinctively blinked as the round left the chamber, reopening just in time to witness the impact - center mass, sending the target pitching forward onto his face in the dirt.

The crack of Todd's shot was still echoing when Jason's round found its mark. In one fluid motion, Jason was already working the bolt, muscle memory taking over as he chambered another round. His target spun violently before crumpling to the ground. The shots, mere heartbeats apart, sparked chaos within the group as they scattered like startled quail. One of them, braver or perhaps more foolish than the rest, blindly returned fire toward Todd's general position, unable to pinpoint the exact source of the initial shot. Todd instinctively ducked behind his log cover, though he needn't have worried - the return fire was cut short as Jason's rifle barked again from his elevated position, the round finding its mark with devastating effect, sending a fine red mist into the morning air around the man.

Todd could see a group of about six run off to the left of the road. While the rest ran to the right. Jason had shot two more times but seemingly missed as the targets were moving quickly. Gunfire erupted from the tree line towards Todd's position. The group to the right of the road returning fire toward Jason at the house on the ridge. Their bullets falling short of his position. Todd slowly scanned the tree line for movement. He caught a glimpse of muzzle flash and put his crosshairs just above the flashes and squeezed the trigger. The bullet ripped the air as it sailed through layers of scrub oak before finding the left lung of its victim.

As Todd fired, his own muzzle flash gave his position away like a beacon in the dark. The raiding party's bullets started to find their mark with increasing accuracy, pinging off rocks and splintering tree bark around him as he ducked desperately for cover behind a fallen log.

"They know where I am," Todd half yelled into his radio, his breath coming in short bursts. "Cover me. I need to move."

"Standby, switching rifles. Move on my shots," Jason replied decisively as he released the sniper rifle and swiftly picked up the AR15 laying in front of him, instinct guiding his movements.

Jason let out what seemed like fully automatic fire, even though it was a semi-automatic rifle, his trigger finger working as quickly as it could to spread hot lead into the tree line. The rapid succession of shots echoed across the ridge like rolling thunder, creating a wall of suppressing fire that lit up his prone position in staccato bursts of orange muzzle flash. Hearing the thunderous cover fire, Todd jumped to his feet and retreated back down the winding trail while keeping his head low, trying to make himself as small a target as possible in the shadows between the pine trees. His heart raced wildly in his chest as he could hear a few bullets zipping by him with their distinctive crack, cutting through branches and leaves overhead, sending splinters of wood and pine needles raining down around him as he moved. His boots found purchase on the familiar trail even in his haste, muscle memory guiding him down the path he knew so well.

Upon Jason's opening fire into the tree line, the group of attackers scattered, some firing blindly while others dove behind whatever cover they could find among the dense foliage. Jason methodically emptied his extended sixty-round magazine into the tree line, the 5.56mm rounds tear-ing through branches and undergrowth. Though he doubted any of his shots found their mark in the chaos, the suppressing fire achieved its intended purpose. Todd was able to make his tactical retreat down the winding trail, disappearing from the attackers' line of sight without giving them a chance to zero in on his position. With fluid movement, Jason ejected the spent magazine from his AR15, letting it drop to the ground as he smoothly inserted a fresh one with a satisfying click. In quick action, he transitioned back to his preferred weapon - the sniper rifle - bringing the scope up to his eye as he systematically swept the tree line left to right, searching for any movement that might betray an enemy's position in the chaos.

Jason counted at least three attackers down, taking a dirt nap, and was silently hoping his cover shots had taken out more. Todd had expertly maneuvered to a new vantage point behind a thick pine trunk, where he could observe roughly half the winding road while maintaining decent cover. He swiftly changed clips and reached for the tactical radio clipped to his vest.

"I'm set, thirty yards north from previous position. What can you see?"

"Three confirmed down, six or seven left. They split up, three are to the right of the road, the others are on your side," Jason responded in a measured tone, methodically sweeping his scope across both groups' positions, tracking their movements through the dense vegetation. "Standby."

Todd heard another sharp crack echo from the ridge as a bullet found its mark, sending yet another attacker crumpling to the ground. "Make that minus one. Two left on your side," Jason announced coolly while swinging his high-powered rifle toward the group on the right side of the road. As he methodically searched for another target through his scope, a fleeting shadow of movement caught his attention - a figure desperately sprinting across the exposed dirt road. Jason's reflexes took over as he swung his rifle quickly and squeezed the trigger, but he could only watch in frustration as the round kicked up dirt and rocks just feet behind the running man. The target had already disappeared into the thick vegetation, now moving directly toward Todd's concealed position.

"You have at least one, maybe two, coming towards you. I missed him." Jason quickly called over the radio. Two clicks of the radio came the response.

Todd kneeled behind a massive ponderosa pine, using its rough bark for support as he steadied himself. He could feel his heartbeat pounding in his ears, the rush of adrenaline making his pulse thunder like a drum. As he deliberately tried to slow his breathing with measured inhales and exhales, he could hear a distinct rustling in the dense scrub oak bushes twenty to thirty feet in front of him. The sound was getting closer, accompanied by the soft crunch of dried pine needles underfoot. He slowly aimed his rifle toward where the noise was coming from, his index finger hovering just outside the trigger guard, ready to engage at a moment's notice. His adrenalin focused him despite the tension building in his muscles.

Just then, a shot rang out, the sharp crack echoing through the forest. The bullet struck the tree a few inches to his head with a violent thwack, sending splinters of bark flying into his face like tiny shrapnel. Pure instinct took over as he squeezed the trigger in response, not even sure if he was aiming at anything specific. He ducked back behind the thick trunk as fast as his neck would allow, his heart hammering against his ribs, just as more bullets struck the tree and zipped past his position with deadly precision. The impacts sent vibrations through the wood at his back, each one a reminder of how close death lurked. He could hear the distinctive rifle reports coming from Jason's position somewhere off to his left, and found himself praying they would be enough to get him out of the desperate bind he was in. However, the incoming gunfire didn't let up - if anything, it seemed to intensify, creating a terrifying symphony of destruction all around him.

Todd frantically grabbed his radio, his fingers trembling slightly as he keyed the mic. "Release the dogs! Release the dogs!" he barked into the handset, his voice carrying an unmistakable urgency.

Hyden heard the desperate call crackle through his radio and exchanged a quick glance with Bruce before they simultaneously released their grip on Bear and Buttercup's leather collars. The two dogs exploded into action, their powerful muscles propelling them down the worn dirt path toward the sound of gunfire, their instinct taking over as they moved with deadly purpose. Todd twisted his body and blindly thrust his rifle around the thick trunk of the tree, squeezing off several rapid shots in the general direction of their attackers, hoping the suppressing fire would force them to duck for cover and buy precious seconds of time.

"Dogs! Dogs come!" Todd yelled at the top of his voice, praying the dogs would find his position quickly.

The gunfire continued in a steady rhythmic pop-pop-pop around Todd's position, bullets thudding into the thick tree trunk and sending splinters of bark flying. He was completely pinned down, unable to move more than a few inches without risking exposure to the deadly fire. Up on the ridge, Jason moved his scope quickly, his eyes frantically scanning the treeline and underbrush, desperately searching for any sign of movement or muzzle flash that would betray the attackers' positions. His anxiety mounted with each passing second, his heart pounding as he realized his friend was likely trapped and in grave danger. Though his trigger finger itched to return fire, he couldn't risk taking a shot - the angles were all wrong, and one stray round could easily strike Todd instead of their assailants.

Todd continued to shoot blindly from around the tree in the general direction of the attackers, squeezing off rapid rounds, hoping to keep them pinned down. Praying help arrived quickly. The bark of his weapon echoed through the trees as he spent his ammunition, his hands still steady despite the dire situation. Just as he was firing his last shot, a streak of black and tan came charging from around the path - Buttercup moving with fierce determination - followed closely by what Todd initially mistook for just a shadow but quickly recognized as Bear, each dog splitting around the tree in full stride with predator precision. Before Todd could fully process the sight of his faithful companions racing into danger, they were already past him, their powerful legs carrying them toward the bushes at breakneck speed, their protective instincts in full display. As they blazed past Todd, their presence filled him with a newfound surge of courage and purpose. He loaded his last clip, stepped out from his position, planted his feet firmly, and began firing his weapon in controlled bursts into the bushes at chest level, providing covering fire for his four-legged defenders.

As the dogs reached their intended targets, the gunshots increased in rapid succession, echoing across the property like thunder. Todd continued to fire methodically in the brush line, his mind quickly calculating trajectories as his brain processed that the bullets weren't aiming for him any longer but were now directed chaotically towards the dogs. Within a split second, the sound of fierce growling and two men yelling in panic and pain was all he needed to hear to know the dogs were on their targets. The sound of Bear's deep, guttural snarl and Buttercup's commanding growl told him his faithful guardians had found their marks and had sunk their teeth in deep. Todd bolted forward to assist his dogs, his boots pounding against the earth as he covered the distance with surprising speed for his age, hoping he could get there before the dogs could be harmed in the violent confrontation.

Todd rounded the corner of the brush line just in time to witness the savage efficiency of his dogs in action. Bear, her powerful jaws locked like a vise around her target's elbow, was methodically twisting and pulling with the relentless force of a medieval torture device. The man's agonized screams echoed through the air as he flailed helplessly, his mind unable to process the brutal attack. Buttercup, displaying her tactical intelligence, had initially clamped down on her target's leg before strategically repositioning for a more devastating assault on his face. The second intruder thrashed wildly, all four limbs desperately fighting for any relief from the shepherd's merciless attack. Without hesitation, Todd raised his rifle and dispatched both men with precise shots, the sharp cracks cutting through the chaos. Even after their targets went still, the dogs maintained their fierce grip, their primitive instincts still driving them to bite and rip at their now-lifeless prey, their muscles working overtime on the perceived threat.

Todd retreated back down the path with small steps, firmly calling the dogs to heel at his side. More threats were still out there, and Todd wasn't about to make himself an easy target by lingering for more attackers to emerge from the shadows. As he reached what he judged to be a safe tactical distance down the trail, he dropped to one knee, keeping his weapon trained steadily on his previous position. The air, thick with tension as he maintained his sight picture, his free hand fumbling briefly for his radio before bringing it to his mouth.

"I'm ok. Dogs saved me. Two down." Todd let out a few ragged coughs as he spoke, his throat still burning from the exertion.

"Thank God," Jason responded, relief flooding his voice, as if a crushing weight had been lifted from his shoulders. "When the dogs attached, the three guys on the right ran back down the road. I don't think there's anybody else on your side, but be stay alert."

"Roger that. I'm going to hold here. Hyden and Bruce, go back to the house and secure it," Todd commanded, his voice steady despite the adrenaline coursing through his system.

"Yes Sir," came the sharp, disciplined response from Hyden. The boys moved with haste, backtracking along the path until they reached the house's familiar silhouette. Entering through the basement door, they methodically sealed both the outer and inner steel doors, the heavy bolts sliding into place with reassuring thuds. Without wasting a moment, they ascended the stairs, their boots thumping on the heated tile floors, taking up pre-planned defensive positions at strategic windows, their eyes scanning the for any sign of movement among the pine trees and juniper bushes. Bobbie sat with Sarah at the kitchen table holding hands, the battery-powered radio positioned between them on the polished wooden surface. Both women's faces were etched with worry, their fingers intertwined tightly as they leaned forward, straining to catch every word through the occasional static. Their tense expressions, highlighting the deep concern in their eyes as they waited for the evening's events to be over.

"I'm moving position," Jason called out, his voice steady despite the tension coursing through his body. "I'm coming down the east face of the ridge. Going to try to get a better angle on the tree line and see if I can spot any movement."

"Copy that." Todd was feeling lucky to still be alive, his hands trembling slightly as he gripped his own weapon, the earlier exchange of gunfire still ringing in his ears.

Jason carefully left his sniper rifle on the ground, ensuring the weapon was secure before picking up his AR15, checking the magazine to ensure a full load. He moved quickly but methodically down the east side of the ridge, his boots finding secure footing on the uneven terrain while watching the last known area of where other targets might be located. The afternoon shadows played across the landscape as he knelt behind a weathered boulder, finding a good position that offered both cover and concealment. The slightly elevated position gave him an advantageous vantage point above where he believed the targets were still gathered, allowing him to scan the dense vegetation below for any signs of hostile movement.

As Todd knelt with Bear and Buttercup, he kept his eyes methodically trained on the area in front of him, his finger resting lightly against the trigger guard. The afternoon shadows danced through the pine branches when Buttercup suddenly started a low, threatening growl deep in her throat. Bear, picking up on the same unseen threat, followed suit as her black fur bristled and her hackles raised along her spine. Todd knew from years of experience that his dogs' instincts were rarely wrong - they sensed something approaching.

Out of the corner of his eye, he caught subtle movement approximately fifty yards away, a shadow that seemed out of place among the afternoon light filtering through the trees. He smoothly and deliberately trained his rifle on the disturbance, his breathing steady and controlled as best he could manage. Two men were trekking to his left, carefully slipping between the dense trees and scrub oak, their dark clothing blending with the shadows as they moved with stealth, never providing a clean shot through the thick vegetation. The dogs' growls intensified into warning barks, the sound echoing off the ridge and reverberating through the valley below, their protective instincts now fully engaged as they sensed the obvious threat to their territory.

As their barking escalated, Todd spotted a flash of movement - both men hastily retreating the way they had come, nearly stumbling in their hurried escape in an attempt to not engage with the dogs. When they reached the edge of where the road met the tree line, they paused and dropped to one knee, frantically scanning both directions along the dirt path before making a desperate dash across. As the lead man reached the center of the road, Jason's well-aimed bullet found its mark mid-torso with brutal accuracy. The impact threw the man forward, causing him to fall and slide several feet across the gravel, his face grinding into the rough surface. The second man, witnessing his companion's fate, immediately froze and thrust his hands skyward in desperate surrender, his weapon hanging from its strap.

Jason kept his sights trained steadily on his target through the rifle's scope and watched intently as the man turned around in desperate circles, his eyes darting frantically across the landscape, trying to figure out where the deadly shot had come from. Neither Todd nor Jason moved a muscle, their stillness making them nearly invisible among the pine trees and scrub oak. After a full minute of tense silence broken only by the soft mountain breeze, the man slowly dropped his left arm down and, with trembling fingers, unslung his weapon from across his body. His movements were deliberate and careful as he slowly lowered the rifle to the ground, placing it on the gravel road with exaggerated gentleness. He slowly re-raised his arms as the universal gesture of surrender. Jason, seeing that the man clearly wanted nothing more to do with the fight, decided to send him a message that would ensure he never returned to Overlook Ridge.

Jason carefully aimed his AR15, steadying the rifle against his shoulder as he peered through the scope. He slowly let out his breath, just as he'd practiced countless times at the range, allowing his body to become perfectly still. His trigger finger started to apply pressure, taking up the slack until he reached that sweet spot just before the break. The rifle kicked against him with familiar force, and the bullet found its target within an inch of where it aimed, the impact echoing softly across the mountain terrain.

In what seemed like slow motion, the man's gun shattered into two pieces as Jason's bullet found the upper receiver, causing the rifle to spin and separate with a metallic screech. Fragments of aluminum and steel scattered across the gravel road like deadly confetti. The startled man jumped back with his arms still raised high, his eyes wide with disbelief as he stared at his now broken weapon on the ground. His tactical vest, which had seemed so menacing moments ago, now appeared useless without a functioning rifle. With his hands held high, trembling slightly in the cool mountain air, he slowly took steps up the road, his boots crunching against loose rocks. Jason watched through his scope as the intruder walked down the road and turned the last visible corner, still maintaining his surrender pose, disappearing into the shadows of the towering pines that lined the winding path.

"I think we are all clear," Jason radioed, his finger steady on the transmit button as he maintained his position behind the rifle. "What do you think about letting the dogs clear the area? They'll pick up anything we might have missed."

Todd didn't like the thought of it, but he knew a dog's life was not the same as a human's life. The mere idea of sending Bear and Buttercup into potential danger made his stomach churn. "Yeah, I think it's the only way." Todd's response sounded depressing, his voice heavy with reluctance.

"Don't worry, I can cover them from here if they find something. I'll follow them with the scope closely, every step of the way. I'll let you know when it's safe to come up to the road." Jason's reassurance carried the weight of his marksmanship skills, his eye never leaving the scope as he spoke.

"Roger that. Ok. I'm letting them go." And with that, Todd gave the dogs the encouragement to go search, watching as Buttercup's ears perked forward and Bear's tail began to wag with anticipation. He patted each dog's head before giving them the command to move out, their muscular bodies tensing with purpose as they began their patrol of the area. The German Shepherd took point, her black and tan coat blending seamlessly with the shadows between the trees, while Bear followed close behind, her heavier frame moving with surprising grace through the underbrush. Todd's heart swelled with pride even as worry gnawed at him, watching his faithful companions disappear into the forest's edge, their training and instincts now put to the ultimate test.

Both dogs ran ahead with focused intensity, their heads down and noses working overtime as they sniffed every inch of ground and vegetation. They came into Jason's view as they reached the dirt road, their powerful forms moving with practiced efficiency. He tracked them closely, watching as they systematically covered the area, running back and forth while investigating each fresh scent. Now and then, they would freeze in place, their ears swiveling like sophisticated radar dishes, catching any suspicious sounds before returning to their meticulous patrol pattern. The dogs moved purposefully across the road and into the thick brush where the left group had been spotted earlier. They worked in widening circles around the area where Jason recalled seeing the figures, their ability clear in how thoroughly they searched every possible hiding spot. After a few tense minutes of observation, Jason gave Todd the all-clear signal, and his friend cautiously made his way to the road, his body language remaining vigilant and his finger never far from his weapon's trigger as he moved.

Jason methodically gathered his tactical gear and carefully made his way down the steep ridge to join his friend. His trained eyes continuously scanned the dense tree line and brush-covered slopes for any remaining threats or suspicious movement, his hand never straying far from his weapon. When he finally reached the road, Todd was standing motionless over the body in the middle of the road, his weathered face etched with concern. The older man's shoulders were visibly slumped, and his usual confident demeanor had been replaced by an air of heavy contemplation, as if the gravity of their situation had suddenly become overwhelmingly real. The weight of responsibility seemed to press down on him like a physical burden.

"Wow. I can't believe all that just happened." Todd's voice sounded surprised and weary, his hands trembling slightly as the adrenaline faded.

"Me either. But we did it. We defended the home stead... again. What are we going to do with all these bodies? We're going to have to open a graveyard if this keeps up." Jason tried to sound lighter, though the strain in his voice betrayed his attempt at levity. His boots scuffed against the gravel as he shifted his weight uncomfortably.

"Well, I don't know. I guess we do the same for them as we did for the others. Except this time, let's put them deeper down and on the other side of the road." Todd's mind was already calculating the logistics, measuring the task ahead with efficiency.

"Do you think we will ever have to explain ourselves? I mean, who were these people?" Jason questioned, his eyes scanning the treeline as if expecting more threats to materialize from the dense forest surrounding Overlook Ridge.

"I don't know, but I think we are going to be sad we didn't kill them all after we see what they did to the neighbors. I'm hoping for the best." Todd's voice carried a grim certainty that made his words hang heavy in the cool mountain air. His usual confident demeanor faltered, as he could only think the worst for the neighbors and beyond that had to deal with this group of bandits.

Chapter 20

A New Beginning

The late afternoon sun cast long shadows across Overlook Ridge as Todd adjusted the solar panels on the greenhouse roof. Below, rows of thriving vegetables stretched toward the glass walls - tomatoes heavy with fruit, leafy greens, and climbing bean vines. The past twelve months had transformed their mountain sanctuary into a self-sustaining heaven.

"Hey Todd, need a hand up there?" Jason called from the ground, wiping sweat from his brow.

"Nah, almost done. Just tweaking the angle before winter hits." Todd secured the last bracket and climbed down the ladder. "Can't believe it's been almost a year."

They walked together toward the main house, their boots crunching on the gravel path. The property had evolved - new garden beds terraced down the slope, a chicken coop clucking with chickens that were traded for with a neighbor, and a sophisticated rainwater collection system feeding their irrigation needs.

"Remember when we first got here? Felt like we were camping." Jason chuckled, gesturing at their expanded compound. "Now look at us - growing our own food, generating power, living off the land."

"Engineering mind never stops working." Todd tapped his temple. "Though I'll admit, some of our early attempts were pretty rough. Remember that first batch of tomatoes?"

"You mean the ones that looked like golf balls?"

"Hey now, they may have been small, but they were mighty." Todd's dogs bounded up to greet them, tails wagging. "At least the pups didn't complain."

Inside the house, the aroma of fresh-baked bread filled the air as it did almost every day. Bobbie and Sarah had mastered the art of cooking from scratch, turning basic ingredients into hearty meals. Solar-powered chest freezers preserved their harvest and game meat, while root cellars stored vegetables through the winter months.

Jason grabbed two cups of coffee and joined Todd on the back deck. "It's been like six months without a single visitor. Hard to believe after those first crazy months."

"Peace and quiet - just what we wanted." Todd sipped his coffee, surveying their domain. "Though sometimes I wonder what's happening out there."

"The radio's been quiet too. Fewer broadcasts these days. Seems people have finally accepted this new way of life."

"Maybe that's not such a bad thing." Todd scratched behind his dog's ears. "We've got everything we need right here. Your family's safe, the gardens are producing, and we've even got entertainment." He nodded toward their media room.

"Speaking of entertainment, Sarah's planning movie night. Says we need to maintain culture up here on the mountain."

"As long as it's not another zombie film. Getting tired of those."

The sound of children's laughter drifted up from the lower garden, where Jason's kids helped with the evening harvest. They'd adapted well to mountain life, learning survival skills alongside their regular studies. Bobbie and Sarah started a homeschool program, and the children were really learning.

"Never thought I'd see my kids so excited about vegetables," Jason mused. "City life feels like a distant memory now."

"They're growing up strong. Learning actual skills." Todd stood and stretched. "Though I still can't get them to appreciate my engineering lectures."

"Give it time. They already think you're the coolest uncle ever - especially after you built them those treehouses."

"Pure engineering necessity. Every compound needs a proper lookout point."

As evening approached, the family gathered for dinner - a ritual that had become the heart of their daily routine. The table groaned under dishes of home-grown vegetables, fresh bread, and preserved meats. Lights using the surplus supply of energy that was being made cast a warm glow over their meal.

"You know what's crazy?" Jason passed a bowl of steaming potatoes. "A year ago, I couldn't tell a zucchini from a cucumber. Now we're practically farmers."

"Speak for yourself." Todd grinned. "I'm still an engineer who happens to grow food. Though I'll admit, I've actually come to liking vegetables."

The conversation flowed easily, punctuated by laughter and the clinking of utensils. Outside, the mountain air grew crisp as darkness settled over their sanctuary. They'd created more than just a survival compound - they'd built a home.

"To think we were worried about making it through the first month," Jason reflected. "Now look at us."

"Just shows to go ya - proper planning and a good team make all the difference." Todd raised his glass. "Though I still say we need to work on that cannabis growth."

The night moon sent a dim light across Overlook Ridge as Jason pulled open the upper deck sliding door. A gust of crisp mountain air rushed past him into the cabin. Behind him, Todd flicked on his flashlight, casting a bright beam across the deck until it found the Starlink pole still standing tall.

"You really think this is worth another shot?" Todd aimed the light at the small satellite dish mounted on the railing. Dust and bird droppings coated its surface.

Jason brushed debris off the dish with his sleeve. "Been six months. Maybe whatever knocked it offline got fixed."

"With no one around to fix it?" Todd's boots thumped against the deck boards as he moved closer.

"Automated systems, maybe. Elon's toys are pretty sophisticated." Jason connected the power cable he'd disconnected months ago when the device had become nothing more than a useless ornament.

The dish hummed to life, its internal motors whirring as it adjusted its position. Both men held their breath, watching the small indicator light on its base.

"Holy crap." Jason leaned in closer. "Todd, look — it's green. It's got a connection to the satellites."

Todd's weathered face broke into a rare smile. "Well, let's fire up the laptop."

Back inside, Jason's hands trembled slightly as he opened his old laptop. The boot-up sequence seemed to take forever, the machine protesting after months of dormancy. Todd paced behind him, his footsteps echoing in the quiet upstairs room.

"Come on, come on," Todd muttered.

The wireless icon appeared, then connected. Jason's fingers flew across the keyboard, pulling up a browser window. "We've got a signal. Strong one too."

"Try the major news sites first." Todd pulled up a chair, the wooden legs scraping across the carpet.

Jason typed in CNN's web address. The page loaded, displaying headlines from that day. Todd's breath caught in his throat.

"Look at the date stamp." Todd pointed at the screen. "These are current. Like a week or so."

"Try another one." Todd's voice cracked with excitement.

They cycled through news sites, social media platforms, government pages. Information flooded their screens—six months of world events condensed into rapid-fire headlines and updates.

"Wow." Jason ran a hand through his hair. "Things are coming back. I mean, not everything is up, but all we need is a few good news sites to figure out what's going on across the world."

Todd took the mouse and scrolled through a news feed. "Looks like they got the power back on the east and west coasts."

"But how?" Jason leaned back in his chair, surrendering the laptop. "We haven't had power, cell signal, nothing for months. The entire valley's been dark."

"Here's something." Todd clicked on a Colorado news link. "Power grid upgrades across the western slope. They are working on a modernization project to restore power. Man, that will be huge."

"Yeah, that would be a real comeback. What about marshal law and law enforcement activities? Be interesting to hear if there's law and order being restored in the cities." Jason's voice rose. "If law and order has been restored, we might could venture out to town."

Todd opened another tab. "Check this out – U.S. Government is standing down control of some of the major cities. The military has been involved in humanitarian aid to cities and such."

The men stared intently at the screen, their faces illuminated by the glow as they carefully read through the scrolling headlines, methodically piecing together the fragments of recent events. Supplies remained desperately tight across the nation, with basic necessities still hard to come by in most areas. Commercial trucking across the country was still at a complete standstill, leaving store shelves bare and warehouses empty. Most gas stations displayed their "No Gas" signs, their pumps covered in plastic. The only financial institutions that remained operational were the ones the Government had forcibly taken over during the height of the crisis, leaving countless Americans still without access to their savings or any form of currency. A mere three refineries out of dozens nationwide maintained active operations, and those were exclusively providing gasoline and oil to the Government for military and law enforcement use. While many major metropolitan areas showed tentative signs of recovery, their situations looked bleak at best - with damaged infrastructure, limited services, and a population struggling to adapt to the new normal.

"Save everything," Todd said, standing. "Download what you can before we lose connection again. See if you can find out anything on the death toll over the past year. It's gotta be high."

Jason nodded as he sat back down in front of the laptop, creating a new folder and saving webpage after webpage. His fingers moved with fast precision across the keyboard while Todd read headlines over his shoulder.

"The world didn't end." Jason's voice was barely a whisper. "Looks like it's slowly coming back. A new dawn."

"Well, if you think about it, the first six months is when all the bad things happened here, really. That's when the bad people were running around with no authorities to hold them at bay. All the people in those big cities dumped into the countryside, causing massive problems in the country towns. Once all the chaos started dying down, it allowed the good people to venture back out and start getting things working again." Jason started downloading PDF copies of news archives.

The laptop screen flickered. Both men froze.

"No, no, no," Jason typed faster, racing to save more information.

The Starlink indicator light outside the window pulsed once, twice, then returned to its familiar dead state. The internet connection icon disappeared from the laptop.

Silence filled the room once again, broken only by the soft whir of the laptop's fan. On the screen, their downloaded files remained—fragments of a world that was rebuilding.

"I bet there are a lot of satellites out of whack. I'm betting there's a window for when the satellites we just used fly by again." Jason stood and walked to the window, staring out at the dark valley below.

Todd closed the laptop carefully. "Mark the time. We need to have someone watch the Starlink connection for twenty-four hours and mark the time when it's up and down. I'm betting you're right. We probably have a window of time once or twice a day to get connected."

The men exchanged glances in the dim room light, their brief window into the outside world already feeling like a dream.

"I think it might be time to go to town and see how things are." Jason sounding hopeful.

"Perhaps. There's no hurry at this point. Let's see if we can gather more information over the next few days if we can get the connection back up. Once we learn as much as we can, we'll decide to leave the property. Deal?"

"Deal," Jason said as he opened the saved folder to shift through the saved websites.

Chapter 21

FINDING COMMUNITY

Todd laid out his tactical vest on the workbench, checking each pocket and compartment with practiced precision. The fluorescent lights in his garage cast harsh shadows across the gear spread before them. He pulled a magazine from one of the pouches, counted the rounds, then slapped it back into place.

"Extra mags in the front right pocket." Todd adjusted the straps. "Keep your radio on channel three."

Jason nodded, inspecting his own equipment nearby. He pulled the charging handle on his AR-15, checking the chamber. "Clear." The metallic click echoed through the garage. "Do you think the roads will be blocked?"

"Can't risk taking the main route into town." Todd grabbed his medical kit, verifying the contents. "We'll take the back roads past Miller's Ranch. Less exposure."

"What about the bridge crossing?"

"Secondary option only. Too obvious a checkpoint location." Todd zipped up the med kit and attached it to his vest. "If we encounter any resistance-"

"Break contact, I know." Jason grabbed a handful of zip ties, stuffing them into his cargo pocket. "No heroes today."

"Exactly." Todd pulled out an old map from his pocket. "Here's our primary route. If we get separated, the rally point is the old grain silo."

Jason leaned in, studying the map. "That's three miles from town. Long walk if something happens to the truck."

"Better than getting cornered downtown." Todd folded and tucked the map back into his pocket. "We move fast, look around, maybe get supplies if we can find any, get out. No delays."

The weight of Jason's plate carrier settled across his shoulders as he adjusted the straps. "How many water containers are you bringing?"

"Four one-gallon jugs. Should fit behind the back seat." Todd checked his pistol, then holstered it. "Enough room for supplies and whatnot if we find any."

"Batteries too." Jason grabbed his list from the workbench. "Radio batteries, flashlights."

Todd nodded, stuffing extra magazines into his vest. "Keep your head on a swivel when we hit Main Street. Last report said the grocery stores in cities are still closed. Shelters are feeding the hungry with government aid."

Jason pulled on his gloves, flexing his fingers. "What's our time limit in town?"

"Thirty minutes max. Any longer increases our exposure." Todd checked his watch. "Sun's up in four hours. We move then."

"Roger that." Jason zipped up his jacket. "You hear from Miller lately? Might be worth checking his place on the way back."

"Radio's been silent since the raiders we had. I fear the worse." Todd frowned, adjusting his chest rig.

The garage fell silent as both men focused on their final equipment checks. Every piece of gear, every weapon, every supply had its purpose. Nothing unnecessary, nothing forgotten. The methodical routine helped push back the gnawing uncertainty of what awaited them on their journey.

"Weather is clear till noon. Should be back well before then." Todd checked the truck's fuel gauge through the window. "Three-quarter tank. More than enough."

The pre-dawn darkness wrapped around the house as Todd and Jason stepped out of the garage. Bobbie stood in the doorway, her arms crossed against the morning chill. The kids clustered behind her, their faces pale in the porch light.

Sarah emerged from the basement, carrying two thermoses. "Coffee. Still hot." She passed them to Todd and Jason. "Be careful out there."

Bobbie stepped forward, embracing Jason. "Be gone only as long as you have to. Not a minute longer."

"Yes, ma'am." He held her close for a moment.

Bear and Buttercup whined at Todd's feet, sensing the tension.

"Load up," Todd commanded. "Get in the truck."

The dogs jumped in the back excitedly, though their ears back and tails beating the truck bed.

Todd placed his drink in the center cup holder. "Remember-"

"Lock everything down after you leave," Bobbie finished. "We know the drill."

The sky had begun to lighten as Todd and Jason climbed into the truck. Through the windshield, they could see their family silhouetted in the doorway, the dogs running from side to side in the truck bed as Todd started the engine. They pulled away from the house, watching in the rearview mirror until their home disappeared as they curved around the driveway.

The truck's engine hummed as they descended the winding mountain road. Bear and Buttercup hunkered down in the truck bed against the cold morning air. Jason scanned the tree line while Todd kept his eyes on the road, both alert for any movement.

Nature had reclaimed the road. Weeds pushed through cracks, and fallen branches littered the shoulder where maintenance crews once kept things clear. Small landslides had deposited rocks and dirt across portions of the road.

"Different from last spring," Jason said, noting the partly collapsed section of road where winter storms had taken their toll.

Todd slowed at Dead Man's Curve. "Road's deteriorating faster than I expected." He navigated around a deep pothole. "If no one maintains the culverts, this is what happens."

They passed the brick house, now overgrown with tall grass. The once-manicured lawn had transformed into a meadow of wildflowers and native plants. The house stood empty, windows dark.

"Remember riding past here all the time?" Jason pointed to the fallen posts along the property line.

"Good times." Todd's knuckles whitened on the steering wheel. "Wonder if they stuck it out, or left a long time ago."

A deer bounded across the road ahead, disappearing into the forest. Bear and Buttercup perked up, tracking its movement. The truck rolled past the old Thompson place where rusted farm equipment sat frozen in time, partially hidden by encroaching vegetation. Bullet holes riddled the house. Showing signs of the struggle from months ago.

"Hold up." Jason raised his binoculars. "Something's different at the intersection."

Todd eased off the gas, letting the truck coast. The stop sign at the bottom of the hill had been stripped away, leaving only a bare metal post. Tire tracks cut through the tall grass leading into the woods.

"Recent?" Todd asked.

Jason studied the ground. "Within the last few days, maybe. Looks like they backed a trailer through there. Let's just push on."

They continued down the mountain at a crawl, noting more signs of change - fallen power lines, washed-out drainage ditches, and the skeletal remains of abandoned vehicles slowly being swallowed by vegetation. After thirty minutes, they reached the edge of Blackhawk Ranch and moved onto the back road that led to town. Along their way, they passed several abandoned vehicles, some completely burnt down to the tires.

At the edge of town, Todd pulled the truck to a stop, studying Main Street through his binoculars. The early morning light revealed a landscape vastly different from their memories. Empty storefronts lined both sides, their windows covered with plywood or makeshift repairs using whatever materials people had found.

"Less damage than I expected," Jason said, scanning the area. "Remember the videos from last summer? Some of the town and cities looked like a war zones."

"Someone's been cleaning up." Todd pointed to neat piles of debris stacked along the curb. "Those are fresh piles."

A small group of people walked past the old hardware store, carrying water jugs. They moved with purpose, heads down, focused on their task. No one lingered on street corners or gathered in groups.

"Roads are clear." Jason noted the absence of the burned-out cars and makeshift barriers that had blocked intersections months ago. "Military must have pushed through here."

Todd drove slowly down a parallel road to Main Street, passing the courthouse where someone had patched bullet holes with cement. The clock tower still showed the wrong time, frozen at 3:47. A string of solar-powered lights hung across the street, suggesting at least some restoration of normal life.

"Look at the building over there." Jason gestured toward the three-story building. Its windows glowed with generator power, and a Red Cross flag flew above the entrance. "They've got that up and running."

"Running's a stretch." Todd observed the temporary repairs - tarps covering damaged sections of roof, plywood reinforcing broken walls. "But they're trying."

They passed the grocery store where a hand-painted sign announced it was closed. A small garden had sprouted in what used to be the parking lot, rows of vegetables growing between faded parking lines.

"Town's adapting," Jason said. "Different from what I imagined."

"Fewer people though." Todd watched an elderly couple emerge from the old post office, which now served as a community center. "Way fewer than before."

The truck rolled past more signs of slow recovery - jerry-rigged solar panels on rooftops, rain barrels collecting water from gutters, and bikes replacing cars on the streets. The town had changed, but unlike the chaos they'd witnessed months ago, there was now an ordered feel to the survival efforts.

Todd eased the truck to a stop across from the Safeway. Where shopping carts once filled the cracked parking lot, makeshift stalls and tables now formed neat rows. A large banner stretched across the entrance:

"TRADING POST & FARMERS MARKET - NO CASH."

"Well, that's new," Jason said, leaning forward to get a better view through the windshield.

People moved between the stalls, carrying baskets and bags. Some held clipboards, carefully recording transactions. Others displayed home-grown vegetables, preserved foods, and handmade goods.

"Look at the security." Todd nodded toward armed men positioned at strategic points around the perimeter. Their weapons were holstered, but visible. "Nice setup."

Through his binoculars, Todd studied the trading system in action. A woman exchanged what looked like hand-sewn clothing for several jars of preserved fruit. At another stall, someone traded ammunition for medical supplies.

"They're using some kind of point system." Todd spotted people referring to hand written paper sheets as they negotiated. "See those cards they're showing?"

"Smart." Jason observed a trader weight out rice using an old-fashioned balance scale. "Better than trying to establish a new currency."

Bear and Buttercup stood alert in the truck bed, their ears perked forward as they watched the activity from a far. The market buzzed with at least a fifty people.

"Might be worth checking out," Jason suggested. "We've got things we could think about trading."

Todd shook his head. "Alright, but we will need to take all this grab off and probably the weapons." He put the truck in park. "Let's take all this off and walk over there."

They carefully removed all the hardware and weapon systems, stacking them neatly on the floor of the cab. Jason methodically emptied ammo from a clip into his calloused hands, the brass cartridges clinking softly as he transferred them to his front pocket. After double checking themselves and ensuring nothing of value remained visible, they exited the vehicle and locked it with a reassuring click.

Todd gave both Bear and Buttercup an affectionate scratch behind their ears, his weathered hand lingering for a moment on each dog's head. "Guard the truck," he commanded firmly, watching as both dogs settled into alert positions, their keen eyes already scanning the busy marketplace across the street.

Todd and Jason walked between the market stalls, taking in the organized chaos around them. Wooden tables groaned under the weight of preserved foods - rows of mason jars filled with vegetables, fruits, and meats. A trader wearing a green vest examined items with a small digital scale, recording values on a clipboard.

"Two points per pound of dried corn," the trader announced to a woman clutching a bag of homemade soap. "Plus another point for the glass jar."

At the next stall, an elderly man displayed hand-forged tools - hammers, trowels, and garden implements crafted from scavenged metal. He bartered with a young couple, exchanging a shovel for what looked like medical supplies.

"Notice how they're tracking everything?" Jason nodded toward a central table where three people managed ledgers. "Must have a system to prevent double-spending."

Todd paused at a stall filled with automotive parts. Batteries, filters, and spark plugs lay arranged by type. The trader showed a customer a worn point card with carefully marked columns.

"Ten points for the deep cycle battery," the trader explained. "Or trade straight across for ammunition - looking for .308 or 5.56."

They passed tables loaded with practical items - candles, soap, matches, and first aid supplies. Each stall displayed a laminated sheet listing point values. Some traders specialized in specific categories - one focused entirely on fishing gear, another on winter clothing.

A woman wearing a volunteer badge approached them. "First time at the market? Need to get you registered for point cards if you're planning to trade."

"Just looking for now," Todd replied, watching a complex three-way trade involving food, fuel, and labor hours.

"Smart system," Jason commented as they moved past a stall offering small solar equipment. "Everyone gets what they need without dealing with worthless cash."

The market hummed with activity - people comparing items, negotiating values, recording transactions. Despite the circumstances, there was an underlying sense of community and order to the entire operation.

The volunteer adjusted her badge, stepping closer to Todd and Jason. "Name's Rachel. I help coordinate the trading post." Her clipboard contained neatly organized sheets filled with handwritten data.

"Have you heard anything about power restoration?" Todd's eyebrows lifted.

"Actually, yes I have. They said the Army Corps of Engineers cleared the main substation last week." Rachel flipped through her papers. "They're working their way down from Denver, replacing transformers and critical infrastructure. Should reach us in a month."

Jason crossed his arms. "What about fuel supplies?"

"Limited diesel shipments started arriving for essential services only." She pointed toward the Red Cross building. "Hospital's running full time now. We're getting regular supply drops - medicine, some food stock."

"Any word on cell service?" Todd watched a trader weighing rice nearby.

"Phone lines are still down, but they've restored emergency services radio networks." Rachel smiled. "Internet's supposed to follow once they get the power grid stable. Military's prioritizing infrastructure over comfort services."

"Makes sense." Todd nodded. "Who's organizing all this?"

"Joint task force - military and civilian administration." She gestured at the surrounding market. "Local council handles day-to-day operations, trading post, rationing. Military provides some security and helps coordinate rebuilding efforts."

"Seems organized," Jason commented.

"Had to be." Rachel tucked her clipboard under her arm. "Chaos doesn't feed people. Structure does. We learned that pretty quick after everything fell apart."

"And the power - you're certain about the timeline?" Todd pressed.

"Engineers already mapped the grid. They're moving systematically, testing and replacing equipment as they can." She pulled out a wrinkled map marked with highlighted routes. "Following the progress, our sector should be next in line."

As Todd and the volunteer talked, Jason approached a stall where glass milk jugs sat in a cooler of ice. The trader, a weathered man in overalls, straightened as Jason drew near.

"That's real milk?" Jason pointed at the jugs. "Not powdered?"

"Fresh this morning. Got three dairy cows producing." The trader tapped the cooler. "Natural, unpasteurized. Good fat content too."

Jason reached into his pocket, brass cartridges clinking. "How much for a gallon?"

The trader's eyes locked onto Jason's hand. "That 5.56?"

"Lake City brass. Thirty rounds." Jason placed the rounds on the wooden counter.

The trader picked up one of the rounds, examining the ammunition with practiced eyes. "Factory loads or reloads?"

"Factory. Still got the crimps." Jason showed him the characteristic markings.

The trader whistled low. "Haven't seen factory ammo in months. Everyone's running reloads these days." He set the clip down. "Tell you what - forty rounds for the gallon. That's fair."

"Thirty." Jason separated the rounds. "Milk spoils. Bullets don't."

The trader considered this, then nodded. "Deal." He carefully counted the rounds while Jason retrieved a glass jug from the cooler.

The milk felt heavy in Jason's hands, the glass cool and slick with condensation. He remembered when a gallon cost just a few dollars at the store. Now it was worth other valuable resources.

The trader secured the ammunition in a locked box beneath his counter. "Pleasure doing business. Come back next week - should have more if the cows keep producing."

Jason cradled the milk jug close as he walked back to Todd. The precious liquid sloshed inside, worth more than gold in their new reality.

As they left the bustling market, they walked in thoughtful silence through the dusty parking lot. The impressive organization of the makeshift marketplace surprised both men. Not only the size but also by the diverse array of supplies it offered - things they could certainly use in the future. They reached Todd's weathered pickup truck and settled into their familiar seats; the springs creaking beneath them. Both men found themselves smiling, sharing a wordless moment of satisfaction as they felt a renewed sense of hope wash over them. Perhaps things were finally starting to stabilize, even if their world remained forever changed.

Todd guided the truck up the winding mountain road, the milk jug nestled securely in Jason's lap. Bear and Buttercup lounged in the truck bed, their fur ruffling in the wind.

"Trading post changes everything," Jason said, watching the town shrink in the side mirror. "Organized barter system means people are settling in for the long haul."

Todd steered around a pothole. "Military presence is promising. If they're restoring power grid sector by sector, means they've got a handle on things."

"Did you notice the gardens? Every empty lot converted to growing space." Jason shifted in his seat. "Town's not waiting for outside help anymore."

"Smart move with the point system, too." Todd tapped the steering wheel. "Prevents inflation, hoarding. Everyone contributes what they can."

The truck climbed higher, engine straining against the grade. Todd downshifted, the transmission whining. "Question is, do we get involved or stay independent?"

"Trading could supplement our supplies." Jason watched a deer bound into the trees. "But it means revealing what we have, who we are."

"And how many we are." Todd slowed for a sharp curve. "Though that milk proves some things are worth trading for."

"Bobbie will be happy about this," Jason smiled. "Fresh milk changes everything for cooking."

They passed the burned-out Miller's place, both men falling silent as they remembered the firefight there months ago. The bullet holes in the walls served as stark reminders of darker days.

"At least now there's structure," Todd said finally. "People working together instead of just taking what they want."

"Order from chaos," Jason agreed. "But we'll need to be careful how we approach it."

Todd pulled the truck into the gravel driveway between the house and garage. Bear and Buttercup leaped from the truck bed, tails wagging as they circled their feet.

Jason cradled the glass jug of milk as they entered through the basement door. The smell of fresh bread greeted them as they climbed the stairs to the main floor.

"You're not going to believe what we found," Jason called out.

Bobbie looked up from kneading dough at the kitchen counter, flour dusting her arms. Sarah sat at the table sorting through the garden seeds.

"Real milk." Jason set the jug on the counter. "Fresh from actual cows."

Bobbie's eyes widened. "How did you-"

"Trading post in town," Todd said, settling into a kitchen chair. "They've got a whole market set up at the old Safeway. Point system for bartering, security, the works."

"That's not all," Jason added. "Military's restoring power, working their way down from Denver. Rachel - one of the coordinators - says we could have electricity in a month or so."

Sarah straightened in her chair. "Actual power? That would be a big change?"

"Army Corps of Engineers is replacing transformers," Todd explained. "They've already cleared the main substation. Emergency radio networks are back up too."

"Cell phone signal are supposed to follow once they stabilize the grid," Jason said.

Bobbie wiped her hands on her apron. "What about supplies? Food?"

"Military's doing regular drops - medicine, basic provisions," Todd said. "But the town's not just waiting for handouts. Every empty spot has been turned into a garden. People are trading what they produce."

"We traded some ammo for this milk," Jason gestured to the jug. "Thirty rounds of 5.56 for a gallon."

"The whole system's organized," Todd continued. "Ledgers tracking trades, point cards to prevent inflation. It's not perfect, but it's working."

Jason called out to the children upstairs. "Kids! Come down here - we've got something special!"

Footsteps thundered down the stairs as Hydan, Jack, Bruce, Rose, and Juliet rushed into the kitchen. They clustered around the counter, eyes widening at the sight of the glass jug filled with creamy white liquid.

"Is that... real milk?" Juliet pressed her hands against the counter, leaning forward to examine the jug.

"Sure is." Jason unscrewed the cap, the familiar sound making Bruce's eyes light up. "Fresh from actual cows this morning."

The five year bounced on her toes. "Can we have some now?"

"I think we can spare a glass each." Bobbie retrieved cups from the cabinet while Jason carefully poured the milk, splashing softly into each glass.

The children lifted their cups with reverence, as if holding precious treasure. Jack took a careful sip, then broke into a wide grin. "It tastes so good!"

"Better than that powdered stuff," Bruce declared, milk leaving a white mustache above his lip that held a wispy mustache.

The kitchen filled with chatter as the children shared memories of milk and cookies, ice cream, and hot chocolate. For a moment, the hardships of their new life faded away, replaced by the simple joy of fresh milk and family gathered around the kitchen counter.

The evening sun cast long shadows across the living room as the family gathered around their dining table, now covered with neatly arranged piles of tradeable items. Bobbie sorted through a collection of preserved vegetables from their garden, her fingers dancing over sealed mason jars filled with vibrant colors.

"These pickled carrots turned out perfect." She held a jar up to the fading light. "We can spare at least six jars."

Jason scribbled notes on a worn notepad. "Mark those as high value. Fresh vegetables are getting harder to come by."

Todd examined a stack of ammunition boxes, counting rounds with practiced efficiency. "Nine boxes of this ammo we can't use, and three of shotgun shells should fetch us some medical supplies."

The kids huddled at the far end of the table, sorting through their own contributions. Jack held up a stack of comic books he found in the closet downstairs, their covers still glossy despite being worthless even before the chaos began.

"Someone might want these for their kids," Jack's eyes lingered on the familiar characters.

"Good thinking." Jason nodded. "Entertainment items are worth more than you'd expect these days."

Bobbie wrapped the mason jars in old dish towels, cushioning them for transport. "I've also got those herbal medicines I made last month. Feverfew, chamomile, peppermint."

"The trading post always needs medical supplies." Todd packed the ammunition into a padded case. "Your herbs might be our best bargaining chip."

Rose and Juliet contributed a pile of outgrown clothes, still in good condition. Bruce added some hand-carved wooden figures he'd been working on during the long winter evenings.

As the inventory progressed, the golden light of sunset painted the walls in deepening amber. Jason stretched, his back cracking from hunching over the notepad.

"Think that covers everything we can spare." He pushed back from the table. "Bobbie, you've got dinner under control?"

"Venison stew's been simmering all afternoon." She waved him off. "Go relax. We'll handle the rest."

Todd caught Jason's eye and tilted his head toward the stairs. Without a word, they climbed to the top deck of the house. The viewing platform offered a panoramic view of the surrounding landscape, with the Rocky Mountains rising like ancient guardians against the painted sky.

They settled into their familiar spots - two weathered Adirondack chairs positioned to face the sunset. The wooden deck creaked beneath them, a comfortable sound that had become part of their evening ritual.

The sun balanced on the mountain peaks, spreading fingers of light through the clouds. Bands of color stretched across the horizon - deep purples, burning oranges, and hints of green where the light played tricks with the atmosphere.

Neither man spoke. They didn't need to. Years of friendship had taught them the value of shared silence. The evening breeze carried the scent of pine and the smell of the kitchen below.

Todd's chair squeaked as he leaned back, his boots propped against the deck railing. Jason mirrored his posture, their routine so familiar it had become choreography.

The sun slipped lower, painting the clouds in ever-changing colors. A hawk circled lazily overhead, riding the thermal currents in wide, graceful arcs. From below came the muffled sounds of the family continuing their work - Bobbie's laugh, the clinking of jars, the children's chatter.

The temperature dropped with the sun, but neither man moved to go inside. These moments, these shared sunsets, had become their anchor in an uncertain world. The simple act of sitting together, watching day fade into night, carried more meaning than any words they could exchange.

The last sliver of sun disappeared behind the mountains, leaving a lingering glow that softened the approaching darkness. Stars began to appear, first one, then dozens, pinpricks of light in the deepening blue.

Todd shifted in his chair, the wood creaking beneath him. The familiar sound blended with the evening chorus of crickets and the distant call of frogs. Jason's breathing had slowed to match the peaceful rhythm of the gathering night. But still they sat, comfortable in their shared silence, watching the last colors fade from the sky.